Engineering
the
Enemy

Designed for easy reading and was printed from new film.

ISBN: 0-6154-5305-8
ISBN-13: 9780615453057

Engineering
the
Enemy
Inside an Al Qeada Cell
The Beginning

Inspired By True Events

For my parents, Sharyn and Bill.

Thank you for not giving up on me.

ACKNOWLEDGMENTS

For technical information, editing and advice I am especially indebted to Ken Haggerty, whose vast knowledge and countless hours submitted in the perpetration of this manuscript can never be repaid.

Also to Jason Tracey whose countless hours editing the raw manuscript was greatly appreciated and to the many other contributors thank you so much for all of your help.

"You can never reach the top
unless you have spent some time on the bottom."

Engineering
the
Enemy
Inside an Al Qeada Cell

Chapter 1

Everyone loves a good fight, even if you can't choose your adversaries.

Less than 24 hours ago I was imprisoned in Upstate New York. Shit. I was minding my own business, cutting down trees and shaping hedges for less than 25 cents an hour. But my day took a strange turn of events as two old acquaintances interrupted my topiary solitude.

A little more than two years ago I was arrested and sent to Federal Prison on charges of money laundering. 'Fuck it,' I thought at the time. I paid the driver and arrived at the destination of my choice.

FBI Agents Clarence Jackmann and Nathan Sinsel, however, couldn't give a fuck about my circumstances, subtlety never being their strong point.

I hadn't seen them since I was sentenced, but here they were again, stamping through the fallen Fall leaves like kids determined to kick the shit out that purple bastard, Barney.

They had chased me down and wanted to rain on my charade.

Chapter 2

"Well, if it's not Marcus Declan," said Sinsel. "How you doing?"

What was I going to say? 'Just dandy?' 'Fine as kind?' I chose the more obvious route.

"Fuck you."

"Now, now, Marcus," said Jackmann.

"Nice hedges," said Sinsel.

I ignored Sinsel's remark. The guy was always a Triple A dickwad.

"What do you want Jackmann?"

"You're getting out of here, at least for a day or so," Jackmann said. "You have to come with us. And please don't be a smart ass. We're not in the mood."

Chapter 3

I'd never seen prison guards snap to attention or shuffle their doughnut-addled midriffs so fast. Events, steel doors, the unique smell of jail-bird piss all became a blur as the agents took me from pillar to post, eventually arriving at a non-descript car outside the prison's main gates.

"You look bemused. Marcus," said Sinsel. "We're gonna let you meet some people and take a quick plane ride. So relax. You may be a free man soon. And, if you're a good boy, you might see a friendly face or two.

"You see Marcus, you've become rather important to the safety of our Nation. Fuck knows how or why. You always seemed to be a prick to me."

I had no choice. It was either compliance or incarceration. I had always been a failure at Conundrum 101, but now, it seemed, one prison cell had been exchanged for another. It would appear I had been ambushed by my past.

Chapter 4

I can't tell you how long the drive lasted. Dull suburban sub-divisions passed by until we reached an airfield.

I'm sure I heard Sinsel mutter something about a decommissioned Strategic Air Command airbase, but I couldn't be sure. I was too caught up in my own bizarre flights of fancy.

"Marcus," said Jackmann. "We're going on a trip."

Pointing to a Bombardier Global 500 in the distance, Jackmann continued in his best conspiratorial monotone.

"There's someone on that plane who wants to meet you."

My limo parked beside the G500 and we stepped from the car. Sinsel asked, "You OK? You look pale."

"I'm fine, I think," I said.

Chapter 5

As I boarded, the smell of luxury hit me first, then a voice.

"Mr. Marcus Declan, it's a pleasure to meet you. I'm Charles Lymes. Your country is in your debt. Oh, and I'm sure you recognize Dr. Baynard. Yes?"

"I need to throw up," I said.

Chapter 6

I moved her legs. 'Heavier than I remember,' I thought to myself as I walked to the window.

It was November and DC already had a blanket of snow.

"What's up with that?" I said. "Never snows in DC this time of year. Fucking global warming."

"Something wrong, honey?"

Ah, yes. My little fruit basket from last night had awoken.

"It's OK. Just gotta do something, honey. Go back to sleep. It's early."

I was in Teek Van Dyne's loft apartment overlooking Chesapeake Bay. He was my best friend. He was also about to become an unwitting foot soldier in the war against terrorism.

My conversation with Lymes, Jackmann, Sinsel and Baynard during our flight from New York had left a sordid embrace on my consciousness.

Lymes had asked me to assist the US Government in matters of national security, specifically to reveal the information I had gathered while in jail concerning a terrorist cell in Canada and its association with the events leading to 9/11.

Looking at Baynard, Lymes said, "Your time in prison has been spent profitably, Marcus."

I weighed my loyalties as an American against self-preservation and the clarion call of better judgment. I had made a deal with the

Government who, with great pleasure and, I suspected, a large dose of malice aforethought, had decided four years earlier to put my butt in jail. Sure, I'd dealt the cards and slept with the Devil before, but what had I gotten myself into this time?

Whatever the eventual outcome, Teek had to be protected from what I had become—a knowing and effective cog in the US's war machine against terrorism in general and Al Qeada in particular.

Chapter 7

I made my way through Teek's apartment. It was a journey of less than 45 steps from my previous evening's sexual conquest to my friend's den. I sat in his leather chair and pondered the concept of freedom that many Americans believe exists in our country. It was a mirage—every jailbird knows that—but sometimes a mirage is the only reality a man can cling to.

I refocused. This was a cluster fuck but the pinned hadn't been pulled. Yet.

I had gained the confidence of terrorists and had been betrayed. Now the Government wanted to know what I knew. But at what price? Lymes had promised me freedom in return for insight, but I wasn't too sure.

'You really are a stupid fucker, Declan,' I thought to myself.

The question was who were the players and who was getting played? Then it suddenly came to me. In this age, the keystroke is king, but did I have enough time to translate my knowledge via a web cam? Could something as easy as a camera save my ass or at least allow me to tell the truth ahead of my schedule with...well, who knows what.

I reached out to grab the marble desktop. It was cold as ice. I thought about what I needed.

I rummaged around Teek's desk for a web cam. I opened the desk drawer. A camera and a USB cable rolled around at the bottom. A wash of euphoria engulfed me having found what I needed. I moved the toggle of the camera to movie, plugged in the USB cord, and placed it on top of a stack of papers.

The stage was now set to tell the world my story. Would it be a blockbuster or a flop? This time I would tell the whole story, and not the amended version I gave to the government's emissaries Lymes, Jackmann and Sinsel and my jail confidant Baynard on the plane that brought me to DC.

My plan was to digitally record all of what I knew concerning Al Qeada, place it within a virus, encrypt it, and send it out to the world. In a few hours I was slotted to tell the heads of every major anti-terrorist organization in the US my story. Could I trust Lymes to keep his end of the bargain? I knew better. This recording was to be my insurance policy and last bastion of hope.

I focused on task at hand and started searching the Internet for what I needed—an encryption program. I was halfway there. The other piece could only come from one person, my favorite professor in college, Geoff Sondon — a computer genius and a guy that never seemed to sleep.

I had his e-mail address committed to memory, launched Outlook, and busted off a flurry of hopes.

Finally. A reply.

I sent a question to verify it was Sondon and not the Feds intercepting the communiqué. His answer verified it was truly him. I responded:

"Geoff, I don't have time to explain right now but I need a program that will break up an encrypted video file into 3 different parts with a public and a private key. The private key has to disassemble/ kill the virus just in case I want to stop it from being released across the entire Internet. I have the DOD-1024 256 bit encryption program, but what virus can I use to disseminate, split, and reassemble the video along with having the option to stop it if I want? Oh, and if that's not hard enough, I also need to give the virus an automatic execution/release date of 72 hours. Can we do this?"

I pressed 'send' and hoped for the best.

Chapter 8

The road was bumpy as DEA Agents Girder and Wilson traveled the long road back from the middle of nowhere Pennsylvania to DC. As they passed the mile marker for Monarch Ridge, VA, Wilson turned to his partner and said, "I think we only have another 40 minutes before we're home."

Girder's only response was silence. He had traveled this exact path hundreds of times only to return disappointed. His new partner's observation only deepened his frustration. After half an hour, Girder pulled into the subterranean parking garage at 700 Army Navy Drive in Washington—the DEA's HQ.

"We should've gotten a dolly," Girder griped as he popped the trunk and started unloading the vehicle of boxes full of evidence pertaining to an up-an-coming legal battle that has the blogosphere alight.

Wilson replied, "If the boxes are too heavy, maybe you should think about hanging it up early ol' timer."

Girder was three months out from retirement and working on what would probably be his last case: investigating the Mafia's involvement in the trafficking of prescription drugs.

During Girder's less-than stellar career spanning 30 years he had only one claim to fame, the one that kept the free booze flowing from the wide-eyed rookie agents: the arrest of Dr. Richard Baynard, a Yalie whom Girder suspected was a Mafia front to help them obtain synthetic heroin. And although Baynard was eventually fingered and Girder's part in his nemesis' arrest proved influential, the portly, grey-haired, Italian-American agent always felt embarrassed by what he considered a screw up on his failure to infiltrate the heart of the Mob.

Now he found himself teamed up with Wilson, a young hot shot just recently transferred from the from the Flagstaff office of the US Marshal Service.

Wilson had made his name going undercover for the Fugitive Investigations division of the Marshal Service to bust a biker gang trafficking Crystal Meth or, as it's known throughout the Midwest and Southern California 'ice' or 'glass'.

Wilson's undercover operation netted the largest meth seizure in US history, when $23 million worth of crystal meth was seized in an 18-wheeler on Route 66 just outside of the Grand Canyons' Cavern's airport. His undercover operation left the Latin MS 13 gang bereft of 500lbs. of pure profit.

For better or for worse, Wilson had become Girders' final opportunity for one final push against the Mob.

Chapter 9

Girder's landmark case—the one that kept him friendly with Jack or Jim—began in South Carolina where Baynard ran a successful pain management practice. Baynard was a first generation doctor but his life was now far removed from his childhood. He grew up in the meager hills of Tennessee in straightened circumstances but he often boasted that his family had been one of the biggest producers of illegal moonshine in the country and had been for generations. He wanted more so he went out and got it but he always remained close to his roots. His friends and family misunderstood Baynard's excellence in school.

Baynard attended Yale University after high school on a full scholarship and graduated summa cum laude. He also became a member of the elite fraternity Skull and Bones. After a stellar academic career, Baynard became Dr. Baynard after attending Yale Medical School. His field was pain management and was soon one of the leading specialists in the country.

Baynard was considered an unconventional doctor—something I believed stemmed back to his family's history of running white lighting and was the reason Baynard became a pain management specialist. His family was the first pain management specialists and Baynard continued his family's work.

I guess the old adage, 'You can take the boy out of the hills but you can never take the hills out of the man,' was never truer Baynard's case.

Christopher Prior

Despite his proclivity for atypical solutions to his patient's problems, Baynard's practice became renowned for 'Gregory House-type' solutions. However, he soon discovered nearly two-thirds of his patients, following prolonged use of pain medication, were developing stomach complications such as ulcers, Gastro Esophageal Reflux Disease (or GURD) and heartburn. He became convinced that either aspirin or ibuprofen (both of which are highly toxic to the lining of the stomach in large doses), were to blame for these potential life-threatening diagnoses. Baynard was so concerned about these side effects; he raised his concerns in a paper in the early 90's at a Pain Management Conference in Chicago.

At the time, the medical establishment ridiculed Baynard's thinking. They all debunked his assertions, opting for slow and steady as they go with the pills the medical profession was comfortable prescribing. This frustrated Barnard no end, prompting him to say at the conference, "The medical establishment is a slow moving cow across the field, and we all know what happens to cows they after they come back to the barn after grazing all day. They get eaten."

Little did he know a drug company, Purdew Pharmaceuticals located in Stamford, Connecticut, was about to develop a new form of synthetic heroin minus the ill-effects of previous medications such as Loratabs, Fentanyl, Oxycodone and others. It was called Oxyconttin. The Sachler's, who had owned the drug company since the late 1800's, approached Baynard with their case and their new 'miracle drug'. For Baynard, this new drug appeared to be medical nirvana and a solution to his professional fears.

Before long Purdew Pharmaceuticals made Baynard an offer he couldn't refuse as the company's sales went into the billions with the release of Oxyconttin. With what seemed undue haste, Baynard, by 1995 had a fellowship and a private plane at his disposal, as he became the public face of the new drug.

I remembered at United States Penitentiary (USP), Lorretto, when he told me he felt like a rock star. Purdew Pharmaceuticals even provided him with money to build a huge facility 'Complete Care' in South Carolina. He was now the crowned, 'King of Pain Management,' but the emperor was wearing no clothes. Oxyconttin was touted to be less addicting, although basically that was lie of the century. The pure nature of the drug created a class of super-addicts. Before Oxyconttin's release onto the market the average per captia use of opiates was 62 milligrams per person for the entire US. Just five years later the average dose rocketed to 629 milligrams.

Baynard's downfall began in 1998 in the hills of Tennessee when reporters started sniffing around a series of overdose deaths in Shelby County. While local authorities remained in a state of exhausted denial, Girder was brought in to throw fresh light upon the case that had become dubbed, "The Tennessee Ten."

Girder rarely found local law enforcement agencies to his liking. "Just too damned stupid," was his (often drunken) viewpoint and he became apoplectic when ordered to work a case in the countryside. The Tennessee Ten were making a mockery of this city boy's comfort zone.

Nevertheless, Girder's respect for old-school detective work, combined with an increasingly hateful desire to, "Get the fuck out of this shit hole," fed his curiosity. By talking to local residents and relatives of the deceased, Girder discovered two patients who overdosed—Florence Girth and Bonnie Stapleton—had received prescriptions directly from Baynard's Complete Care practice. Girder investigated the case purely because of the fact the women traveled from Tennessee to South Carolina to buy their drugs. "That's the damndest thing," he often thought to himself. To the best of Girder's knowledge there were 27 other places where these women could have had their prescriptions filled or had their medical conditions dealt with.

Girder flipped two of Baynard's patients who admitted to being the source of distribution of the drugs that led to the deaths. They admitted the doctors at the pain management clinic in South Carolina were fully aware they had no medical reason to be prescribed Oxyconttin but they were given prescriptions regardless. In short order, all the patients turned on the doctors, and the doctors, one by one, turned on Baynard. This was a textbook Federal prosecution and the Fed's wasted no time—Girder's case was solid. And even though Baynard himself had not written any of the prescriptions related to the deaths, he was fingered as the person behind all of the illegal distribution prescriptions as Girder would later self-righteously proclaim.

Following Baynard's conviction, Girder pleaded with his boss Frank Miller to let him continue his investigation. His boss asked the obvious question, 'Why?' Girder's response was that even though Baynard was headed to jail he still wanted to implicate the Mob, too. As far as Girder was concerned, Baynard was a prize-winning dick that wouldn't keep his mouth shut and would eventually screw up and tell someone in jail about the connection.

Miller relented. 'Give the old bastard one more chance at glory,' he thought and said, "Ok, go with it."

Girder's mind was not on the glory he would receive but on busting the Mob and getting drugs off the streets. His younger brother overdosed as a teenager and that was why he worked for the DEA and the reason he stubbornly made countless the trips to stalked the good doctor.

Chapter 10

However, Girder's latest surveillance sojourn had again netted him nothing. For six months, Wilson and Girder bugged Baynard's 'phone calls to his wife and kids and the myriad conversations with the criminals that encircled him on a daily basis by placing wires all of the areas in the prison where Baynard hung out. Girder was slowly coming to his senses: the investigation was going nowhere.

Flopping onto the couch in his office Girder noticed a sealed manila envelope. The handwriting was unmistakable. It was from his boss Miller.

"Shit," thought Girder. In his experience internal mail from the boss was rarely a good sign and today's missive proved no different: Girder's crusade was being "terminated" as of the end of the month. The seen-it-all-before vet had less than a week to prove Miller's initial skepticism wrong.

Oblivious to his partner's potential meltdown, Wilson brought up the final load of recorded tapes from the parking garage and saw the look on Girder's face. Wilson asked, "What's up?"

"They are shutting us down," Girder said.

Wracking his brain for any angle to revive this near cadaver of a case, he asked Wilson,

"How many tapes haven't we listened to?"

"Well we have this batch from Fort Dix," Wilson replied.

"What else?"

"We got those two trips back to South Carolina for Baynard's appeal."

Girder blew out a sigh of resignation. "No good. Baynard didn't talk to anyone in a county jail."

Wilson walked over to all the surveillance tapes from the previous six months. "What about these FCI Loretto? We never listened to any of those," Wilson offered hopefully.

Sensing his partner's rising sense of optimism, Girder cut him short. "That's because there weren't any wise guys housed there," he said. "The place is for meth chemists and stock brokers. That's all. Nothing for us there."

Wilson had had enough of the old man's griping and offered a last ditch suggestion. "Listen we only have six days until Miller shuts us down. I vote we revisit the Loretto tapes tonight."

Girder wearily nodded and pulled open the box. Each of them grabbed a tape, went to their respective desks and hit the tape recorder's play button.

Hours ticked by as they heard Baynard talking about what he ate for dinner, fights he saw in the yard—the usual mind-numbing minutiae that fills an inmate's daily life.

"Jail bullshit," stated Wilson as he pulled off his headphones and threw them on his desk.

At the same time, Girder lifted his finger in the air as if to quiet a particularly noisy five-year-old child.

Wilson said, "What? Do you have something?"

"I dunno," said Girder. "But our Bulldog's in his cell talking with someone about Al Qeada."

Girder quickly popped the tape from the machine and looked at the recording's date.

"This tape was recorded during Baynard's final week in Loretto. Grab the doc's transfer records," demanded Girder.

Wilson scrambled over to his desk and shuffled through the mountain of papers. Finally locating the documents, he handed them to Girder.

"What's on the fucking tape?" Wilson snapped.

Affecting what could only be described as his come to papa voice, Girder blurted, "Baynard is talking to this guy and he's telling Baynard about Al Qeada's next target."

"Are you serious?" Wilson said. "How the fuck did we miss this!"

"Who the fuck knows," responded a now highly animated Girder, "And yes, I'm dead fucking serious."

Chapter 11

Girder realized the information was credible because after 9/11 he was temporarily reassigned to the Joint Taskforce on Terrorism (JTT) to play up the drug angle for sleeper cells in the US.

Girder explained what the guy on the tape with Baynard was squealing about.

"Remember the Northeast power outage in 2003 when Michigan, Ohio, New York, New Jersey, Connecticut, Massachusetts and Ontario, were without power. The blackout left an estimated 55 million people literally in the dark. The official story was the Ottawa power facility was hit by lighting.

"But I know the real story. A Buffalo sleeper cell, or the Buffalo Six as we called them, was supposed to hit the Robert Moses Niagara Power Plant in Niagara Falls, N.Y. But after the authorities arrested them, a secondary cell from Hamilton, Ontario picked up where they left off. The second cell couldn't get into the US to hit the Niagara Falls Plant so they hit the Ottawa plant instead."

Girder checked the time. It was just after three in the morning when he picked up the phone and woke Miller up.

Still half asleep, Miller wearily ordered the agents to hand the tapes directly to Steven Foley, the Director of the CIA at the Langley by six that morning.

Amazed they hadn't been fired, Wilson and Girder continued to listen to the low, monotone voice of the unknown source. As the minutes crept towards their deadline, the partners became increasingly confident that the (as yet) unknown person in Baynard's cell had done what every government on the planet had tried to do since 9/11: successfully infiltrate Al Qeada.

Girder and Wilson packed up what they considered to be possibly the largest breach of Al Qeada to date and made their way to the Beltway.

The drive to Army Navy Drive & Fern Street, Arlington, took less than 20 minutes. As Wilson sat calmly beside him, Girder reflected on what may lay ahead.

Recalling his time with the CIA when he was part of the JTT, he'd always felt the CIA had a different take on the way the good fight should be fought. When working off American soil, the CIA bent or ignored local laws. This rubbed Girder the wrong way because he lived within those laws, often being forced to let criminals walk the streets free because of his own morality. He knew that every honest law enforcement officer during their career has their character tested, often forced to ask themselves, 'Do I bend the rules to make the bust?' The CIA made no such distinctions. They were an end-always-justifies-the-means kind of organization. "Pissants," spat Girder.

Girder and Wilson arrived at the Langley complex and after a series of ID checks, the guard directed them to swing around the guard booth and follow the red line to an underground concourse.

As Girder slammed the Suburban into park he noticed two armed sentries approaching the vehicle. As Wilson began to exit, Girder grabbed his partner's arm and pulled him back in. "I think that we should wait until these fine gentleman come to the car," he advised.

The sentries, now standing by the passenger's side of the car, motioned to Wilson to roll down his window.

The smaller of the two sentries said, "We know why you're here, but if you can wait in the car until your escort arrives it would be greatly appreciated."

Wilson quickly realized that it was clearly more of an order than a request and rolled up the window. The two DEA agents watched as their vehicle was inspected. The larger of the two sentries pounded on the back window and motioned to pop it open. Wilson obliged. Through the cabin the sentry spoke in a firm, demanding tone, "What's in the boxes?"

Just then the agents' escort arrived and yelled, "I'll take it from here boys."

Turning his attention to Girder and Wilson, he said, "OK, grab what you have and follow me."

The agents trailed the escort through the entrance, past the sentries, and into the elevator that began its descent—much to the agent's surprise. The assistant expressed his amusement with a wry smile and said, "Everyone assumes they're going up."

"Fucking pissant," thought Girder.

They finally stopped 20 floors down. The two agents were laden with a box each while Girder's load also contained an accordion-type legal folder. They exited the elevator and shadowed the assistant down the hallway and entered a conference room. They were instructed to sit and wait.

As Wilson fumbled through the tapes and Girder arranged his papers, a short fat man who leaned to one side, trusting a cane with a staffiture of the American eagle to support his ample frame, quietly but stiffly walked towards them. Girder was positive this gentleman had never attended any of the Taskforce pow-wows.

Now in his own warren of dreams and devious ways, CIA Operative Charles Lymes introduced his authority with a simple question, "So what is it that you have for me gentleman?"

Girder thumbed through his notes like a kid giving a presentation in high school, and explained they had come across an individual who claimed to have inside information regarding Al Qeada. Lymes sat unemotional as Girder explained what he and Wilson had unearthed.

After his presentation Girder patiently waited for Lymes' response. Wilson, however, had had enough of the pretense.

"So what do you think, sir?"

Lymes looked at Girder and said, "What makes these recordings creditable to you?"

Girder spoke up, "I was assigned to the JTT after 9/11. During one of the briefings the taskforce were instructed to keep confidential the fact that an Al Qeada sleeper cell in Canada was responsible for the Northeast power outage."

Lymes casually nodded both in agreement and acknowledgement. Girder continued, "But on the tape, sir, the man talking with Baynard tells the same story but gives insight to the fact the Canadian cell was only mobilized because the Buffalo Six cell had been exposed and arrested."

Wilson pushed the tapes to Lymes and said, "Listen for yourself."

Lymes's interest was now peaked. Thinking that maybe the agents had stumbled upon something valid, he pressed a button on his desk to summon his assistant. As Lymes' lackey popped the tape into the tape player, Girder and Wilson were asked to leave the room. "Mr. Lymes would like to listen in private now."

It would be three hours before the agents were summoned to return.

Lymes, immediately, upon their entrance said, "Have both of you listened to this tape?"

They replied in unison, "Yes."

"Who else has listened to them?" demanded Lymes.

"No one," Girder replied. "When I realized what we had uncovered I called my boss Frank Miller and here we are."

Lymes said, "You are not to disclose this to anyone. This material is highly sensitive and a matter of the highest order for national security."

Girder and Wilson nodded in agreement.

"So where is this Dr. Baynard now?" Lymes questioned.

Wilson said, "He's still in the Federal Bureau of Prisons (BOP) at the Fort Dix USP facility."

Lymes wrote it down and said, "I want to thank you for bringing this to my attention. I will take it from here. Please leave a copy of your credentials with my assistant."

Girder and Wilson were devastated. They had been politely cut out of the investigation.

Lymes picked up the phone and spoke, "Get me the head of the NSA and the Superintendent of the BOP."

As the agents exited the office, they witnessed Lymes tapping his pen, deep in thought. But Girder was sure he heard Lymes mumble, "Baynard? Why do I know that name?"

The assistant pointed to two sets of papers on the edge of his desk. "You must sign these before you leave. Please read them carefully."

The papers were stamped: 'NATIONAL SECURITY-CONFIDENTIAL,' and 'UNDER PENALTY OF TREASON.'

Through the door they overheard Lymes say, "Listen, I have tapes confirming an insider in Al Qeada. I need you down here now."

The assistant went to close the door. He turned back to the agents and handed them pens. "What you've just overheard is also covered under those gag orders you're signing," he said.

"Goddamn fucking pissants," muttered Girder as his career hit the brick wall he had become so familiar with.

Chapter 12

FBI Director Bryan Greene paced the situation room where he was overseeing a hostage negotiation in New York via satellite. The agent in charge was a colleague and a close friend, Clarence 'Shooter' Jackmann. Greene's assistant approached his side. "This just arrived for you, sir," she said.

Greene replied, "This better be important."

She handed him an envelope, it read 'FOR YOUR EYES ONLY—TOP SECRET.' Greene immediately knew it was from the NSA.

He took the file and swiftly moved to his office. He rarely, if ever, received packages directly from the NSA.

Greene opened the package and emptied its contents. Out spilled a letter that read, 'RE: Unknown prison inmate has credible information relating to Al Qeada. He has infiltrated a verified sleeper cell.'

Greene pondered the 'RE:' if this was credible, it could be the break he had been searching for since he was named Director two years ago. Penetrating a terrorist cell was the law enforcement community's Holy Grail.

His assistant came back into his office and stated the situation in New York demanded his immediate attention. 'This palatable Al Qeada information would have to wait,' he thought.

The New York crisis centered around James Trishaw. Intel had discovered he was unemployed, facing foreclosure and in trouble with the IRS. "Usual shit," was all Greene could say as he surveyed the man's hapless situation.

However, Trishaw, on this fine morning, had entered the Federal Reserve Bank in Lower Manhattan claiming to be a suicide bomber.

"That fucker," as Greene now called him, had barricaded the front doors and locked down the building. He was holding 73 people hostage.

Greene reentered the crisis center only to hear the cackle of Jackmann's voice coming through speakers, "I'm going in."

Greene screamed, "Stop him! For Christ's sakes."

It was too late. Jackmann had made his move, he was past the barricades and was at the front entrance.

Shooter was addicted to being an agent. It gave him the same rush as when he was an Olympic wrestling hopeful while at Northwestern University in '92 before a back injury put an end to his dreams.

Jackmann's partner, Nathan Sinsel, was a former Navy Seal in the late 90's but after a stint in Somalia and North Africa he had had enough with pointless missions. He loved the work he did as a soldier but he felt like he was more the strong arm for big oil than for the American people interests. So he left the military naive with a feeling of underused bravado. He felt the FBI could feed his need for adrenaline but at the same time release him from the pointless devastation.

Sinsel's partner was now perched at the front door of the bank. Trishaw yelled, "Get the fuck back, mother fucker." Jackmann pushed through the barricaded turnstile doors and into the foyer; he was now face to face with the perpetrator.

Jackmann placed his gun on the foyer floor to put James at ease. They spoke for nearly 45 minutes before ice packed on the roof of the building shifted and fell to the street below, startling the already shaky perpetrator.

He yelled, "You lied. You're just trying to distract me while those bastards out there try to kill me."

Shooter tried to reason with the man but it was to no avail. He witnessed the man's desperation. But when Shooter saw the anger leave the perpetrator's face and turn to a pleasurable acceptance he knew what was coming next.

Greene could only look on via the satellite on the internal cameras and assume he was about to witness his friend's death. The situation room became eerily quiet.

Shooter focused on the detonator in the man's hand. A wire ran down the course of his arm to his chest. For the first time Jackmann could see the bomb and, perversely, saw his chance. He reached for his service weapon on his leg and drew up on the man. Trishaw's thumb pressed down on the plunger as Jackmann squeezed off a round. The bullet missed and ricocheted off the foyer's marbled walls. The plunger sank and nothing happened.

Trishaw and Jackmann glared at one another in surprise. James, realizing the bomb was a dud, lunged at Jackmann with a knife. Shooter quickly squeezed off another round, this time at the man's knees. The second shot found its mark. As the man fell, the knife nicked Jackmann's left arm as he cuffed the would-be terrorist.

Greene was livid. As he watched the action unfold, his mind returned to the envelope waiting for his attention.

He looked for the signature of the sender, Charles Lymes. Greene had heard the name before. Lymes was a legend with nearly 50 years in the intelligence business. He started in the early 60's. Recruited by the CIA, Lymes was known as a cowboy in the Beltway, but his service record was a laundry list of successful operations.

Greene picked up the phone and dialed.

Chapter 13

Green next called his agents in NYC. Sinsel handed Jackmann the phone and said, "It's Greene and he's pissed," as the paramedics tended to his partner's arm.

The Director laid into Jackmann but the agent wasn't in the mood for a scolding. Instead, he half-turned the phone away from his ear and walked to his car with Sinsel. Halfway there Jackmann stopped and pressed the phone close to his ear trying to hear over the commotion. Jackmann flipped the phone closed and addressed Sinsel, "We're headed to DC immediately."

"Why?" Sinsel asked.

"We're getting a promotion," Jackmann said.

"Promotion?"

Jackmann tossed the keys, with his good arm, to Sinsel and said, "You drive and I'll explain on the way.

As his partner explained the impetus for their quick departure, all Sinsel could really think about was the Director's secretary, Terry Dell. They had met before—a brief, flirtatious evening at Komi at Dupont Circle that Sinsel hoped would end with them both in their birthday suits. He was new to civilian life and all the codes that melt within the Beltway's existence. He wanted her badly that night but it ended in nothing more than a failed mission. She was the one that got away.

Chapter 14

Shooter and Sinsel arrived at the J. Edgar Hoover FBI Building and made their way to the 14th floor where they were met by Sinsel's love potential interest, Terry Dell, and asked to wait. She was what guys in college term a "Butter Face." Jackmann rolled his eyes at his partner's sober version of beer goggles.

Greene appeared and barked, "The two of you in my office. Now. And Sinsel. Keep your hands off my secretary."

Jackmann and Sinsel trailed the Director into his office. Greene pulled his chair close to the desk and tossed the envelope from the CIA to Jackmann.

Greene said, "Shooter, what you have in your hands could quite possibly be the largest break in terrorism known, and the source, if you can believe it, it's locked up somewhere in the BOP, we think."

Sinsel asked, "So, who is the source?"

Greene answered, "That's just it. We don't know, and that's why I'm giving you two a promotion. Charles Lymes, from the CIA, requested I put my two best agents on this; I need you to find the source. Don't screw it up. There are a lot of eyes on this one.

"The break was uncovered by two DEA agents surveilling a Dr. Richard Baynard. They stumbled across this while working a case trying to link the Mob to the illegal distribution of prescription narcotics. Their investigation recorded a conversation between the doctor and an unknown individual. This individual, who ever he is, has

Christopher Prior

creditable information relating to the Buffalo Six terrorists and other cells left out of the sweep in Buffalo."

"Shooter, you were in Buffalo during the sweep right?" Greene questioned.

"Yeah, I was."

"That's the reason I choose you and your partner. You know the players and Sinsel has dealt with the CIA in Afghanistan and Operation Desert Storm. That's it boys, you're to meet with Charles Lymes, a heavy hitter within the Company. He's a fucker so if he offers to shake your hand, just be sure to count your fingers afterwards. Good luck gentlemen."

Chapter 15

Jackmann and Sinsel arrived at the CIA around 40 minutes after leaving J. Edgar Hoover Building on Pennsylvania Avenue. They walked into the marble entrance noticing the gold stars on the wall representing the agents who had given their lives in the line of duty.

They made their way to the reception desk, checked in and after a wait of 15 minutes, were finally escorted to the office of Lymes.

His office had neither a name plate nor department heading. This made both of them uneasy. Their escort swiped his badge and the lock popped. The door opened and the agents were directed down a hallway. Suddenly a voice crackled in a garbled tone, "Please come in." It was Lymes.

"So you two are the best agents Director Greene has? Sit down and tell me what you know."

Jackmann briefly reiterated what Greene had told them just an hour ago.

Lymes added, "The asset, this unknown person speaking with Baynard, is the source. He either befriended them in jail, knows the terrorists themselves, or shit maybe he has international dealings in the Middle East. As a precautionary measure I had Baynard transferred this morning to United States Penitentiary (USP) Administrative Maximum Facility (ADMAX) in Florence, Colorado to prevent him from contacting anyone. The BOP was not informed as to the rationale behind his transfer, so let's keep it that way."

Florence is a supermax prison. It is unofficially known as the Alcatraz of the Rockies. It houses the prisoners who are deemed the country's most dangerous and in need of the tightest control.

Florence was constructed as a response to two incidents that occurred on October 22, 1983, in which inmates murdered their escorting corrections officers at the United States Penitentiary in Marion, Illinois. Relatively lax security procedures allowed each prisoner, while walking down a hall, to turn to the side and approach a particular cell so an accomplice could unlock his handcuffs with a stolen key and provide him with a knife. Two officers were killed in two separate incidents by this tactic.

"The DEA recorded the conversation at the FCI Loretto. Here is a list of all the inmates who were incarcerated with Baynard at the time. The source could still be in BOP custody so tread lightly."

Looking directly at Jackmann, Lymes simply said, "This is my operation, so no cowboy bullshit like you pulled up in Manhattan. Understood?"

Lymes slid some papers across to Jackmann and said, "Here is a work up on the voice of the unknown inmate. The voice analysis and our linguists have determined the source is from the Midwest, Upstate New York, or Ohio.

"It's the real deal, gentlemen. This person knows the players, the targets, and the training facilities here, in Europe, the Middle East and South East Asia. He knows Al Qeada. We need him found."

Chapter 16

Jackmann and Sinsel returned to FBI Headquarters to report to Greene. The ideas swirled around the room as Greene called into to his office two extra agents—Duffy and McGovern soon stood beside their colleagues. Greene made the decision to split up the work load.

As Jackmann and Sinsel left Greene's office to track down know associates at the Federal Correctional Institute (FCI) Loretto and Duffy and McGovern would head out to see if Baynard's well was dry or not.

As all four of them left their only order was, "Keep me in the loop, boys. I don't trust Lymes or the CIA and neither should you!"

They headed to the FCI in Loretto PA, Shooter knew that it would be a four hour journey. Plenty of time to ponder the whys and wherefores' of the CIA handing over a juicy lead like this.

Greene for once was right thought Jackmann. Lymes couldn't be trusted.

Sinsel drove, Shooter pondered as to why the CIA would hand over their best lead. While Lymes knew something he didn't.

It took six hours to arrive with a multitude of near death experiences. On more than one occasion Jackmann grabbed the O-shit handle above his right arm.

Shift change was occurring at the prison when they arrived. They sat at the front gate for twenty minutes; it was nearly 1 AM on Nov. 25th, almost a day after the discovery by the DEA of an al Qeada insider.

The agents knew that arriving at the prison at this late hour would make the Warden, Teddy Ackerman, suspicious. They had their goal and were under strict orders not to divulge the nature of the investigation. But if Ackermann did harbor any suspicions he hid them well. The dynamic duo were greeted like old friends as walked into Ackerman's office.

"So this must be important if you two risked life and limb to get here in this shit storm?" the Ackerman said. "This is the most snow we've had all season.

"Your boss, Director Greene, informed me that you would be coming, but he didn't give me any details."

"I'm sorry, sir. But we can't give you anymore than what the Director gave you," Jackmann replied apologetically.

"So how can I help you?"

"We're looking for an inmate that was here about six months ago, a Dr. Richard Baynard," Sinsel said.

"But Baynard is no longer here. So that leads me to ask you 'why are you two here?'"

Considering, the hour, thought Jackmann, it was a pretty good question, "Baynard came up in an open investigation of gang activities and we're looking at each of the facilities Baynard has been housed in. We think he may be part of the Bloods."

"Baynard? I remember him. We don't get a lot doctors here. He ran our Higher Learning Program and he cleaned my office. The guy was like 50 years old. I find it hard to believe he was involved in gang activities, especially the Bloods."

"Yes sir, that was our initial reading of the situation, too, but we believe he is and we need to speak with any inmates that were friends of Baynard's and any correctional officers that oversaw him," Jackmann said.

"The doctor, huh? If he was involved in gang activities at this prison, it would be in his file," the Warden pulled Baynard's file and handed it to Jackmann. "As for questioning the inmates, that will have to wait until morning—lights out was at midnight. The first count is at 5:30 AM. You can question whomever you like then,"

"Okay sir. Who's in charge of surveillance here at the facility?" Sinsel asked.

"That would be Captain Keger, but he doesn't arrive until first count,"

"Look, you guys have already had a rough trip. Why don't you catch a couple hours of sleep here and you can do what you need to do in the morning."

Although the thought of being so close to the people who would gladly eviscerate them in a blink of an eye was an uncomfortable one, the agents were in no mind to argue with the invitation and wearily followed Ackerman. The Warden showed them to two cells in the prisoner segregation wing. "I know it's not the best accommodation, but it will save you from having to travel 50 miles to the nearest hotel in Hollidaysburg."

Chapter 17

In the morning Sinsel and Jackmann met with Keger. The plac-ard on the door read, 'Inmate Supervision and Discipline, Captain Keger.' Sinsel knocked on the door and Jackmann opened it.

Keger welcomed them form behind his desk. "Good morning agents Jackmann and Sinsel, how'd you sleep?"

Jackmann had a knot in his back the size of mount McKinley, and Sinsel's eyes could barely focus.

"Not too good sir," said Jackmann, "We actually feel like shit I can't believe these guys here sleep of those mattresses."

"Any chance you've got coffee Captain?" Sinsel asked.

"All in good time boys, now then the Warden left me a list of the things you two are after. I've arranged for you to meet with Baynard's immediate supervisor from the school, a civilian teacher, who over-saw Baynard, the C.O. in charge of Baynard's housing unit, and the custodial supervisor Baynard worked for," the Captain stated.

"You know I ran Baynard's name through the gang affiliation program and I got nothing. So, in an effort to better assist you, I have asked our surveillance coordinator to bring up all the tapes of the common areas, yard, and hallways, while Baynard was here. It's prob-ably 5,000 hours of tape."

"So where do you want to start?" Sinsel asked Jackmann. He replied, "At the beginning, let's go right down the list."

Over the next four hours they questioned civilians, custodial staff, and the C.O.'s who oversaw Baynard on a daily basis.

Jackmann and Sinsel quickly learned the civilians, C.O.'s, and inmates were useless. None of the inmates who admitted to knowing Baynard fit the profile they had from Lymes. They headed back to Keger's office with nothing.

"Any luck?" the Captain asked, already assuming they had none.

"Nope. We're going to have to watch the surveillance tapes," Jackmann replied.

The Captain got up from behind his desk and asked the agents to follow him to the video surveillance room.

A civilian technician ran the department and he explained how the system worked. As Keger left the agents, Sinsel let out a sigh. It was a daunting task.

The hours ticked by as Jackmann and Sinsel scrutinized the tapes. Each time they saw Baynard they printed a hard copy of the shot tape. After four hours, they amassed an enormous stack of print-outs.

The agents had what they needed and left the surveillance room. For the next two hours the agents peppered Captain Keger for information on the inmates in the pictures with Baynard.

Most notably, they had questions about a tall, thin white man with glasses who appeared about 50 years old, a heavily tattooed skinhead about 40 or so, and a twenty-something kid who resembled Clark Kent.

"It could be any of them," Sinsel said, "especially Superman."

Oblivious to his partner's sleep deprived cynicism, Jackmann continued to stare at the grainy black and white images before his eyes. "Who's this?" he said pointing to Baynard's bespectacled friend.

By now Keger was bored and deep within his renowned couldn't careless attitude. Squinting at the picture, Keger yawned, "That's Jack Halford. He's one of your FBI agents."

Jackmann's suspicions were dead on. "He's one of ours? Why was Halford undercover?"

"I don't ask too many questions when you guys place somebody in my prison, so I don't know. Maybe you two can solve that particular conundrum, but as for the other guy, I have no idea. Why don't you ask Baynard?" replied Captain Keger.

"I think that's exactly what we'll do, replied Jackmann."

Chapter 18

Jackmann and Sinsel return from Pennsylvania at 5:00 AM in the nation's capitol. Agents Duffy and McGovern would follow shortly about a half hour later with their report on Dr. Baynard.

All four made a b-line to their Greene's office only to see an open desk with their boss nowhere in sight. Instead they were greeted by Operative Charles Lymes sitting in a couch to the right of the Greene's vacant desk. The two agents brought Lymes up to speed as they frantically searched though computer databases for the whereabouts of Scrog and then it hit Jackmann. It was a bolt from the blue and blast from the past. The guy in the picture was Marcus Declan, but skinnier, so he couldn't be sure. There was something about that Clark Kent look that struck a chord. Jackmann put his name into the database, too.

They discovered Declan first but they were out of luck. He had been released from BOP custody six months earlier and to further confuse the situation there was no indication as to his whereabouts now.

Jackmann recalled Declan also had State prison time to do in New York. But, as he hoped, if Declan's time had been run consecutively instead of concurrently with his Federal time, it was possible he was already out. Jackmann put a call into the New York District Attorney to look up the information on Declan's New York conviction.

He slammed the phone down. "He's not in for another hour."

They turned their attention to finding Scrog. The BOP database didn't have him listed as being an inmate. So they were stuck again. Lymes, fed up with this quartet of stupidity, decided to get it from the horse's mouth. He immediately called to wake up the US Attorney Matthew Yota to obtain information on Scrog's conviction.

Yota told him that it would be about 20 minutes until he could get access that info. As they awaited the return call they were sorely disappointed after Yota told them there were no records or case file for him. Lymes apologized for waking the US Attorney, who was now in his office in sweats by slamming the phone back on the receiver never waiting for a response from the man he just woke up.

They were stuck and didn't know what to do. They had surveillance photos of Scrog from FCI Loretto, but there was no record of him ever having been there. Sinsel said, "What did this guy do, just up and disappear?"

Greene entered his office and asked, "What's up?" While Jackmann got his boss up to speed, McGovern and Duffy ambled in. "Baynard knows who's in the pictures but won't talk unless we tell him why we want to know," said Duffy.

Greene mused upon Duffy's information for a moment and then asked, "So what's up with this Declan?"

"We have to wait until six before the New York DA, Linus MacManus, gets to his office then we'll have Declan's records."

Greene then asked, "What about this mystery Scrog guy?"

"That's just it," said Sinsel. "We can't find him anywhere. No arrest record, no conviction record and, he's not in BOP custody."

"Well the guy just didn't go up in smoke," Greene said. The word smoke triggered something within Jackmann. His mind, purely by training, went into out of the box thinking. He knew most of the time the answer is usually right in front of you. He thought 'smoke' and leading him to his college days and of the ridiculous assertion that Bill Clinton, 'didn't inhale' when even Jackmann himself had partaken.

"I got it," he said.

"Got what?" Greene asked.

"I bet Scrog is DEA. Who else besides the FBI has the authority to place informants in the BOP?"

Lymes called Girder to see if he could shed some light on the situation. The call went straight to voice mail and Lymes wasn't the type to leave a message.

Jackmann got a hold of MacManus and had Declan's location: Butler Correctional Facility, outside of Syracuse, NY.

Not surprisingly, Girder returned Lymes call post haste. After listening to Girder's info the agent was dismissed with a calm, 'Goodbye and thank you for all of your help' after about three minutes. Charles then informed his attentive audience, "Scrog was a DEA plant sent in to investigate the prison."

"That means Declan has to be our man," Jackmann said with relief.

"What about Baynard?" Duffy asked.

"We won't use him unless we have to," Greene said.

Again the name Baynard triggered something in Lymes' mind. He knew only one person with that last name but it must have been 30 years ago. He had a feeling it had to be the same person. It was far too much of a coincidence. Lymes asked for a photo of Baynard from McGovern, he studied the photo it was the same man.

Lymes then told the group, "I'll deal with Baynard and you guys grab Declan."

Greene called the warden of Butler prison work camp, Gerald Toth, and told him he wanted Declan segregated immediately.

"No can do," Toth informed Greene. "Butler Correctional did not have a segregation unit. But there are parole hearings later today."

Toth explained if Declan was placed on the call out to see the parole board he would be pulled from his work detail and would be as isolated as the warden could make him.

Greene had no other option than to agree to the warden's work around.

Chapter 19

The dawn of November 25th had already cracked open the dark clouds over the Potomac when Jackmann and Sinsel found themselves once again in the company of Greene and Lymes.

As they filed their verbal report, Greene quietly accessed the database Halford was actually Phillip Stayton who was incarcerated in FCI Loretto to gather information on medical staff having sex with the inmates.

Greene dialed Stayton's handler in the Baltimore, MD office and was soon informed Stayton was back out on assignment. This time he was in Texas another federal penitentiary.

"Place him in segregation," ordered Greene. "I've two agents would like to talk to him."

Greene now summoned Duffy and McGovern into his office. As they arrived, he spoke, "Jackmann and Sinsel, you two get moving on Stayton, Lymes and I will get these two up to speed."

It was 10PM when Jackmann and Sinsel boarded an FBI plane to Texas. Meanwhile Duffy and McGovern flew to USP Florence ADMAX in Colorado where Baynard was sequestered.

Duffy and McGovern studied Baynard's case file and the information Greene, Lymes and the DEA had uncovered. They planned on breaking Baynard's silence.

Upon arriving at Florence, they both realized this was no regular prison. It was an ominous penitentiary. Prisons are built to restrain the body but this facility was designed to handicap the mind. Duffy and McGovern followed their escort to Baynard's cell.

Baynard appeared visibly frazzled. The solitary confinement ill prepared him for visitors yet alone those intent on interrogation.

As the agents question Baynard, it was clear, that although the doctor knew the persons in the pictures but he was unwilling to divulge their names. Baynard repeatedly interrupted the agents and demanded to know why he was placed at Florence.

Baynard angrily proposed a deal.

"Tell me why you need to know the names, and then I'll tell you."

All three had reached an impasse. The agents had no authority to expose that information. While Baynard reminded defiant, Duffy and McGovern went out empty handed.

Meanwhile in Texas, Jackmann and Sinsel were sitting with Agent Stayton at FCI Big Springs. Jackmann slid the printouts of Baynard from Loretto to Stayton. One by one Stayton ran through the pictures. Then finally there came the break.

"These last two hung around Baynard all the time," Stayton said. "The skinhead knew Baynard from Tennessee, I think. He grew up where the Doctor did or something like that. He had this crazy garble when he talked. I think he got stabbed in his throat. His name was Billy something, Billy Scrog. I think?"

"Okay, what about our Superman guy?" questioned Jackmann.

"Where the Hell was he from?" Stayton thought aloud, "Maybe Upstate New York or thereabouts. Wow, that's kinda weird that you referred to him like that 'cause that's exactly what everyone called him, Superman," Stayton replied.

"Do you remember this 'Superman' guy's real name?" Sinsel asked impatiently. Without a second's hesitation, Stayton replied, "It was Declan. Yeah, Marcus Declan was his name."

"You're sure?" Jackmann asked, almost pleading for it to be a mistake.

"Yeah, I'm sure. Why?"

Sinsel butted in, "Because Declan was the stockbroker Jackmann here busted about a year ago on stock fraud and embezzlement. He was from Upstate New York."

Jackmann studied the picture more carefully again and thought, 'That guy's too buff compared to the fat bastard I arrested. Shit, he must've weighed 320 pounds then.'

Sinsel moved on, "Did you ever hear Baynard talk about Al Qeada?"

Stayton replied, "Al Qeada? No. I never heard him say anything of that nature."

"What about Scrog or Declan?" Jackmann asked.

"No. But I remember my handler sending me a memo regarding the two terror cell guys from Upstate New York who were transferred to Loretto while I was there. The memo read something along the lines of keep a close eye on them along with my other investigation of the medical staff," Stayton replied.

It was long past midnight when Jackmann and his partner thanked Stayton for his help. They had something to go on now.

Chapter 20

Lymes studied the security shot photos of Baynard from his cell at Loretto and other various areas of the prison. The CIA's most trusted spook was 99.9% positive it was the same man he knew 30 years ago and took his time dissecting Baynard's case file as they prepared to fly to Colorado with McGovern and Duffy. The assistant rarely saw his boss ogle files in this manner, he was sure there was a connection between his boss and this doctor but he didn't dare ask. He knew better.

Greene had no such qualms though. He intruded into Lymes's intense dissection of the file and asked, "So what's the deal? You have the look that says you know this guy?" The assistant awaited his boss's response to the question he never dare ask.

"Yes, very precocious of you, Greene," Lymes growled and left the mystery hanging for a moment. As a top dog spook, Lymes liked to keep his dirty laundry to himself but also liked to elaborate on his own self importance.

"I liked him, his eyes were intense," Lymes explained, "There was something about him. I encountered him in Africa when he was recruited from Yale and rose to the rank of general in the Rhodesian Army. Seeing Greene's incredulous look, Lymes took pity on the boy—a monumental effort for a man so devoid of charm.

"I know, Greene. I know. But you must remember these were the days when our country's best and brightest headed to ease their yen for the Yen or, in this case, Baynard's preference for the Rhodesian Pound."

A smile came across Lymes' thin, rapacious lips as he cleared Greene of any further misconceptions.

"Baynard took the road less traveled. He returned from New Haven, Connecticut from first year at Yale with an idea implanted in his brain, by Wilfred Derbick, a highly decorated, ex-Special Air Service (SAS) officer. If there's one thing the Brits know how to do well is kill their enemies. They've been adept at various forms of covert ops since the damn Crusades."

As far as Lymes was concerned, the SAS, a highly secretive military group, was just another Limey group of troubadours who reveled in their lineage of comfortable assassinations.

Lymes continued, "Derbick trolled Yale and other Ivy League schools for recruits for the Rhodesian Army. They had plenty of soldiers but few officers and with Derbick's promise of great riches and power Baynard was sold. Drunk on the vision of becoming mercenaries, Baynard put his desire to become a doctor on hold to fulfill his dreams with his buddies."

"Baynard researched Rhodesia and found that Cecil Rhodes was someone to be admired. Rhodes grew up poor just like Baynard but still some how managed to found the DeBeers Mining Company by sheer will and initiated the Rhodes scholarship at Oxford. Cecil Rhodes was a 'Robber Barron' of the first order building empire of wealth and power through diamond and gold mining by creating a mining monopoly in Africa. He eventually amassed enough power and money to establish his own country from what was once part of Zimbabwe, hence the name Rhodesia. Baynard, like any man, had dreamed a similar dream and Rhodesia offered Baynard the excitement that was lacking at Yale. Lymes's trip down memory lane had longer legs—he decided to paint the picture of the world back in the 60's and 70's for his enraptured audience of one.

"In the hippie and disco years Africa was in disarray along with the rest of the world especially the UK. The UK had huge economic problems caused by a large trade deficit, a currency disaster, the 1973 oil crisis created by Organization of the Petroleum Exporting Countries (OPEC) and the topper was the UK government for lack of a better way to put it had become the economy. Nearly 60% of all people work for the government.

"They were forced to borrow five billion dollars from the International Monetary Fund (IMF) to keep the country afloat and caused high inflation and a recession.

"So with the UK too caught up with their own problems, the US decided to capitalize on unstable nature of the situation along with others. Making matters worse the Rhodesian government enacted Unilateral Declaration of Independence (UDI) and created a civil war in 1965 that lasted till 1979.

"Vis-a-vie I was placed in Africa. The CIA saw an unbelievable opportunity. So the UK who had dominated the continent since the colonization of the southern tip of Africa in 1652 was now forced to suppress the civil war. The central part Africa was turned into the Wild Wild West.

"Rhodesia had become a haven for expatriates. Seventy years after Cecil Rhodes' death there was still plenty of money to be made over the control of diamonds and gold.

"Baynard's intellect and the backing of his childhood buddies allowed him to move up the ranks quickly. But it wasn't until he became a general in the Rhodesian Army that he landed on the CIA's radar screen.

"I watched as Baynard won battle after battle but on one occasion he and his troops were set up to take heavy losses in southern Rhodesia just outside Salisbury for lack of any intelligence agencies at his disposal. This was something I could not let happen given our, the US's, interests so I stepped in. So I sent a surveillance packet of rebel movements to Baynard detailing for him the forces he was up against. They outnumbered Baynard's men 20-1.

"Baynard now realized he was undermanned and out gunned. He devised a pretty clever plan. He had his men dig foxholes and covered them with local foliage. Baynard's plan was to allow the rebels to pass and attack them from behind. It was a risky plan but I liked it. So I monitored the situation from my CIA headquarters on the other side of the city of Salisbury.

"Little did Baynard know that if he was defeated in the battle, the CIA's operations in central Africa would be placed in jeopardy. So as a precaution I sent in helicopter gunships to the area just in case things got ugly.

In the battle, Baynard was shot and required medical attention. His first lieutenant, a native Rhodesian, radioed for help but Baynard was near death. Meanwhile I had intercepted the communiqué and order one of the gunships to pick me up so I could extract Baynard myself. It seems like yesterday."

After regaling Greene, Duffy and McGovern with his exploits in Africa that would make Conrad shudder, the plane to Colorado was ready. Lymes shook Greene's hand and told him, "If this is the same man I knew 30 years ago, I'll get what we need."

"I hope so. I hope so."

Chapter 21

Lymes reflecting on his own sense of purgatory, I had reached the prison's admin building and waited for the parole board to begin. Trying to stay focused, I visualized my old life before jail, and what it would take to get back to even. There were so many aspects of my pervious life I had to face, if or when I got out.

To my left sat Cisco, a Puerto Rican from Brooklyn. He was 43 and had spent more time spent in jail than anyone else I crossed paths within the system. He was a Latin King, the largest and most organized Hispanic street gang in the United States and a lifer. Cisco was one of those guys that obviously loved jail.

Next to Cisco was a white guy. From the look of him he was definitely a pedophile or what inmates called a 'tree jumper'. In jail everyone knows who the pedophiles are by their haircuts. The prison barbers purposely fuck up their hair so they can easily be identified and beat up.

Across from us was a young black kid who was definitely heading home. The board always let the young ghetto kids go. They knew they would be back in the system soon on another charge. It was funny to me. Freedom came easy to the young street thugs. They thought they were getting out, but what they were really getting was a chance to tighten the rope around their necks. It was job security for the penal system.

Next to him was a 60 year old white guy with nine convictions for drunk driving. There was no way he was getting out.

Christopher Prior

Cisco said to me, "Superman, you're goin' home. You're one of those 'one time' dudes they send upstate. I've seen it thousands of times. They always send you 'white collar' motherfuckers home."

Since the age of 17 Cisco had spent no more than a year on the street before getting locked up again. There had to be some weight to what he was saying. My expectations rose.

As with all the others, a C.O. exited the parole hearing room and called my name. On the surface I looked cool but inside, my blood was pumping. I thought to myself, "Best for last, right?" I squeezed past the corpulent C.O. towards my possible freedom.

Chapter 22

For Lymes, uncertainty was as distasteful as cheap, motel room toilet paper. Over the years he had interrogated hundreds of 'assets', confident of achieving what he would casually call, "The 'correct' outcome." None like this one, though the flight to Colorado gave time to reflect. He knew Baynard personally and the thought made him uncomfortable.

After landing at Fremont County Airport he descended the plane's steps with agents Duffy and McGovern, he allowed himself a subdued grin. Was this the time to take a trip back to his 'glory days', or was he about to meet a career-ruining playmaker.

Those thoughts played on his mind as he arrived at Baynard's cell and was face to face with the man whose life he had saved 30 years earlier.

Dispensing with formalities, Lymes blustered, "Dr. Baynard, how are you today?"

Baynard couldn't care less. Engrossed in a book that made him think of home named Blood & Whiskey: The Life and Times of Jack Daniel, he remained in bed with his back to his guest. Slowly, he turned to see who was speaking. Adjusting the only pair of glasses he owned, he replied, "Round two, huh? You might as well just turn around. And three of you? What'd you think, three's the charm?"

There was only one place to sit in the cell, a stool attached to the white iron desk adjacent to Baynard's bed. Lymes parked himself on the desk, accidentally knocking over some of the doctor's toiletries. Baynard took issue with this lack of respect and sized up the man sitting across from him.

"So, you came in here to knock my shit all over the floor? Is that how you get your rocks off?" Baynard growled.

"Actually, I'm here to take you down memory lane," Lymes said.

"It's obvious you don't remember me. Not surprising really, considering the shit storm I rescued you from. But I remember you, Doctor. I remember you as a man who didn't need any fucking toiletries. I remember you as a killer and leader of men."

"I never killed anyone in my life," Baynard spluttered, assuming this odd little man was referring to the 'Tennessee Ten'.

"The guy I knew led thousands," Lymes said in a proud tone. The voice now sounded familiar, but Baynard still could not place it.

Lymes read Baynard's mind and explained, "The years have treated you better than they have treated me. That's why you can't place me. But I'm sure you remember the CIA gunships that saved your ass."

Baynard's memory made knelt before this old white man.

"You were in Rhodesia?"

"So you remember me now, General. I was the one who ordered CIA forces to extract you," Lymes said.

"You were in the helicopter that grabbed me? You're CIA?"

Lymes smiled and pulled out a digital voice recorder, placed it beside himself and said, "This is the reason I had you moved here."

Lymes tapped the face of the tape recorder and pressed play.

Ten minutes later, Baynard made the connection, nodded to Lymes and said, "I remember the conversation. That's Marcus Declan."

Lymes settled into a less uncomfortable position and waited for the pleading to begin.

"So what happens now?" Baynard asked. "Do I get to get out of this place? If you already have the tape why do you need me?"

If Lymes' grin was subdued previously, he now allowed himself a full-on malevolent grimace.

"You see, my friend, intelligence value drops when it's disseminated and unfortunately for you, you're in the know, and that makes you a liability."

Lymes continued, "To answer your question, you're coming with me. But what happens later depends on Declan."

"Quid quo pro, only less so," thought Baynard as Lymes motioned him out of the cell. The doctor obliged and as they walked the hallway to the entrance of the prison, Lymes turned to the doctor. "Why didn't you use the Al Qeada information to your advantage?" he asked.

Baynard contemplated the question and said, "Honor among thieves."

Chapter 23

I entered the hearing room around 9:30am at Butler Correctional only to witness the three members of the parole board packing up their belongings. It was my first chance to get out of jail so I wasn't sure what I should expect, but this didn't seem right. I asked, "What's going on?"

The C.O. from the doorway answered, "Take a seat Declan. They will be with you when they're ready."

If I'd considered the morning's events confusing up till this point, I was about to be at the parole board.

I sat only to watch the members place their folders and miscellaneous papers in their briefcases and silently leave the room. 'Okay, that's fucked up,' I thought.

After 20 minutes, a door swung open and standing there, like a nightmare turned reality, were my BFFs: Jackmann and Sinsel.

"What the fuck are you two doing here?" I screamed. "Did you conjure up more charges? Add more time, maybe?"

"There's no parole hearing for you today, buddy," Jackmann gloated. "But I think you're going to want to hear what we have to say. So why don't you take a seat, cut out the histrionics and I'll explain why we're here."

Jackmann grabbed a file from his briefcase and set it on the table. "We're here about your time in the Feds," he said, "I need to know about some of the people that you had contact with while you were in BOP and in Erie County."

I knew what he was asking. He wanted me to snitch on someone. The question was who? Sinsel grabbed a picture out of the file and slid it towards me.

It was a surveillance photo of the yard at FCI Loretto with Tihir, Mukhtar el Barwan, and me. I played it cool and said, "It's a picture of me in the yard, so what?"

Next, Jackmann revealed a file about six inches thick from that damn briefcase of his that made me nervous. He slid them to me and I cursorily glanced through them. Flipping the pages I said, "They look like my US Marshal Transfer and BOP housing records, so what?"

Jackmann stood up and pointed to the highlighted sections on the US Marshall Transfer record and said, "The entire time you were in the Feds you were transported with the Buffalo Six. You went from the Erie County Holding Center to Batavia INS Hold, and then transferred via plane by the US Marshalls to the Metropolitan Detention Center for Fed reception. Finally, you were all bused to USP Lewisburg in Pennsylvania. At Lewisburg, the Six were split up, but Tihir, el Barwan and you were transferred to FCI Loretto."

I stared at Jackmann and said, "Thanks for the memories, but I still don't know what you're getting at?"

Jackmann continued, "Listen Marcus, we are investigating all the people who had contact with the Buffalo Six and your name was on every single record we've come across."

Jackmann pulled out another hundred pictures of me with the terrorists from various prisons and said, "You must have had conversations with them."

I paused to think of an angle. What did they know? Was Jackmann purposely being vague or was he just providing me with enough rope to hang myself? I asked, very cautiously, "What is it that they would have told me? What are you looking for?"

Jackmann almost seemed genuine when he asked, "This is a matter of national security and we're here for some help. We can make it worth your while to talk with us, plain and simple."

I knew they were fishing and replied, "Listen, just because these guys just so happened to be where I was, doesn't mean they talked to me about anything that can help you.

We talked about the Buffalo Bills, their bench press and other work out stuff, Beef-on-Weck, chicken wings, etc...Basically, the usual jail bullshit. I don't know how that's going to help your investigation."

The agents were being tight lipped and I followed the same course. They watched my mannerisms. I stared blankly ahead. I could see by their expressions that they expected some sort of reaction from me. I didn't give them the satisfaction. This forced Jackmann's hand. He tried one more play.

"In a couple of hours the heads of all US intelligence and law enforcement agencies are meeting at the Pentagon to disseminate information needed to prevent another attack from occurring. The FBI is charged with approaching possible material witnesses with a certain criteria that you have met."

"Is there an imminent attack or something else about to happen?" I asked. Jackmann replied, "That's what we are trying to find out."

"So what do you want from me exactly?" I asked.

"We are prepared to vacate your sentence if you choose to assist us," Jackmann stated.

Sensing my less-than-enthusiastic mood, Sinsel's pissy attitude broke the silence. "You mean to tell me you have nothing to say? We've checked up on you and your family. You have two family members serving in Iraq and you still have nothing to say?"

Jackmann interrupted and said, "Wait a second, Geoff. Let's just give him a chance to do the right thing this time."

This Pentagon meeting, Jackmann and Sinsel's presence, the photos and their offer had totally thrown me off guard. I needed time to process everything. I knew what they wanted, but what did they know?

"Your country needs you and the possible intelligence you've acquired could help your country," Sinsel said. "Doesn't that mean anything to you?"

I pondered the question. I had no love for the government regardless of worldly implications. I got shafted by them during the prosecution of my case.

"So what's the exact deal you have for me?" I asked. I wasn't really ready to trust anyone from the government, but I wanted to hear their offer.

Chapter 24

I listened as they offered me a deal that I just couldn't pass up: freedom, with strings. All deals come with riders—little strings. You just need the best pair of scissors to dislodge them. The government needed me, which was a very advantageous position to be in. I signed the deal and had them promptly fax it to my lawyer, Patrick Mallory.

The documents read: Marcus Declan is hereby released from the legal requirements of his sentence from the State of New York by issue of the Governor. Any and all time remaining, including the obligations of parole after incarceration, is hereby negated. Marcus Declan is hereby released into the custody of the FBI to forward the knowledge of an investigation deemed to be of National Security under USC 997 section 1227. The person in question, Marcus Declan, will afford all knowledge of relevant crimes and information to the aforementioned matter pursuant to the implementation of this document. He is only to be emancipated when the criteria set forth is fulfilled to the satisfaction of the FBI If all requirements are not met, this legally binding contract under the Homeland Security Act will become null and void. The person in question, Marcus Declan, will immediately have all charges re-instated and will complete his court ordered sentence/obligation.

It was signed by the Governor of New York, the Director of the FBI, and little old me.

If the cat was already out of the bag, why not make the deal? What did I have to lose? At least it would relieve me from cutting down trees for a few days. For all intents and purposes my photographic proximity and inquisitiveness had garnered me a pardon. Sinsel's disdain for me was evident. Did they know I had uncovered all of Al Qeada's secrets? If they did know, they didn't let on. Jackmann, however, was focused on the task at hand, to take me from upstate New York to DC.

I asked Sinsel to cuff me as we exited the hearing room. Without the cuffs, if the deal fell through, I would be back here labeled a snitch. As the metal tightened around my wrists, I said, "Enjoy it Sinsel, this will be the last time you ever have your little bondage time with me."

We exited the admin building and got into a navy blue Chevy Suburban half-ton LS.

"Fucking government likes to travel in style," I said to no one in particular.

The destination was Syracuse—a town I knew well and about an hour's drive away. I had agreed to the agents' little deal, but I attached my own rider. I had a taste for style and I wanted out of these prison clothes as soon as we were clear of Butler. Grudgingly, they obliged me.

We passed the city limits and were soon pulling onto Marshall Street, headed for J. Michaels. For a moment I took in all the sights, the sounds and thoughts of what it was like to be so close to my alma mater. I had forgotten so much. "Remembrance of things past," I happily misquoted Proust.

Jackmann pulled the Suburban over and parked. I exited the vehicle flanked by each of the agents. They had no trust in me. The feeling was mutual.

"Listen, if I wanted to run I would have run at Butler," I said. "The fence at Butler was only four feet tall and didn't even surround the entire prison. So relax, ok?"

Jackmann and Sinsel backed off a bit. I said, "Hi," to a couple of girls and they giggled. My ego told me they were interested but I was still in my prison garb, the most probable impetus for their outburst. The three of us entered J. Michaels and I headed to the men's department.

A navy blue thin pinstripe suit with a matching blue shirt caught my eye. I picked out a tie and handkerchief, grabbed a pair of black socks and loafers then went to the dressing room. I changed into my new attire and addressed myself in the mirror. 'Now that's the guy I remember' I thought.

T pressed the prison clothes into the salesman's hands presented myself in front of the three way mirrors only to see Jackmann and Sinsel ogling me. Noticing their stares, I adjusted the handkerchief and tie, like a 1920's gangster, and said, "That's what I'm talkin' about!"

Surprisingly, they both found this funny. I turned to them and said, "Let me take care of this and we're out of here."

"This one is on us," Jackmann replied, I didn't disagree.

An hour later we pulled into a little airport, drove onto the runway, and boarded the plane to DC. It was a Gulfstream G4 private jet.

"You two must be moving up the ladder to be able to pull a plane like this for duty," I said "A tad above your pay grade isn't it?"

Jackmann and Sinsel simply directed me to take a seat. Still reeling from the day's events, I made myself as comfortably confused as I could be as we headed for DC.

Chapter 25

The roar of the engines drowned out the minutiae of what may lie ahead of me. Jackmann had a "Washington Post" and I asked him for it. He extracted the sports section, and handed me the rest. It felt weird to have this morning's paper in my hand. The Department of Corrections staggered, by at least three days, all the incoming literature just to screw with you.

A small but important detail leaped off the front page. Tihir, one of the Buffalo Six and my escort into the world of Al Qeada, was on the cover. He was up for appeal. All the pieces fell into place but it seemed all too coincidental.

But was it Jackmann and Sinsel's plan to misinform me? Was the paper real? Or were they trying to get me to react?

I pretended to engross myself in the paper as I began to weigh my options and contemplate my angles. What was I going to say in Washington? The truth? Hell, I could end up in a place like Abu Ghraib or worse. What did they actually know? After the Pentagon, could I just walk out free? Who makes that call? All questions aside, I wanted to know if their story of surveillance photos and possible information was the true reason for the end of my incarceration or was something else afoot. Did someone betray me?

Seeing the "Post" brought Teek to the forefront of my mind. I wished that I could talk to him right now. We always were on the same page and I'm sure he would give me the advice I needed.

Christopher Prior

Teek and I grew up playing travel hockey together and in high school we both played lacrosse. Lacrosse ended up being my ticket out of Buffalo. It was the early 90's and Buffalo had already been in decline for about a decade losing tens of thousands of people every year. Not one of my friends from my high school, St. Francis, stuck around to watch the inevitable. We all wanted out. We all wanted opportunities and Buffalo was a cul-de-sac of hope.

Teek's father, an ex-Underwater Demolition Team (UDT) Navy SEAL, was a lacrosse guru and taught our group of friends how to excel in the sport. We had a kick ass senior team, easily winning the NY State championship title in the early '90's.

I received scholarship offers from William and Mary, VMI, Butler, UMASS, the Air Force Academy and the Naval Academy. The Naval Academy was my preferred choice simply because my cousin and close friend Evan Tanner was enrolled there. Eventually I decided the regimented society didn't blend well with my personality, and I chose Butler University instead. The irony that I attended Butler and was imprisoned in Butler was not lost on me. I received a free ride to both.

In college my entrepreneurship blossomed. Back in Buffalo I used to throw keg parties to make money but at Butler the students weren't interested in keg parties. The kids had cars, girls, whatever they wanted.

I, on the other hand, grew up in a middle class household of divorced parents and was at school on a scholarship. With all the money circling around in college, I wanted some too. I uncovered an unexploited business opportunity in the market place. I began selling fake ID's. Together, Teek and I built an empire. Together, had found a den of fools to exploit. Was this a dyslectic version of my life?

I was floating aimlessly in a sea of doubt. I asked myself one question: Why would the government offer me such a sweet deal? At face value, it appeared I had lucked into a bargain and all I had to do was speak about my inane conversations with the Buffalo Six. It didn't compute, though. I knew there was more to Jackmann and Sinsel's tepid assurances. They were just puppets masquerading as top dogs.

Someone had betrayed me, and I needed to know who.

Chapter 26

My only bastion was my mind. I soon organized a list of potential backstabbers or patriots depending what side of the fence you were on. Tihir topped the list for me. But el Barwan with Patrick Mallory our mutual lawyer was a very close second. Baynard, Jack Halford, Jose Padiigizus, and Mike O'Connor were jail buddies but would they follow the code?

Tihir and el Barwan would unlikely cozy up with a government they had sworn Jihad against. But with ever the present threat of getting old another decade behind bars went by, they clearly had the potential to be the rat.

Mallory, on the other hand, was an arrogant sleaze bag which made him good at his job. He persuaded me to sit on the information because he thought it would only lead to a larger headache for me. It made sense at the time. The question was, did Mallory figure out what I did in Erie County Jail? If he did, then he might break attorney client privilege to punish me for stealing his documents.

The next person I told was Dr. Richard Baynard. I trusted him because we knew the same guys from New York and I knew his case. Baynard was probably one of the most interesting characters I ever met. Talking with him at Loretto made me feel like I wasn't in jail.

However, Baynard was getting old and looking at least another decade behind bars, he clearly had the potential.

Jack Halford was another guy I knew from FCI Loretto. Baynard introduced Halford to me when I arrived. Halford and Baynard had been thick as thieves until I came to Loretto. I think Halford was envious of my friendship with Baynard. Halford was forever asking questions.

Halford was in jail for setting up illegal tax shelters in the early 90's. His crime did not catch up with him until he moved to DC to become a principal at Booz Allen. He claimed he implemented guidance systems for surface to air missile systems and satellites, a rocket scientist in other words.

I was not convinced of his authenticity so I had Teek perform some due diligence. His story checked out but I still wasn't fully convinced. I knew satellite communications; one of the many things I learned from Geoff Sondon. I gave Halford enough rope to hang himself. The yardarm was burdened quickly. This could only mean one of two things; either he was a jailhouse snitch, or worse, an informant for the Feds.

The last two potential snitches were from New York State Corrections. I had gone from Loretto to Erie County to Wende and then on to Reception at Elmira. Receiving a 04 number representing 2004. The Elmira prison cell tiers were like something out of a movie. There were rats as big as pot belly pig and inmate attacks daily. I spent two and half months on the Tiers, scared out of my mind, waiting to get transferred out.

I had no deodorant for the entire time I was there. Every day consisted of four to five bird baths in the sink in my cell. I showered a total of eight times in two and a half months. The noise from inmates yelling down the cavernous main corridor never ceased. I was on edge every time I came out of the cell, twice a day for yard and three times a day for chow. I made a couple of friends. One guy in particular was Jose Padiigizus, who went by Jesus. I told him about Tihir and el Barwan to pass the time and keep my sanity. In total, there were 13 stabbings and two deaths in that 10 week period. I was eventually reunited with Jesus when he made it to Butler.

The last person I told was Mike O'Connor. He was about 15 years older than me reminded me of the old Irish guys that hung out at my dad's bar in Buffalo. He was from Long Island and had been a NYC Fire Fighter. Mike and I became good friends.

He was upstate on vehicular manslaughter and D.W.I. Mike was coming home from a NY Islanders hockey game on the LIE (Long Island Expressway) which was covered in snow and ice. Admittedly, he was pretty drunk on Jack and Cokes after being out with his fellow fire fighters. Mike lost control of his car, just as a car was merging into traffic off the ramp. The driver, a Pakistani, slid into the traffic sideways in front of Mike. There was nothing Mike could do. He T-boned the car on the driver's side and they both careened into an off-ramp divider. The impact crushed both sides of the victim's car and he died on the scene. It was an accident but they threw the book at Mike. He was NYC fire fighter and he should have never been drinking and driving. He pled guilty and was sentenced to five to 15 years.

Mike and I spun the yard and talked all the time. I gave him stock tips which he did really well on. One day I confided in him. I wanted to get his take. Mike was an on duty NYC fire fighter when the 9/11 attacks occurred. His firehouse responded to the tragedy. After telling the tale to Mike he tried to pressure me to tell someone. I told him no way. He had been in jail long enough to know the code.

I always told the story like, "Listen to what happened to me on the way to the store. You're not going to believe who I was locked up with." It was small talk to pass the hours in jail. At this point, flying in a luxury plane, still a prisoner, my options were limited. But then again, perhaps my BBFs could be helpful. I was determined to pry more information out of Jackmann and Sinsel.

Chapter 27

I had to come up with an 'in'. I was located in the middle of the plane, and Jackmann and Sinsel were both seated in the front. I asked Jackmann, "Hey, does this plane have a bar or something?" Jackmann hesitated to answer and said, "Why?"

"I'm thirsty, a water or soda will do," I said. They looked at each other and Sinsel said, "I think it's in the back."

I headed to the back of the plane and rifled through the cabinets. I found a bottle of Captain Morgan's, Coke and some ice. I always sailed with the Captain. The ice hitting the glass got their attention. Mission accomplished. I poured a glass of liquid courage. I strutted back towards my seat waiting for a reaction.

"A drink huh?" Jackmann questioned.

"What are you my mother or something?" I baited him.

"I just don't think given the circumstances being inebriated is appropriate," Jackmann replied.

"Well I'm not the one on duty," I said and took a swig.

I handed back the 'Post' to Jackmann, minus the front page, and said, "So how legit is that document I signed back at Butler? How do I know you guys didn't make it up just to get me to come with you? You guys still haven't told me why I am really here. After all you guys deal in falsehoods all the time," I said.

"Listen, the US is trying to stay ahead of the terrorists and you 'for good or for bad' have had enormous interaction with the only

Christopher Prior

captured cell. The government is desperate, which is why they are willing to deal with you," Sinsel retorted.

"So the mundane conversations I had with Tihir, el Barwan, and the other terrorists are going to bring down Al Qeada?" I baited them again.

I could tell Sinsel wanted to let the cat out of the bag and lay into me. Their reaction had given me a brief peek at their hand. I pressed further.

"So can I use this phone over here to call my lawyer?" I asked.

"I'm afraid we can't let you do that Marcus," Jackmann stated.

"Why not?"

"Like we told you back at Butler, we are just in charge of bringing you to DC and that's it," Jackmann said.

I knew they would never let me use the phone but the point was to get them talking. As I turned in my seat, I let one final thought settle into their minds.

"If you're not going to let me talk to my lawyer, you might as well turn the plane around right now because I'm not saying a word to anyone. We're talking about my safety here. You think I trust you? Someone has to know where I am and what I am doing."

I backed the agents into a corner. Jackmann got up and grabbed the phone. As he dialed, he stared me down. My threat, no more than a bluff, had its desired effect.

Five minutes later Jackmann came to my seat. "Listen, I can't let you use the phone on the plane. Maybe you can call your lawyer once we land in DC. Will that do?"

"I guess," I replied. "It's not like I have a choice in the matter."

Chapter 28

I took another mouthful of the booze. The burning in my throat reminded me of what real liquor tasted like. In jail they made alcohol using a garbage bag, orange juice, sugar, dinner rolls, and tap water. The concoction was left to ferment, and when finished, it had a viscosity of puke. I drank it once and hurled.

I had a look around the plane and all I wished for was a parachute to escape. During college my friends and I learned to skydive. Back in those days if it was dangerous we tried it. But there was an ancillary reason in those days. It was out of necessity.

Our necessity was our need to launder the copious amounts of money we made selling fake I.D.'s in college. At the time I knew little about international finance so we hid our money the old fashion way—in cash. Teek, our crew and I would take a commercial flight from a city in the mid-west to costal Texas or Florida, each of us wearing a money belt holding $100,000. We staggered the bills so the metal strips in the money were not lined up or it would set off the metal detectors. Using all 30 members from our I.D. crews, we could extract just over $3 million per trip.

Teek and I would then charter a private flight out of a city, like Panama City or Corpus Christy and the other guys would take a commercial flight to the Cayman Islands. Once there one of our main guys, Carl, was in charge of renting a boat for a day. He would navigate the boat to the prearranged GPS coordinates and pick us up once we jumped out of the plane. Using chartered flights was the key to staying off the radar of the authorities. We controlled the flight manifests so we could make our trips undetected.

Off-shore monies were the best monies. They were tax free and secure. I thought to myself about the life that I had led up until now. I lived like there was no tomorrow and my actions had no consequences. When you're young, ignorance is bliss.

But reality, today and the quickness in which the FBI scooped me up made it impossible for me to orchestrate such an elaborate plan for escape. I would have loved to see Jackmann and Sinsel's face as I exited the plane at 30,000 feet.

Most people don't have the choice when it comes to jail time. But I wasn't 'most people.' I had become an expert at counter surveillance due to my previous career as a forger. It was a necessary skill for self-preservation. In fact, I had only myself to blame for my incarnation.

In the fall of 2002, as a stockbroker, I had run into a brick wall. I had spent nearly eight months trying to get back what I lost on 9/11. At the time I was running a hedge fund and in the three days preceding the attacks I lost 72% of everything. That was 72% of not just my client's money, but mine as well. Those three days were the most devastating of my life.

By the 14th the realization had sunk in. I had lost millions dollars. I ran the hedge fund like a stock club, in which I was the only one that had a vote. Getting clients to sign up was effortless. My pitch was, 'If I made money, they made money.'

I owned 53% of the entire fund. The remaining 47% was distributed over 400 clients, all friends or friends of friends. Once again I was the emperor, this time of a legal business. 9/11 threw my kingdom into uncertainty. The villains were at the gate.

Nothing was wrong until quarterly reports were due to be issued to my clients and the Securities and Exchange Commission (SEC). I had the choice to tell the truth or lie. I had lost 72% of the fund. I had been beating the market for five years now, and didn't believe anything, not even 9/11, could best me. My ego basically took over. I turned into a gambler instead of a stockbroker—the worst possible transformation.

I sent out a fudged first quarter report and luckily no inquiries came up. It wasn't until the third quarters of less than accurate numbers was I under a fully-fledged investigation.

Already a step ahead, I had started to siphon off money from the fund and place it in a, U-Store It storage unit. I did this while being watched by Jackmann and Sinsel of the FBI. I was even so bold towards the end I would place a business card underneath the windshield wiper of their surveillance car.

I had amassed millions of dollars in cash with my siphoning within months. Filling twenty duffle bags with the illegally wrought monies, I was prepared to leave for good. I had my exit planned but then, my father intervened.

My dad and I had made plans to go to a Buffalo Sabres game on Oct. 21st, 2002. It was to be one of the last times I would see him though he didn't know it. Then out of character my father made a surprise stop at my house. I was in the shower so he let himself in and upon entering he saw the bags lined up. His curiosity led him to open one up. Like father, like son, I guess.

When I came out to the living room I found my father with the most disappointed look on I had ever seen on his face. He composed himself and asked one question, "What is all this?" I simply said, "I'm leaving for good."

We talked for an hour and finally something he said rang true. "If you go on the run now, you'll be on the run for the rest of your life." He was right.

I hired the best lawyer in town, an influential guy, Patrick Mallory. It was the toughest decision I ever had to make: go to jail now so I could have a life afterwards.

Mallory told me jail is like a vacation to another country. "You don't know the customs and you don't know the language but to survive you better learn quick."

I chose to go to jail but I didn't choose to be poor. Mallory suggested I had something to come out to after jail. I had a friend, Paul Romano, who sold mattresses for a living. His goal in life was to start his own mattress business. He was an excellent salesman and made over $100,000 per year, not bad for a legit guy in a city like Buffalo.

My first reaction was to reach out to Paul to set up a meeting to talk. Success breeds success and I could trust him.

We initially met at a local strip club named Seductions on Lundy's Lane. Paul floated to me the idea of he had in his head about creating a mattress topper made from the pressure relieving memory foam material. He was certain they would sell. His idea sounded promising.

I dug in deep and found a manufacturer who would produce and drop ship the mattress toppers Romano desired. Allowing me to forgo building a factory or a warehouse. All told, it took about two months for me to complete the finished product, the website, and seal the manufacturing contracts.

I sent the first unit to Paul. He sold the topper within an hour of receiving it. My mattress business was born.

Two days later I received a 6:00 AM wakeup call. It was the FBI and SEC. They were there to arrest me for my illegal stockbroker activities but as the cuffs clad in place, I felt happy. At the time, jail had been only an abstract concept of fear and the possibility of self-loathing. I just had to survive what lifestyle imposition.

The cuffs were placed on me all I could think about was that I was happy I had started the mattress business was my space foam landing once I was out.

At my bail hearing, the prosecutor insisted to the judge that I was a flight risk. Mallory replied in kind with, "Mr. Declan was well aware of the FBI surveillance. He could have run at anytime but didn't. His arrest by government agents was completely unnecessary. We had a plan in place to turn him over to the authorities if they felt it was warranted."

The Judge then directed his attention directly to me and asked, "Is this true Mr. Declan?"

My response was quick and a lie, "Yes, that is true your Honor."

In support of his desire to keep me off the street the prosecutor stated, "While searching Mr. Declan's residence we came across over a hundred photos that appear to be from various cities around the world. Yet we cannot find any instance where Mr. Declan was issued or used a US passport. Honestly your Honor, Mr. Declan is a convicted manufacturer of fraudulent identification. For this reason alone, besides the merits of the pending indictments which include international wire fraud, grand larceny, 52 SEC violations, and a scheme to defraud stock holders, we the prosecution believe that Mr. Declan is a flight risk."

The Judge asked what I had to say about this. I replied, "Your Honor, the pictures are photo-shopped. They're fakes. I used them to impress clients nothing more."

The judge, unimpressed, ordered each photo be investigated. He then added, "The suspect is remanded. We will revisit the issue of bail after the FBI authenticates the validity of these pictures and Mr. Declan's claims."

Three weeks later the rouse was up. The pictures were real and bail was out of the question.

I summoned Mallory and told him to get Teek to the Erie County Holding Center. Signed in as Mallory assistant, I transferred the power of attorney of the mattress corporation to my friend. We then realized it would be more advantageous to have his sister, a single working mom, and therefore a believable member of society as the figure head for the business. My safety net now lay within the capable hands of my best friend, his sister and good friend Paul Romano.

Over the next two months, while in jail, I slowly introduced Teek as the point man to the manufacturers and distributers. This was only possible because of my connections at the holding center. My job as a library clerk in the prison gave me access to fax machines, a photocopier, a phone, and the internet. I was able to help out with the day to day operations during the transition.

There soon came a point where my day to day involvement became less important. Anyway, I had more important things to worry about, like my trial.

Teek and his sister ran the business well, even making it into, Business Week in the spring of 2003. They sent me a copy. I was on top of the world. My future was secure. They had a full page write up with a photograph of them jumping up and down on one of the newly designed mattress toppers.

A part of me was envious, 'I'm supposed to be there too.' The business's success made me think of my mother and something she always told me, "Marcus, you could fall into a river of shit and come out smelling like a rose." Maybe she was right, but probably not. Truth has a habit of being misinformed and my present predicament was proof of that.

I had made the flight from New York to Virginia many times. At this point in the trip I should have been able to see the Chesapeake Bay. To every destination there is a certain geographical signature and what I saw below didn't match up to where I was told we were going. I asked Jackmann and Sinsel, "How long until we land in DC? We've gotta be close."

Their indifference spoke volumes. Maybe they thought I wouldn't notice the difference. I looked out the window. We were either headed into the Midwest or coming out of it, which one I couldn't tell.

Jackmann rose from his seat and said, "We're going to Denver."

"Why are we going there?" I questioned.

I could tell Jackmann had no intention of acknowledging my question although I was enjoying our continuing version of entente cordial.

"Well, at least when we get there I'll start getting some answers to my questions," I said.

Sinsel chimed in and said, "Oh, you're going to get some answers. Lymes will make sure of that."

Jackmann's head spun towards Sinsel. Acknowledging the slip-up I said, "Lymes, huh?"

"Just shut the fuck up," Sinsel said. I just sat wondering, 'Why Denver?'

Chapter 29

The weather in Denver had turned down right mean. During our approach the jet hopped an air pocket and dropped 50 feet throwing my stomach into my throat. Jackmann, Sinsel and I all had a 'what the fuck was that?' look on our faces. I peered out the window only to see a blanket of white.

The pilot came over the speaker, "Y'all better buckle up back there, we're hitin' a little chop."

I thought to myself, 'oh really?' as a picked my cracked glass off the floor and buckled in. Jackmann and Sinsel did the same. The next 15 minutes felt like rolling around the inside of a clothes dryer. I pulled my belt as hard as I could.

As we made our approach we dropped again. I started to think we might not make it out of this and said, "So who's the Big Bopper, who's Richie Valens and who's Buddy Holly?" They didn't appreciate the reference to rock'n roll deaths. I noticed the pilot's windshield was completely white too.

Jackmann yelled up at the pilot, "How close are we?"

"About quarter mile out, we'll be on the ground in two minutes."

We all braced ourselves for the landing. As I stared out the window a wave of calm came over me. I always functioned best under pressure. I thought if it's my time then so be it.

The clothes dryer morphed into a kamikaze-like run for the next two minutes. Left then right then down and left again until we hit the tarmac hard.

The pilot steered us to a slew of private hangars. The plane came to an abrupt halt and then progressed into the hanger and lowered the stairs.

Jackmann and Sinsel exited leaving me behind to watch a semi circle of Chevy suburban's park in the hanger. Our greeting party was what I considered to be a circus of conspiracy.

An older man, who assumed was Lymes, emerged and walked toward Jackmann. Behind him followed a clean-cut younger man carrying a large box with handles and an attaché case. The two men stopped in their tracks and turned back to the car. Lymes motioned for another individual to exit the car—'Dick' Baynard—my buddy from jail.

I watched as Lymes pointed with his cane towards the jet and asked a question. Lymes tapped his cane on the cement floor of the hangar, it was time to go, but not before telling Jackmann and Sinsel to uncuff the doctor. Baynard wrenched his wrists. I knew that feeling well. Handcuffs left a bitter taste.

As Lymes boarded it was obvious he was old, battered, and disheveled. I found him creepy. His assistant lumbered to heave the box over each of the seats as the two of them shuffled their way to the back. Lymes simply ignored me.

He was as serious as they come. He wasn't a Bureau agent that was for sure. He was intimidating and appeared to be a veteran, in a sinister way, of worldly affairs. Lymes sat in the last row of seats, no doubt to prohibit my eye-balling him. I would have to wait to confront him until after we were in the air.

I turned my attention to the soon to be punched in the face Dr. Richard Baynard.

Did Baynard know I was on the plane? Why did he rat me out? If he gave me up, why was he still in custody? Questions erupted in my brain. I heard the jostling of the G4 steps. Baynard was close; I ducked below the headrest of the seat in front of me. I was five rows back. I heard the footsteps getting closer and I readied my fist. Looking down the aisle, I saw a foot, and I sprang from my seat like a jack rabbit and socked him.

It wasn't Baynard, it was Sinsel and I knocked him out cold.

Baynard stood frozen but said, "Oooooh...shit."

While Sinsel lay on the aisle floor unconsciousness. Jackmann pushed Baynard aside to get to me. The plane's engine started up. Jackmann leaped over his partner and went to grab me but I gave him the wax on wax off treatment. As I turned to ready myself for a second attempt, we both heard a voice.

"Enough Mr. Declan. Why don't you take a seat! You too Jackmann," Lymes commanded.

I offered my assistance to the fallen agent, and apologetically said, "It was supposed to be Baynard."

My explanation didn't seem to place a dent in the tension as Jackmann helped his dazed partner back to their seats. Baynard bravely sat to the right in the same row as me. As the plane taxied out of the hangar and proceeded to take off, we looked intently at each other.

Chapter 30

Baynard and I were locked in a staring contest. Who would flinch first? Jackmann asked the pilot if there was a first-aid kit aboard. The co-pilot tossed it to Jackmann.

The plane seemed sparse even with the addition of Baynard, Lymes and his assistant. Lymes sat in the far back while sat in the remaining eight seats. I was to the left in a seat facing the front of the plane while Baynard sat directly across the aisle. In back of me Jackmann tended to Sinsel.

I watched as Jackmann rummaged through the kit. I thought, 'I've just assaulted a Federal officer. But that was the least of my worries. My rubber-necking allowed me a peek at the man himself. Lymes was sitting calmly going through papers he had strewn about his table. Everyone was busy and I had my chance.

"What the fuck are you doing here?" I said in a low whisper as I leaned in towards Baynard.

Baynard looked up over the seats to the front and to the back and said, "Apparently the same thing you are."

I peered over the seats at the two agents. Jackmann had been waving smelling salts under Sinsel's nose. After the fourth or fifth pass Sinsel pushed Jackmann's hand away and said, "Ok, ok, ok. Geez!"

Sinsel popped up from his seat a minute later, still a little un-stable and set his bearings on me. I had been in tougher spots upstate and I just sat there coolly. Sinsel's face was painted with anger.

He got within a foot of me and fell, tripped by Baynard, letting out a whimper. I wondered what he would do this time.

Then from the back we heard, "I thought I told you two to knock that shit off. Sit down Agent Sinsel.

"We can finish this when we land," Sinsel hissed as he returned to his seat. Lymes had saved me from a shiner for sure.

But what I wanted to know now was why Baynard would betray me. So I asked him again, "Why are you here Baynard?"

"I really don't know," Baynard said.

"Maybe because of this?" I said. As I held up the Washington Post and pointed to the picture of Tihir one of the terrorists from Buffalo.

"You ratted me out," I said.

"I didn't man, I swear."

"I don't believe you. I never told anyone else about the terrorists. So it has to be you."

"I didn't tell anybody," Baynard stated in his defense.

"Man, if our friends in New York knew what you did?" Baynard knew I was referring to our mutual Mob friends.

"But I didn't."

"So, did they offer you a deal?"

"Yes, but my deal hinges on your deal," Baynard replied.

"What? How do you know I have a deal?" I asked loudly giving up on the pretense of keeping the conversation private.

"You have a deal with the CIA," Baynard said and motioned toward Lymes.

"How'd you know that? And how'd you know he's CIA?"

"Lymes told me about your deal."

"They picked me up over some pictures of me with the terrorists."

"They must have shown us the same pictures, but I didn't rat you out," Baynard said, "I was moved by the US Marshalls to Florence ADMAX on Administrative Segregation a couple days ago. A day later two FBI agents showed up and presented me with pictures of you and the terrorists. I knew the score but didn't throw you under the bus."

Like teenagers in childhood playground standoff, Baynard and I simply glared at each other. The disbelief and mistrust was obvious to everyone who gave a damn. Seconds later, a pile of folders landed in my lap.

"What's this?" I said.

The assistant said, "It's the reason you're here."

"What do you mean?

Then Lymes spoke for the first time, "Mr. Baynard didn't rat you out. You ratted you out."

This spun my head like a top and I replied with, "I never told anyone other than Baynard about the terrorists."

"Why don't you look for yourself," Lymes said, "Everything you want to know is right there."

Chapter 31

The cover read, 'DEA Surveillance.'

I thumbed through the documents which were transcriptions of numerous conversations. I glanced over at Baynard. I had more then a few questions, what does the DEA have to do with the terrorists and me? Could the Buffalo Six's cover story be true? Were they in fact drug dealers?

The DEA surveillance documents looked like a movie script. One person says this, another says that, and so on. I scanned through it quickly not really reading entire conversations. I turned to Baynard and asked, "Do you know what this is?"

Baynard replied, "Nope, it's the first time I've seen it." He said this so off the cuff I believed it was the only truthful thing he has said so far.

Heading after heading read 'Baynard and unknown individual speaking at FCI Loretto.' They had it all. Every conversation I had with Baynard about the terrorists was there.

I turned to Baynard and asked, "How did they get all this?"

"I don't know."

"Every conversation you and I had about the terrorists is here," I said.

In that moment all my assumptions went out the window.

The question was: is their knowledge limited to my conversations with Baynard or is there more? They were fishing for more information but I don't think they had any clue what that was.

Christopher Prior

What I knew they would jump at the chance to read the illegally obtained legal papers of el Barwan. I stole them from the interview room at The Erie County Holding Center. They contained el Barwan's confidential lawyer conversations, notes on his case, and I learned the true extent of his involvement with Al Qeada. Did they know I had obtained this?

These were things that were never placed into the official court documents on the Buffalo Six. The devil was in the treasonous details.

I asked Baynard, "Did you know they were still investigating you? How could you let me tell you all this shit in your room? We could have gone anywhere in the prison? That's fucked up."

Baynard replied, "I didn't know they were still investigating me. I had figured they were done with me after they locked me up."

I nodded my head in agreement. It made sense.

"So what did you mean by your deal hinges on my deal?" I asked.

"That's just it. I am here because of what you told me. I reckon they're trying to isolate the people who know what you know," Baynard explained. "Am I the only one you told?"

I had a ready made response, "Yeah, you are the only one that I told."

"If you tell them what they want to know, I think we are looking pretty good," Baynard stated enthusiastically. I responded, "Don't worry, I'll make it so we get back what we lost, or should I say what they took.

As I sat back in my seat, I realized what Lymes said was true, I had ratted myself out. I had a big mouth and in the past it had gotten me into some tight spots, but none as tight as this. I felt Lymes lurking with intent behind me.

Chapter 32

"So Mr. Declan, your file said you were assessed as intelligent, but it's obvious you're not smart enough to keep your mouth shut."

It was a jab at me. Lymes moved from looming over me like a malevolent gargoyle to lean on the arm rest of a seat across the aisle.

"So who are you?" I asked.

"I am Charles Lymes, but you already know that."

"Ok, so you're what...the guy that running this little shindig?"

"Yes and your help is desperately needed."

"Who do you work for?" I asked.

"You already know that, too. Maybe you haven't figured out as much as I thought you have." Christ, he reminded me of some Alex Trebek double talker.

"I just wanted to hear it from you," I said.

"So are we really headed to Washington or are Baynard and I headed to Abu Ghraib?"

Lymes snickered and replied, "If I wanted you there you already would be there. I don't think you realize what you have done Marcus. You entered the world of Al Qeada on a whim. I've listened to the tapes. You gained the confidence of the most prevalent terror cell in America. This is something we have been trying to do since before 9/11. You made us all look like bumbling fools."

The adulation made me weary.

"I need to ask you one question before we go any further Marcus. Is Baynard the only other person that you told?"

I mustered the best poker face I had, looked Lymes directly in the eyes making sure I positioned my body language and eye movement with that of an honest person. Looking from the top left to him directly, I said, "Yes, Baynard's the only person I told. I believed at the time I could trust him, which I know now was well placed trust."

Lymes replied, "You're right. The first agents we sent in were met with a brick wall. We had surveillance photos from FCI Loretto and showed them to Baynard. All Baynard wanted to know was why the agents wanted the identity of the individuals in the pictures with him. He wouldn't give up the names."

Baynard looked up from the transcripts to give me an 'I told you so' look.

"What does the DEA have to do with any of this?" I asked.

"The information was brought to my attention by two DEA agents investigating Baynard."

This statement got the doctor's attention. "Why were they still investigating me?" Baynard inquired.

"They were looking for a link between the New York Mob families and you, Dr. Baynard, as their major supplier of prescription drugs. They figured you would eventually slip up," Lymes replied.

Baynard and I both looked at each other. The DEA's attempt to ensnarl the Mob was pointless. We both had Mob dealings and we knew better than to open our mouths about that kind of information.

I asked Baynard, "Did you tell anyone? How about Halford? I know that you two were close?"

Baynard went to answer but Lymes beat him to the punch and said, "No. Baynard didn't tell Halford."

How do you know?" I asked.

"Because Halford was a snitch in the BOP," Lymes said. Baynard and I shared a smile. We had discussed that very possibility.

"So, I know the basics from the tapes but I need to hear it from you Mr. Declan. Are the things you told Baynard truthful or did you use artistic license?" Lymes asked.

I answered with a request, "Before I answer that, I want to know exactly whom I am to meet with in DC, and what happens to me after I talk. Basically, what assurances do I have for my own safety and what does Baynard get out of all this? And perhaps more importantly, how do you and Baynard know each other?"

Chapter 33

Baynard looked to Lymes like a lovelorn puppy gone bad.

Turning to Baynard with mock affection Lymes said, "I guess you should be the one to tell him Richard."

Baynard took the invitation to elaborate on what he had previously told me at Loretto but with one important new addition. He told me about his rescue in Rhodesia by Lymes.

I asked if my deal would be honored even if the information I was able to provide was nothing more than what was on the tapes. Lymes said yes. I asked Lymes about Baynard's situation.

"Baynard's deal is a little more complicated," Lymes replied. "But anything Baynard would receive out of this meeting of the minds hinges on what you say in Washington."

Obviously Lymes's instinct told him there was something far more useful not on the tapes.

Maybe I was giving the opposing team too much free press. Lymes, from the look of him, had been playing this game long before I was born. His deep set wrinkles and furrowed brow said everything I needed to know. I had to choose my words carefully. "Explain to me exactly what is going to happen at the Pentagon," I asked Lymes.

As his face took on a sour puss demeanor, I realized Lymes was concerned more about protecting his back than my life. His reply possessed a perfect glaze of venom.

"Ever since this information came to the attention of the NSA, they have been investigating its validity. Up until now every piece of information you, Mr. Declan, told Baynard was verified as credible. Over the past three days we tried to track you down, all the while investigating the claims made on the tape. I'm bringing you to meet with the heads of the US intelligence community. I am basically here to persuade you to help us."

I threw Baynard an incredulous glance. After all, the government put me in jail. All things are negotiable and everything has a price.

"So there's going to be a room full of NSA, CIA, and Homeland Security guys and they're just going to pepper me with questions?" I asked.

"I wouldn't say 'pepper' you, per se, but they will have a lot questions for you to answer," Lymes said. "That's for sure."

"How long will this meeting take?" I asked.

"Well, that all depends on you and what you say," Lymes came back with two questions. He knew he had me by the balls.

My final question was, "After this is all done, am I free man? What about the conditions in those papers I signed that stated that I had to meet the criteria to the satisfaction of the FBI?"

"Yes, you will go free as long as you fulfill those conditions ," Lymes said, "And I, not the FBI, have the final say on whether or not you are in full compliance. I guess that makes us three peas in a pod, you, me, and the doctor here.

"And if I comply, Baynard gets the same deal?" I asked.

"Like I said, it's more complicated, but I can make it happen. Especially for an old friend," Lymes replied.

Just to have some fun Lymes threw a final curveball for the day, "So, where is your first stop going to be if we release you?" he said, "Your buddy Teek Van Dyne's house perhaps?"

Chapter 34

It worried me immensely Lymes knew of Teek but did he know all of our dirty little dealings? Teek and I had been involved in so many. Did Lymes know that Teek was running my mattress business? Did he know about the ID's? Did Lymes know I supplied Teek with the monies to propel his construction business? Did Lymes even care about any of that stuff? He was a spy after all, not a cop. I had to assume that he knew it all and that it all mattered.

Lymes' awareness had dangerous implications for me. All that I worked for from the age of 18 was resting on the careful choice of my words. I could lose everything. All the money I made selling ID's, Teek's construction business, the mattress business and not to mention all the money I had hidden off shore while being a broker.

Lymes asked, "So does that explain everything you wanted to know Mr. Declan for now?"

"Yeah," I answered. I made sure to distance myself from the reference to Teek. I would never knowingly bring anyone down with me, especially Teek; I lived by my devotion to my loyalties. Betray them once, and you'll regret it for the rest of your life.

It was now Lymes' turn to question me. He began, "Well, I would like you to start at the beginning. How did you know the terrorists? Did you know them before jail? How did you come to have the same lawyer as one of them? How did you become the only person to have contact with them at Erie County Holding Center? How did you manage to get them to trust you? Take it slow, one answer at a time."

I began, "No, I didn't know the terrorists before I went to jail. They had lived on the other side of the tracks. Buffalonians all know it's a poor area and mostly populated with towel heads and I don't look like I like Falafel's."

My plan was to give Lymes what I gave everyone else, the watered down version of the story. I could only hope what I gave him would satisfy his hunger. I didn't like the idea of being a snitch.

As I spoke I noticed Baynard and the agents were listening intently too. I felt like I was telling a story at camp. I focused on Lymes though, keeping eye contact with him, watching for the smallest inkling he wasn't buying my story.

I continued, "Patrick Mallory was an old family friend and that's was how I came to have him as my lawyer. He and my father grew up together. They both attended South Park High School and, more recently, would run into each other playing golf at South Shore Country Club."

I told them how my father intervened and convinced me to take the heat. This surprised Jackmann. He never thought I was anything more then self-centered and greedy stocker broker with no conscience. I don't think Jackmann had any idea I was about to run weeks before he and his partner arrested me.

Lymes asked, "Did you know Mallory was taking el Barwan on as a client?"

"Of course I did. Mallory knew I worked in the law library and was privy to all that happened in the Holding Center. Plus, Mallory and I had many mutual friends who worked at the prison; there would be no way to keep it from me," I said, "Mallory taking on el Barwan as a client worried me. I wanted reassurance I would not be placed on the back burner. Mallory scoffed at the notion and assured me he could handle both. He clearly lied to me. If you trust a lawyer, you deserve what you get." This statement provided everyone a moment of levity. Jackmann chimed in and said, "Why do you think you got screwed?"

I paused to answer and said, "Why do you think? Any deal that lands you in jail is no deal at all."

Chapter 35

The next question was obvious.

"How did you become the only person to have contact with the terrorists at the Erie County Holding Center?"

That was a complicated question to answer. I had to worry about implicating family members and friends; people who had gone out on a limb for me during my incarceration. They had real lives, wives, husbands, kids, pensions, real responsibilities, unlike me. My life was ruled by the ability at any time to pick up and go.

I told Lymes, "After Jackmann and Sinsel arrested me in Buffalo I was housed downtown at the Erie County Holding Center. I was supposed to be placed in a regular dorm but at intake I ran into one of my friends. He immediately called a relative of mine Aunt Sarah. She was one of the head guards' downtown and I was placed in the trustee dorm instead. By that afternoon I had a job serving food in the mess hall. I only worked two days in the mess hall before Sarah had organized my promotion to the law library."

"The library was located on the second floor. It was a place for guards to meet that weren't running units upstairs. It was like a little clubhouse. I would listen to them speak about their days off and the things they did on the outside. The guard who ran the library was an avid fisherman and when we went to rec on the roof of the prison we could see him out on Lake Erie in his boat.

"The library itself was small. The room was only 20 by 40 feet. There were bookshelves against every wall and rows of free standing racks in the middle of the room. Tucked in tightly were 2 round tables. But more importantly, the law library was only two doors down from Sarah's office, so I got to see her everyday which made being in jail easier. You know, a friendly face and all that.

"My workday consisted of handing legal books to the burgeoning masses of jailhouse lawyers—a cottage industry in prison. It made me laugh to watch guys who barely made it through grammar school try to beat the system. It was a form of mental masturbation."

Lymes asked, "So when did you meet the Buffalo Six?"

I explained, "I had been a clerk for about a month before el Barwan was arrested and placed in Erie County. El Barwan and the rest of the Buffalo Six were placed in Administrative Segregation for their own protection. They were locked down 23 hours a day. Their only hour free from their cells was spent in the law library with me.

"Sarah pulled me aside in the library one afternoon in late November and said, 'I have reports some of the inmates want to try and take out the terrorists. In fact, I had two kitchen inmates arrested this morning for trying to poison their food.'

"Did they die?" I asked.

"No, but they did get pretty sick. I sent them to Erie County Medical Center (ECMC) to get checked out. And this is the reason I pulled you aside, I can't have any more incidents like this I could loose my job. So I have to ask you this question.... Is it going to be a problem for you to work in the library while they are in there?

I said, "Are you serious? Can't believe you asked me that? I'm a stockbroker. I think I have enough of my own problems right now, don't you think?" I could tell that she felt bad lumping me in with all of the other inmates.

"My aunt, now reassured, allowed me to continue to serve as their law clerk after the attempt on their lives. It was quite a production every time they would come to the library. The guards would lock down the entire jail to move them. We called it the shackle-shuffle. Once in the law library, the terrorists were unshackled and left with me. In jail, you're always sizing up the other inmates to see who is a threat and who is not. They were polite and courteous and went about their research and commiserated in Arabic."

Lymes asked, "Ok, but how did you get them to trust you?"

"Well, I don't go all the way on a first date. I take it nice and slow. Having the same counsel as el Barwan allowed us to bond over our hatred of Mallory and the depths of his sleaziness.

"Word on the street was the Buffalo Six always had the best weed and coke in town. I reached out to a couple of drug dealer associates to confirm this information. I was told it was true."

Jackmann asked, "How did you get a bunch of drug dealers to come in and talk to you in jail?"

I replied, "They didn't have to come in. I called them."

"So what your telling us is that you called known drug dealers on a from jail phone and they talked to you? Bullshit I don't believe it. They wouldn't be that dumb." Jackmann said.

"Who said I used the prison phone," I stated.

"Well I just assumed that's what you used," Jackmann replied.

"And that's the problem. You assumed. I used a cell phone a guard buddy of mine smuggled in," I told them.

"I don't believe it," Jackmann said. "Neither do I," Sinsel added.

I answered, "It happened. I asked for a phone and within 24 hours it was in my hands. It was a prepaid drop cell phone. I left the charger in the law library among the myriad of cords that went to the fax and copy machines. It blended in perfectly. You would have had to know it was there to see it. The phone, on the other hand, I had to bring down with me every day and back up to my cell every night."

Sinsel asked, "You didn't get caught?"

"The guards were friends, so I was never checked. Plus, they all knew what was going on, it was it was my own little personal don't ask and I won't tell policy."

"Considering I was in jail, I had it pretty sweet. Almost every day I ate food my aunt would bring me in: pizza, wings, or a sub. But the best part was the access to the internet, fax, and photocopy machines in the library's office."

Jackmann and Sinsel were amazed. They assumed, I think, I was chained in some lower level dungeon or something. By the look of their faces, it seemed to make my arrest less of a victory for the good guys and more of just a big time out for me. It clearly rubbed them the wrong way.

"The best time for me to use the cell phone was with the terrorists in the law library. The guards were prohibited from entering because the terrorists were afforded extra privileges. That meant no oversight while at the law library i.e.: no guards. I gave them the books or forms they needed and retired into my office to talk on the cell phone. There was a regular land line but that was traceable and the cell phone wasn't. The Buffalo Six knew I was talking on the phone but they kept their mouths shut about it. Tihir even asked if he could 'phone home' once.

"Tihir was the most talkative of them all. He was what I would characterize as the most Americanized. Outside, he partied hard and dated a white girl. I think he might have had a child with her, but I don't know for sure. The terrorists learned the rules of jail quickly. I was their only access to the rest of the world and I used it to my full advantage. It was obvious to them I had a lot of friends in jail. I walked around the jail freely under the guise I was delivering legal papers to other inmates.

"As their cases moved towards sentencing, they started to clam up. I had to make a move to get more information. My plan was to obtain access to el Barwan's privileged lawyer documents."

That's when Jackmann spoke up, "When did they tell you the info you told Baynard? All the stuff about their cells' target and knowing Mohammad Atta."

I replied to Jackmann, "I am getting to that."

I looked at the five of them on the plane. They were all like kids sitting around a campfire listening to a story waiting for the ghost to jump out of the woods.

"What I did next was against the law." Looking directly at Jackmann and Sinsel I asked, "I have full immunity right?"

Jackmann said, "Yes," what I thought was a reply tinged with venomous abandon.

Regardless I turned my attention to Lymes.

"It doesn't matter once you hear it you won't be able to use the information against the terrorists anyway," I said, "It would be inadmissible in court."

This statement really drew them in. Perfect.

"Why?" Sinsel asked.

"Cause I obtained the info illegally and I would never stand up in court to verify it to help you."

"I arranged for a couple of inmates to have a staged fight on the same floor as the law library. This sent the entire jail into lock down mode. Inmates were forced into their cells.

"And that was what I needed nobody around to see what I was up to. Second, I scheduled a meeting with Mallory for the very same day as el Barwan. Everything hinged on this. I was betting on Mallory's laziness. He would bring both my and el Barwan's files together. Why make two trips right?"

My audience was starting to understand. Lawyers are lazy. If they can double book meetings and make twice the money in one trip well, why not. The stage was set.

I went on, "I enlisted the help of couple of inmates to start the fight. My guard friends informed me Mallory had two large boxes with him. One contained el Barwan's name and other had my name. The two inmates started the fight. With the fight going on, the whole jail went into lock down. Mallory was pulled out of the interview room while el Barwan never made it out of Special Housing Unit (SHU). I was left in the law library free to do what I wanted. All I had to do was go into the interview room, grab the box with el Barwan's case files, bring them down to the law library, and use the photocopy machine." Lymes was fully engaged with the results of my devious my plan.

I continued, "It was almost too easy. I had el Barwan's entire case file. I was hooked on finding out as much as I could about the Buffalo Six."

Lymes asked, "So what you're telling all of us is that you have photocopies of el Barwan's legal files from his case?"

I replied, "I have everything."

Jackmann said, "You're right. We won't be able to use any of the information in court, but it would be a great insight to read what's in there. Where are the files now?"

I casually said, "They're in my locker at Butler."

Lymes said, "So all of this information on the first terrorist cell arrested and convicted in the US is just sitting in a jailhouse locker?"

I replied, "Yep."

Lymes leaned over to his assistant and whispered something. His assistant got up and made a call.

I asked Lymes, "What's your assistant doing?"

Lymes replied, "He is having those files transported to DC. Did any of the Buffalo Six know you had el Barwan's files?"

"It would have been pointless if they found out, right? No one knows I copied the files, not even the guards that helped me. I kept everyone in the dark. I didn't want them to know what I was up to."

Christ, Lymes seemed nascent at this information. National security was on the line, unencumbered information was paramount.

"After I read el Barwan's files I had the tools to further the investigation," I said.

Jackmann sarcastically asked, "What investigation?" As if to say the FBI were the only people capable of getting at the truth.

I replied, "What would you call it?"

He gave no answer.

"After photocopying the documents in the box I returned them to the interview room and went back to the law library. Neither Mallory nor the terrorists caught wind of the investigation." I used my fingers to do air quotes to satisfy Jackmann.

Chapter 36

I had given them a peak behind the curtain but now it was time to pull them all the way back.

"In Erie County I had laid the ground work. After that we were all transferred from the Holding Center to Immigration and Naturalization Service (INS) Detention in Batavia, NY. We spent about a month there and then we were all transported back to Buffalo to board a US Marshall Transport flight to Metropolitan Detention Center (MDC) Brooklyn for Federal Reception.

"During the flight the terrorists and I realized we were headed to real jail now -prison," I said.

"There's a huge difference between being in a county jail as opposed to being in the Bureau of Prisons (BOP). First, people in country jail are still fighting their cases they're not looking for any trouble. But when you get to the BOP people are sentenced to life they got nothing to lose by fucking with you. That's the difference between the two.

"We flew from Buffalo to New York City, landing at Newark, New Jersey International Airport, and then were loaded onto buses headed to the MDC facility. That's where I got another dose of reality."

"What do you mean?" Lymes asked.

"I entered the bus first followed by Tihir, el Barwan and the rest of the Buffalo Six. I sat down and almost immediately saw, written in black magic marker, 'Osama will save us' along with some Arabic writings. I pointed to the message with my shackled hands and said to Tihir and el Barwan, 'What's up with that shit? Listen, I've pretty damn good to you guys so if this is my time to go, I want to know.' Tihir and el Barwan both seemed just as surprised. We just hoped we would make it to MDC Brooklyn."

Sinsel asked, "You must have really been worried if you wanted to make it to jail?"

I answered, "Yeah, I'm riding on a bus with terrorists and then I see some crazy Arabic writing. Let's just say I was happy to get my cell. We were sent to cell block D on the 14th floor. Shit was popping off on that block daily. Fights, stabbings, you name it.

The Buffalo Six and I were shook. Inmates were talking about what they would do to terrorists if they came through MDC Brooklyn. Even Muslim inmates were ready to kill them. I pulled the Six aside and said, 'Listen, we're in New York City, what do you think is going to happen if any of these guys find out why you are here? You guys would be fucked. I've kept your secret and I'll keep your secret. So, if you guys have my back, I have yours. After all, the government put me in here too.

"After that, I ate with them, hung out with them. I asked them questions about their faith. It was all part of my campaign to amass as much knowledge as I could. After all, this might had been the last place I would have contact with them."

"Not long after our Brooklyn dodge the Buff Six and I were moved to the oldest prison in the United States, United States Penitentiary (USP) Lewisburg. Lewisburg sits on the top of a mountain in Pennsylvania but you would have never known it on the inside. The walls blocked out every tree and every blade of grass. The lack of greenery could drive anyone crazy.

"The Buffalo Six and I were stuck in the Transfer Unit. The bunk beds were stacked three high. Sleeping there felt like existing in a Costco Hell with rats the size of small dogs to enliven the night.

"I knew we would be transferred elsewhere, but it couldn't come soon enough for me.

"After three weeks we were placed on the transfer callout. You never know where you're going until you get down to the staging area.

Which really sucks cause you don't know if you're in for a long of short trip. They do it like that so the bus isn't ambushed.

"We waited with 15 other inmates as each person was called into the processing area. The Buffalo Six figured this might be the last time they would see each other. They huddled in the corner and said their goodbyes. It struck me as weird they had been kept together as long as they were. The BOP, as per policy, usually split up co-defendants after sentencing. Unless the BOP was watching them to see if they would talk about their cases it was an odd to say the least. It wasn't protocol.

"Processing for transfer in the Fed's starts by handing over your prison issue I.D., then you're fingerprinted, your picture gets taken, you're strip searched, x-rayed, and given clothes. Finally, you get your I.D. back and are sent out to the bus to be you handcuffed and shackled. The last indignity is when you are black boxed. A hardened piece of plastic goes over the loose part of your handcuffs so you can't move your hands at all.

"I was processed last and directed to the third bus of seven. The sign on the top of the bus read, 'Federal Prison.' I wished it displayed a happier destination.

"The bus was already full. It was like being back riding a very dangerous high school bus. I saw el Barwan first but the seat next to him was taken. Further back I saw Tihir sitting alone. The seat next to him was open, I staked my claim. A minute later the C.O. came on and announced we were headed to FCI Loretto. A Hispanic inmate spoke up and said, 'Where the hell is Loretto?' The C.O. answered, 'The middle of nowhere Pennsylvania. Now all you assholes shut the fuck up or you're going to the box as soon as we get there.'

Chapter 37

"When we got to FCI Loretto we were told it was a converted Franciscan Monastery. It wasn't much to look at. In fact, it reminded me of college dorms with a Catholic flair for the gothic.

"Once off the bus we were ordered follow the C.O. into yet another processing area. Tihir and el Barwan were right behind me. The whole procedure was repeated again. I was given my dorm assignment and told when and where I could get my draft bags and new issue clothing. The same drab forest green pants and shirt.

"In the Draft Room is where I first met Dr. Baynard. He introduced himself and Jack Halford, and extended his help in getting me situated to my new surroundings. I was wary of his offer, but the good doctor seemed on the level. He told me his cell number and after I dropped off my things I went to see him. I forgot all about Tihir and el Barwan."

"A week went by and Tihir and el Barwan hadn't emerged. I began to ask around if anyone had seen them, but no one had any answers. Baynard explained sometimes when there aren't enough beds new transfers are placed in the Administrative Segregation Unit until a bed opens up.

Baynard then interjected saying, "I asked him why he wanted to find these guys so bad? Are they part of your case or something?"

"Right. I told you we were all from Buffalo and been bounced around the Fed's together.' That was when Baynard asked what they were in for?"

Christopher Prior

"I lied to you buddy. I told you they were in for drugs.

"I followed Baynard around the whole first week. We discovered we knew some of the same people and had in fact done business with the same Mob families. Of course I checked out Baynard's story."

I turned to Baynard to ask him, "You checked out me out too, right?" He nodded yes. "I was told Baynard was 'a stand up guy' which was code in Mob language for I could trust him.

"Two weeks into Loretto, Baynard introduced me to the most powerful guy in the jail. He was an inmate named: Richard Mozilla, the leader of the Dominican Power (DP) gang. Mozilla ran all of the work details and room assignments. To get in good with him was to be doing very well. I took Baynard's suggestion and anted up the gratuity. By the second week I had my own room with a shower. Jail house moves.

"Three weeks in, I finally ran into Tihir and el Barwan in the yard. Man, were they happy to see me.

"Baynard and I were in the weight pit working out when I looked up and saw Tihir and el Barwan walking down the hill from the main building. When Baynard finished his set I racked the weights, and we went to meet them. I made introductions and asked if they needed anything.

"They smelled horrible so I told Tihir and el Barwan to follow me to my room. They were shocked when we got there. I had a little TV and tons of food. I offered them something to eat. They gobbled down three bags of potato chips and a couple of Snickers bars before I pointed to the shower.

"Once clean they said the guards fucked with them hard in the box. Luckily, el Barwan was able to get word out to Mallory and that's when the warden released them.

I knew if anyone realized el Barwan and Tihir were the terrorists it would mean bad news for me. It was cluster fuck waiting to happen. But I need answers and pushed the thoughts of being shank'd to the back of my mind.

"So they took me to their housing unit. It was awful. In the Fed's you only get a better place to live by good behavior or, like me, you buy it. I told them to start get'in proactive about a job before one was given to them."

This prompted Sinsel to ask, "So, it's like the real world?"

"Sure, if you don't find yourself a job, believe me they'll find one for you. And you're not gonna like it.

"I told Tihir and el Barwan I could hook them up with a good job but it would cost. Mozilla gave me a little taste for each person I brought to him. The more and more I did for the terrorists', the more I earned their trust and the more they confided in me.

"Eventually, Moz came through giving el Barwan a job sweeping the gymnasium and Tihir was given the same job as me, which essentially was doing nothing. The actual job was to roll down a bunch of plastic garbage bins to the compactor. The other inmates, also 'friends' of Moz's little syndicate, would throw the garbage into the compactor. Mozilla's guys did all the work. I could tell Tihir got a little kick from the luxury. My money was on Tihir to spill his guts about Al Qeada. He seemed like he was eating up every part of my plan."

"Isolating el Barwan was a gutsy move," Lymes said.

I replied, "It had to be done. There was no way I would have gotten either of them to talk when they were next to each other. They had to be separated."

Jackmann and Sinsel nodded their heads, while the latter asked, "How did you know to do that?"

Lymes and crew were getting into the story which made it more fun for me to tell. I've always felt a captive audience was an audience you could manipulate and control.

So I went on, "I worked on Tihir for about a month before he began to open up. I suggested he write a book about what he had gone through. He loved the idea until I told him about the 'Son of Sam' law, which prohibited inmates from benefiting financially from writing about their crimes.

"Prison is boring and it was my pet project to get everything out of Tihir and el Barwan. At first all they revealed was official information from their cases. I started to think maybe there wasn't any more to be told. Maybe their story of being young, impressionable kids sent on a wayward journey to a country far away was true. I decided to make one last push to get more information.

"I walked up on Tihir and el Barwan hanging out in the yard about a month after we got to Loretto engrossed in conversation. I asked them what they were talking about, and they said, 'Friday's prayers.' Tihir explained Friday is the Islamic day of rest and asked me to join them at the prayer service. The Catholic in me said no way, but the sadist in me said grab a rug."

"After that I began attending more and more Muslim events. Learning about the five pillars and other Muslim acts of worship. I played it light and told both Tihir and el Barwan I was just interested in learning about their religion. I asked them questions about what things meant and how those things differed from Western faiths.

"I read texts on religion, the Koran, or anything that I could get my hands on." Reading them until it became rote."

Baynard interrupted and said, "That's why you had me bring you all those books while we were at Loretto."

I thought, 'Yeah. No shit Sherlock.'

"Inmates were required to read law library books within the library, but with Baynard's help I was allowed to keep my investigation secret. I was fully committed. At the same time I was getting nothing good out of Tihir or el Barwan until."

Chapter 38

Patrick Mallory felt the buzz of his phone in of his Armani suit left inside pocket.

He just received a text message from his office secretary marked—

URGENT: Just received fax from NYS state prison warden's office concerning Marcus Declan. Call office immediately.

His natural reflex was to think, 'What he had gotten himself into now?', but dealing with Mr. Declan would have to wait.

Mallory was in court and about to give his closing arguments in a salacious murder trial. His current client sitting beside him in an orange jump suit was accused of killing his entire family. Mallory had taken the case 'Pro bono'. However, his new found charitable façade was cracking.

His client, Terrance Raddar, a black man was accused of killing his entire family after a fight following a family picnic. Tempers flared when members of Raddar's family, began to rag on him about having a white wife. It didn't matter that they had been together for 15 years, nor did it matter that they had five children together ranging from ages one to 12 years old. The man's family members were relentless so the couple decided to leave the party. But the ride home was the same as the family picnic but this time it was the couple fighting each other while their children watched from the back of the car.

It wasn't long before they were home where the fight continued. The children ran immediately to their bedrooms with the sounds of their parent's hateful words filling the hallway. They had heard their parents fight before but not like this. Fueled by emotion and intoxication the man's wife said the one thing to him that he never thought he would hear from her, "Stop acting like a nigger!" And that's all it took.

Suddenly everything was quiet in the house. Raddar's wife and children heard him walk into the back room where he kept his weapons locked in a safe and went out side and grabbed three large cans of gas he used to fill up the tanks of the lawn mowing equipment for his business. He proceeded to dump and pour the gas around the base of the house and on the siding. Then he started the house on fire with his family in it.

When Raddar's wife and children tried to get out he screamed, "If you try and get out I will shoot you down!" And that's exactly what he did. His wife and children tried to escape out a window and he shot them all. Even a cynic such as Mallory couldn't comprehend the malice of his client. 'A jobs a job, though,' he tried to convince himself as he looked in the mirror every morning.

Meanwhile, Marcus's father, William, was on his way to Butler Correctional facility to surprise his son with a visit. Marcus and his father, who normally went by the name 'Whitey', had bonded throughout his imprisonment. Whitey understood what his son had done was wrong but he was still his son and he would always stand by him.

Marcus's family hailed from Upstate New York and his parents had been divorced for nearly 10 years. His father was a retired salesman for a large company that provided safety equipment to airports. His mother, Olivia, lived in West Palm Beach in Florida and worked as a nurse at a local hospital.

There was no doubt Marcus came from a good family but he was the proverbial 'black sheep'. His younger brother, Paul, who lived in Ft. Lauderdale, didn't know what to make of his older brother Marcus.

Whitey had decided to make this surprise trip during the week because he had made plans to visit Paul, so the 'normal' bi-weekly weekend visits, to Butler Correctional to see Marcus would have to be moved up.

Plus, now that he was retied Whitey didn't travel much, and he missed driving through Upstate New York during the fall. So Whitey went to Costco to pick up some of the things Marcus loved to eat and wear to give to him during his visit. New York state prisoners are allowed to receive packages of up to 60 pounds of either food or clothing each month. There were two caveats though. First, all food must be factory sealed. Second, all other items such as sweat pants, sneakers and towels must be of the approved color and type because of the gangs who wear specific colors to signify their allegiance to their set.

As Whitey eased his Ford Edge onto the interstate 90 and settled into he three hour trip, Whitey, was oblivious to what a surprise he was going to be in for.

Chapter 39

After spending the better part of the morning in the car and drinking four cups of coffee, Whitey decided to take a 'constitutional' and pulled into a local rest stop to use the bathroom and grab some breakfast. He hated going to see his son without eating some real food first as the only choice in prison visiting rooms was vending machine crap. That type of food always gave him a terrible stomach ache.

Satisfied with what resembled waffles and grits, Whitey went back to his car and returned to the road. As usual he aimed to arrive at the jail early. It was just his nature and a hangover from his days as a salesman, but being early for visitation in jail had two advantages. He could visit with his son longer and avoid the long lines. He pulled into the visitor's parking lot and popped open the back of the Ford Edge.

Out tumbled six plastic bags of groceries but he gathered them up, he remembered to take two Benjamin's from his bill fold and tuck them in his shirt pocket. He was by far the first to arrive which meant he could slip the guards the money to let in the extras. Normally, Whitey was opposed to pay into graft but this was for his son. He felt secure paying off the guards because he knew the officer he was paying was from Buffalo too. "It's never what you know, it's who you know'" me muttered to himself, refusing to allow his self denial any countenance. Whitey was old, old school.

Christopher Prior

He made his way into the lobby of the prison and set the food down on the counter where inmate packages were received. Whitey pulled out his cell phone and made a call. As the steel door to the package inspection area swooped open. Standing there was Officer Zimbra. He was Mr. Declan's man in Amsterdam à la 'Pulp Fiction's' Marsellus Wallace.'

"Hey, how you doing Whitey?" Officer Zimbra asked.

"Not too bad, Zimmy. How are you?" Whitey replied.

"Tired as Hell. I feel like a fucking Zombie. Just worked a two doubles and I got five more hours until I can head back home."

"Wow, so how many hours is that?" Whitey asked.

"20 hours each day with a four hour break in the middle," Zimmy said.

"Well you're a better man than me," Whitey said.

"Hell, you drive here just about as much as I do," Zimmy said. "Maybe you should get a job here."

For Zimmy, it was the same old shit. Prison guard humor sucked.

"No thanks. I'm retired," he replied.

"Hey got a question Whitey, Why are you here in the middle of the week? Don't you usually come to see Marcus on the weekends?"

"Yeah I usually do but I'm flying down to see my other son, Paul, to go golfing and I would have missed seeing Marcus," Whitey said.

"Wow, you're good to stand by your son like that, 'cause I tell you we don't have many people that travel as far or come as often to see their people in jail," Zimmy said.

"Hey Zim, it is what it is," was Whitey's reply.

Chapter 40

As he waited, Whitey grabbed up the local news paper sitting next to him on the table. The front page story screamed: **'Terror Plot Foiled!'**

As he read the story, he casually noted that a plot to attack the football stadium in Denver, Colorado was foiled by the US Customs Agents. Two men were captured trying to enter the US though Michigan on expired visas. As border agents rifled through the vehicle they found detailed, written plans for the attack in the Mile High city.

Marcus's father took a deep breath and sighed. He hated his son had done this to himself and that he had to be in there with people like those in the article and worse. He put down the paper and sat with his legs crossed as he looked at his watch. There was another 15 minutes until he could see his son and hug him.

Whitey looked around the beige room with its bars and metal detectors. He thought to himself, 'Only two more years until Marcus comes up for parole and he can get the out of here.'

Over to Whitey's left hand side the door opened from the visiting room but today something was different. Normally, on the 20 plus other visits he had made, he would get up and walk in. But this time Officer Zimbra was accompanied by a man wearing, what Whitey considered, a damned expensive, bespoke suit.

As the men made their way over to Marcus's father, William stood up and asked, "What's wrong?"

The suit was Warden Gerald Toth whose personality was limited to toothy smiles and downtown bon homonie—a characteristic in men which always made Whitey uncomfortable.

"Hi Mr. Declan," Toth said in his usual effusive manner. "I sure would like it if you'd accompany me for a second, sir."

"I'm not going anywhere until you tell me Marcus is OK," Whitey demanded.

"Please sir, I would rather discuss this in my office so if you would be kind enough to follow me this way," Warden Toth said as he motioned with his hand.

Whitey looked to Officer Zimbra as if to say, 'Please tell me he is still alive', but with his boss there Zimbra just couldn't take the chance to assure his friend.

"Please Mr. Declan. Just follow the Warden and he will explain what has happened," Zimmy said.

"Mr. Declan...this way," the Warden asked.

Now in Toth's office each of the men took a chair. The Warden at his desk and Officer Zimbra to the left hand side of Marcus's father.

"Let me start by telling that your son Marcus is fine. Nothing has happened to him at all. He's in good health," Toth said.

"So let's see him then," Whitey demanded.

The Warden looked over to Zimbra and then back to Whitey and said, "That's going to be the difficult part, sir."

"Why?" Whitey asked.

"Because your son is no longer here. He was removed yesterday morning by two FBI agents," Warden Toth said.

"What the fuck do you mean he's not here?" Whitey yelled.

Zimbra leaned over and placed his hand on Whitey's arm and said, "Listen, Mr. Declan, Marcus is with the FBI that's all we know."

Warden Toth confirmed with a nod.

"So what the Hell does that mean? Where in the Hell is my son? He's your responsibility. He's State property and that means you're charged with his safety. So if anything happens to him...," Whitey left the threat hanging in the air.

Having been a warden for over 15 years and dealt with far more nefarious threats on a daily basis from inmates, Toth brushed aside the father's obvious frustration. Rising from behind a desk that overshadowed even his ego, Toth replied, "Listen, Mr. Declan. The only thing I can tell you is that I was given written orders by the Governor of New York State to release your son. That's all I have."

He extended his hand to the confused father. "I'm sorry I don't have more information for you, sir. I'm as in the dark as you are."

Whitey hesitantly shook the Warden's hand in a daze. Zimbra escorted him out of the office.

Walking together down the hallway back to the visiting room, Whitey asked, "So what do I do now? Who the Hell has Marcus fucked off this time?"

For a moment, Zimbra's mind returned to his ineffectual rookie year as a guard when the answers to questions were too painful to contemplate. "I don't know, Whitey," he quietly replied. "I just don't know."

Chapter 41

As my father returned home with a desire for beer and an end to the shitstorm he'd just encountered, my BBF's, Baynard and I continued to bond.

"One day Tihir and el Barwan were completing their daily prayers while Baynard and I spun the yard," I explained." Except the Latin Kings wanted to play soccer and no amount of praying was going to prevent the Kings from bending it like Beckham.

Baynard chimed in, "I remember that day, I was with you and Mozilla. They closed the whole fucking yard after that."

"At first it didn't seem like anything was going to happen, but we weren't the only ones watching. The work out pit was full of African American Muslims, mostly guys that converted while in jail. It was like 9/11 was a blow horn to recruit lost young black men. I never understood why so many of them converted in jail; I think they were just happy to be learning something other than guns, drugs and killing. They were like fuckin' sheep.

"But the shit really went off when one of the Kings grabbed the sajjāda rug from under Tihir while he was praying. I knew what was coming next. It was on and popin'. I broke away from Baynard and Mozilla and headed for the middle of the playing field. With every step, I was asking myself if I was crazy. Getting in the middle of someone else's beef was more or less a death wish. But if I saved their ass, Tihir and el Barwan would owe me.

"I heard Tihir and el Barwan telling them to return the sajjãda rug. Then one of the Latin Kings reached down into his sock and I knew what was coming out: a banger to air out Tihir and el Barwan. They were outnumbered and now out gunned. The gang surrounded Tihir and el Barwan to block the surveillance cameras. I had a hoody on which I immediately pulled off.

"I was in the thick of it now and confronted the King with the biggest desire to slice up a Muslim or two.

"You have to understand, I'm no fucking hero—this was all about self preservation—so I admit my, 'What's the problem here?' query struck everyone as naive, suicidal and hilarious at the same time.

"Fuck you, cunt," was the reply as I heard the head King screaming, 'Air these motherfuckers out.'

"Tihir was the King's first target. I grabbed for the shank with my balled up hoody and got it tangled up in the fabric. I felt a couple of hard blows to my back and head and I fell. I just laid there on the ground.

"The Muslims from the weight pit all made a beeline to our little party. As I stood back up, the riot horn shrieked and I realized the shank I grabbed had cut the inside of my right arm.

"With the Muslim contingent in the mix, the melee quickly dwindled to a juvenile pushing match. Call it whatever you want, but I saved Tihir and el Barwan's lives that day."

Jackmann asked, "So how bad were you hurt?"

I answered, "Pretty bad. Luckily the shank missed all the major tendons and arteries in my arm."

Lymes remained unimpressed. "So if you didn't go to the infirmary, how did you take care of the wound?"

I motioned with my head and pointed to Baynard, "My friend, Dr. Baynard, of course."

Baynard said smiling, "He needed about twenty zippers so I stitched him up with a sewing needle and dental floss. I used smuggled in whiskey as a disinfectant."

Wincing at the memory, I explained the personal consequences of the fight. "After that day, Tihir and el Barwan couldn't do enough for me. They were like lovesick puppy dogs on dope. From then on they answered my questions and vouched for me to the rest of the Muslim fraternity. Instead of looking at me like I had a dick for a nose, I began to be greeted with 'Assalamo alaikum' which means 'Peace to you.' It was a sign of respect usually only reserved for other Muslims."

Chapter 42

"A few days after the incident in the yard, Tihir and I were walking to work and I explained to him that today was surveillance tape day, which meant the last month's entire phone recordings were to be disposed of. Tihir and I walked to the Admin Building. Once inside we were shown about 50 boxes of audiotapes stacked against the wall. Tihir and I loaded up the boxes and were escorted to the regular garbage collection point.

"On the way, Tihir quietly asked, 'So these are all the tapes of our phone conversations with the outside world, huh?' I nodded yes and muttered 'Quid pro quo, baby' and thought nothing more of his question as for the next three hours our lives revolved around smashing and pulling apart each and every one of those damn tapes while the guards lazily watched us. After Tihir and I finished we went to 'spin the yard.'

It was a cool day, with a slow, swirling wind catching the conversations and recriminations of the inmates and blowing them around on a whirligig of fruitless hopes and desires. I thought to myself.

"But as we sat perched on the hill overlooking the site in the yard, Tihir opened the flood gates about his dealings with Al Qeada.

"Tihir thanked me for what I had done for him and el Barwan. I replied, 'You would have done the same for me, right? His eyes bore the answer I wanted to see.

"He knew I was leaving soon to start my New York State bid. He asked me how many days I had left at Loretto and I told him 40.

Christopher Prior

He surprisingly said he would miss me, and added it was tough to find trustworthy people in jail, explaining that ever since he and el Barwan came to FCI Loretto he felt as though they were drifting apart. I told Tihir it was just jail getting to him and warned him not to isolate himself from the one person he was going be with for his entire sentence, because that my friends is a long ass time to stand alone.

"I felt for Tihir, though. I had six weeks left in the Fed's, and a two to four in the State and I would be free. Rummaging for the best cliché I could find, I simply said, 'Listen man, you can do the time. Don't let the time do you.'

"He was quiet for about 10 minutes after that pearl of wisdom. 'I just don't know if it is worth it now, he mumbled. 'What if more shit goes down again like the other day? What if someone finds out why I'm really in here? I'll be screwed man, I tried to kill Americans.' I agreed with him, but didn't let it show. He was, to all intents and purposes, royally fucked.

"I kept trying to ease his desperation and finally said, 'Listen man, I'm the only one who knows who you guys really are or what you've done so as long as you and el Barwan stick to your cover story you're both gonna be good.'

"Tihir remained impassive, but said, 'You're right Marcus. However, I don't understand how you can be so optimistic?' I replied to Tihir, 'What choice do we have, buddy?' This made him smile.

"By this point he seemed at such a low ebb. 'Fuck Sisyphus,' I thought. 'This guy's got nothing on that poor sucker.'

"Our time together that day was coming to a close. In an hour they would blow the horn to close the yard. I had to push him one last time. 'Tihir, I know you're troubled. And we both know all the fucking prayer mats in the Muslim world aren't going save you from the inevitable. So take a load off, man. What's on your mind? After all, who the fuck am I going to tell?'

Lymes and company had been in the dark until this very moment and I was about to flip the switch.

Chapter 43

Everything that I had told Lymes, Jackmann, and Sinsel to date had been leading up to this point, but I had a question I wanted answered before telling them what I had uncovered about Al Qeada.

"What was it, in the transcripts, that made you believe what I was telling Baynard was true?"

Lymes simply stated, "The North East Power outage."

This statement surprised Jackmann and Sinsel prompting Jackmann to ask, "Why that?"

Lymes replied, "There was no way that Mr. Declan could have known it was a terrorist attack unless he had first hand knowledge of it. The President sent a memo stating any mention of the power outage as a terrorist attack would not be tolerated."

Lymes further added, "And the Canadian Government agreed to keep the incident quiet."

"So did you catch the cell responsible for the attack in Ottawa?" I asked.

"No," Lymes answered.

This answer gave me the current insight of the government's knowledge of Al Qeada. Quite simply, Lymes and the CIA and the rest of the US government were too busy attacking the head of Al Qeada. They just didn't understand the intrinsic interdependence of each cell. They missed it by a mile. Men bound by religion were a determined force.

Jackmann asked, "So how did you know that a terrorist cell hit the Ottawa power plant?"

I answered, "Tihir told me, but we're getting ahead of ourselves, gentlemen. Let me tell you the story as it was told to me."

I think the off the cuff nature in which I replied caught them by surprise, what I was about to tell them now would change the course of my life forever, so I chose my words carefully. I thought about how well my social engineering experiment had paid off getting Tihir to tell me everything he knew about Al Qeada.

"More or less, the Buffalo Six were manipulated by three men. Alnahban, Dosari and Derwish who were in direct contact with the upper echelon of Al Qeada."

"Who do you mean by upper echelon?" Jackmann asked.

"Khalid Sheikh Mohammed (KSM) and Osama bin Laden. It doesn't get any higher than that does it?" I said.

"When I further investigated," I said.

"Investigated?" interrupted Jackmann inferring the FBI were the only people able to get to the bottom of something

"Yeah what would you call it?" silence.

"From the places and the people Tihir mentioned to me in the yard, I was able to assemble the puzzle piece by piece. These guys lived in their own little world separated from the rest of the city of Buffalo. It was like little Bagdad down there."

"Yeah it was," Jackmann said, "The whole area is made up of old row houses that used to house the steel workers from Bethlehem steel plant."

"Yeah when the plant used to be running," I said. "Now it's a shit hole."

Lymes spluttered, "What do you mean by that?"

I replied, "There's nothing down there."

"Maybe that's why they did what they did?" Sinsel stated.

"Who knows? But what I do know is this they were torn between who they were and who they thought they should be. The truth is these guys were major drug dealers living it up American style, but that conflicted with their religion."

They weren't the only ones I thought to myself.

I know from personal experience you can't lead two separate lives and keep them apart forever. The guilt and the lies take a toll. If you add the pressure of indoctrination into the largest terrorist network backed by the religion of their youth, you get an explosive situation.

"Tihir explained this guy named Derwish was smart and well spoken—traits Tihir and the rest of the Buffalo Six were lacking.

"Derwish had a command of an extreme version of Islam. It was called wasabi and they're obsessed with eradicating all who are not wasabi. The West is definitely not wasabi."

Lymes smiled and smugly chimed in with, "It's called Wahabi."

"Well it doesn't matter if I put the wrong emPHAsis on the wrong syLLAble," I replied quoting Mike Meyers in 'View from the Top'.

"The Buffalo Six ate that extremist shit up."

Thinking back I specifically remembered the happiness in Tihir's voice while he spoke about that time in Buffalo. I think he felt he was now becoming the Muslim he was supposed to be.

"The Buffalo Six hung on every word coming out of Derwish's mouth. Goya was so enthralled with Derwish he moved in with him.

"But Goya was soon replaced by a guy named Alnahban as Derwish's right-hand man. This was confirmed also by the files I stole from Mallory—an important fact that will make sense shortly."

Chapter 44

"A year passes and Derwish tells the Six and Alnahban he was going to make good on what he's been preaching. He is leaving to join the fight in Afghanistan with the Taliban." I remembered this time period because it was when I siphoning all the money out of the fund.

"This meant the students were left without a teacher but not for long. Before Derwish's departure he made Alnahban the head of the tight-knit unit. Alnahban put Goya in charge of staying in contact with Derwish through e-mail and satellite phone.

"In April 2001 this guy Dosari, showed up in Buffalo. Dosari's arrival reinvigorated the cell with new blood and even crazier ideas. Dosari told the Six and Alnahban he had just come from fighting with Derwish in Afghanistan and it was Derwish that sent him to Buffalo. Derwish knew Dosari would be able to get them to join Al Qeada."

I suspected to capitalize on American Muslim's desires to help in the fight in the Middle East.

"Dosari proselytized during the Dars (Friday prayers), evoking their duty as Muslims to fight for those that couldn't do it themselves. Dosari beat into them tub thumping chants like, 'You could be next. You must train for the upcoming Jihad.' In short order, the men from Buffalo were convinced of their destiny and decided to travel to an Al Qeada training camp.

I took a breath to break the momentum. Lymes could wait for me. Sitting there impassively, I laughed at the thought of the Six entrenched in the Middle East. When I was in jail with Tihir he had shown me pictures of him at home. He looked like Apu from the Simpsons in the episode where he is a playboy. Decked out in an open unbuttoned shirt, hairy chest and gold chain. I just couldn't imagine him in a towel head getup.

"Mr. Declan anytime today would be nice," sneered Jackmann.

"Ok, so the Six, Alnahban and Dosari, came up with a convincing story to cover their tracks. It was decided to tell anyone who asked they were traveling to Pakistan to study with the Islamic evangelical group, Tablighi Jamaat, a story the FBI believed until you, Mr. Lymes, intercepted an e-mail from el Barwan while he was in Bahrain."

Lymes nodded his head in agreement and said, "Their true destination, of course, was Al Farooq—an Al Qeada camp."

I went on, "Exactly. All this planning and travel took about a month."

Jackmann looked astonished, "One month? That's it? I guess this Dosari was pretty good?"

I replied, "Yeah that's what I thought too."

I pondered the timeline. It was fast but was it believable? Maybe it was because they were all soccer players and played on the same team. It could have been that fact that they were drug dealers and they had to trust each other.

"Dosari's split the group of seven men into two groups to avoid the risk of alerting authorities. Tihir, Gallad, and Mohammad left first and they were followed shortly after by Alban, el Barwan, Goya, and Alnahban.

A smart move I thought.

"The first group didn't go directly to the Al Farooq they went to some halfway house somewhere in Pakistan; I don't remember exactly, maybe Kandahar."

Lymes face showed he was internally scrolling through his rolodex of Al Qeada hide outs in his head but he offered no additional info. So I continued.

"The second group was met at the airport by Derwish, who they hadn't seen in a year. Derwish promptly pulled Alnahban aside for a private conversation. After that little pow-wow control of the newly arrived recruits were split into two smaller groups. He told them this was a direct order from bin Laden.

"El Barwan, Goya, and he [Derwish] travel directly to Al Farooq to meet up with the others, while Alban and Alnahban would travel to the same safe house in Kandahar that Tihir, Gallad, and Mohammad had just arrived at.

I could just imagine the trip. They get to where they are going and then they are redirected somewhere else. I would have been pissed.

"This is important because this is where Alban met bin Laden for the first time."

"What do you mean for the first time? Are you saying he met with him more than once?" Lymes asked.

I thought why did he care if bin Laden met with him more than once? 'Note to self, I thought. Did he know what I knew?'

"Yes he did, but let me explain ok. Osama at the safe house called for Alban and Alnahban to become martyrs by saying, 'Men will hold their souls in their hands.'

"In Alban's court case he stated publicly he was freaked out by the meeting with bin Laden and all the talk at the Al Farooq camp of terrorism was the reason he left the camp early. And even though he states that 'fact' in his court records it was a lie. But you guys bought it anyway."

This little gem I discovered from el Barwan's court documents I stole.

Lymes looked confused and asked, "What do you mean?"

Maybe he didn't know what I knew.

I answered his question with more questions, "If Alban was so freaked out, why didn't he leave right after his meeting with bin Laden in Kandahar? Why did he then go on to Al Farooq? Riddle me that."

While Lymes sat pondered, Jackmann and Sinsel each possessed a look of such bemusement I almost felt sorry for their torment. Baynard, however, just looked bored.

Chapter 45

"One thing stuck me as odd, though, once Alban and Alnahban finally arrived at the Al Farooq camp. They found Tihir, Gallad, Mohammad, el Barwan and Goya had been ordered to wait outside the camp until they arrived."

Jackmann shot me a confused look and we both looked at Lymes for answers. Lymes said, "It's standard procedure for Mujahedeen," offering no other explanation.

'Ok,' I thought, 'That's cool. I was like how was I supposed to know that?'

"At Al Farooq they were kept as a tight-knit unit often being supervised by bin Laden himself. Tihir told me this created tension among the other recruits. Tihir and the rest of the Buffalo Six were fully into what they were learning at the camp. Tihir lit up when he talked about the various subjects they were taught, handling guns, rocket propelled grenades (RPG's) and bomb making."

"It was like they went to an evil Disneyland," Sinsel added.

But all I could think of was, 'this Kingdom was far from magic.'

"While at the camp the Six witnessed the towel-head equivalent of the merging of two Mob families."

This statement made Baynard laugh—he was the only one.

"This guy, Zawahiri, the leader of the Egyptian Islamic Jihad, and bin Laden inspected the new recruits, especially the Six. There, bin Laden and Zawahiri decided to combine forces merging the Egyptian Islamic Jihad with Al Qeada."

Lymes looked at me like this was obviously old news but to Jackmann and Sinsel it seemed appropriate to tell them.

"This is where the official story and the real story diverge, and why Alban's story for leaving early was bullshit."

"Why was it bullshit?" Jackmann asked.

"In Alban's trial, as he told it to the government, he got freaked out saying that it was all too much. He wanted to go home to see his family but was denied. Seeing no other way, Alban faked a leg injury to expedite his exodus home."

"But what really happened was Derwish informed Alban his request would be granted on a condition: he must first meet with bin Laden. The remaining six members hoped Alban would be persuaded to stay but, to their dismay, Alban was allowed to leave. Tihir and company thought Alban had pussied out."

As would have I, I thought.

"Now down a man, Buffalo Five,—Tihir, Gallad, Mohammad, el Barwan, and Goya—continued training at Al Farooq. A couple of weeks later, about June '01, they were summoned to a private meeting with bin Laden, Khalid Sheikh Mohammad, Dosari, Derwish and Alnahban.

"At this meeting preparations for future and ongoing initiatives concerning Al Qeada were discussed in Arabic. Tihir wished he had been more fluent because this conversation put in motion the reason he was in jail. at least that's what he told me.

"Alnahban and Derwish pulled aside Tihir, Mohammad, and Gallad telling bin Laden had decided they had completed enough of the training and due to Alban's departure, if they didn't leave immediately it would attract too much attention because they all came there together jeopardizing Al Qeada's ongoing missions.

"Tihir had one parting obvious question, 'What's our mission?' Alnahban explained el Barwan and Goya would supply them with their target when they returned to the US.

"The remaining four, Derwish, Alnahban, el Barwan, and Goya were split into two teams Derwish with Alnahban as team one and el Barwan with Goya as team two continuing training with the same fever."

Chapter 46

"Meanwhile Tihir, Mohammad, and Gallad arrived back in Buffalo, but not before the FBI questioned them at JFK Airport. Their cover story continued to hold, but Tihir said they felt rattled after the questioning."

I remember when the FBI questioned me—it was not the most pleasant experience I've ever had and I wasn't a terrorist.

"The answer to Tihir's question came one month later with the return of Goya and el Barwan. Tihir told me back in the day on the soccer field in high school, both he and el Barwan always seemed to be in sync, but something had changed, it seemed as though el Barwan was holding something back. The Ron Jaworski Stadium days were over. Goya and el Barwan had returned with a new purpose in life.

"Goya proudly told the group el Barwan was chosen by bin Laden himself for a secret mission. El Barwan remained tight lipped as Goya informed Alban, Tihir, Gallad, and Mohammad that Khalid Sheikh Mohammed (KSM) arrived the day after they left. KSM, alongside bin Laden, watched them train for the next two days. Goya explained he and el Barwan were pulled aside for private meetings with KSM and bin Laden.

"Goya said at the meeting they talked metaphorically of a big meal and were asked questions of martyrdom. Bin Laden stated, 'It will be so big that you will not be able to withstand it.'

Jackmann asked, "You remember the exact quote?"

Christopher Prior

"Listen when someone tells you something that came directly out of the mouth of the world's most wanted man, you don't forget it," I replied.

Jackmann nodded in agreement.

"Four days into their extra training, Derwish and Alnahban were escorted to meet with KSM and bin Laden again. At this final meeting Derwish spoke for the al Qeada leadership. He informed Goya and el Barwan they would be leaving separately due to US military operations in the area. This perplexed Goya and el Barwan but neither questioned it. According to Tihir, bin Laden's last words to them were, 'My request will soon become clear to all of the Buffalo Six.'

Chapter 47

"The real reason for Alban's early departure was secret and had remained just that."

"Like I said before, they thought Alban had pussied out. El Barwan knew Osama had sent Alban on a special mission so he told him to let the cat out of the bag.

"Alban explained that his story about being homesick and injured was a cover to conceal his true mission. The real reason, he explained, was that bin Laden had personally handed of two video tapes by bin Laden. He was instructed upon leaving al Farooq, to take one tape to a safe house in Kandahar while he was to return to Buffalo with the second tape.

"So finally, the Six knew the truth? But what was that truth? And what was on the tapes?" Lymes asked.

"Tihir asked the same question."

"The first tape he dropped off in Kandahar had excerpts from the USS Cole bombing and other al Qeada propaganda. The second tape was ordered not to play it until he returned to Buffalo.

"Once home, Alban discovered the tape revealed the phone numbers of Al Qeada contacts in the US along with instructions to transfer funds to said members. There were numbered bank accounts and times when the funds were to be transferred. Also he was to make fake I.D.'s for each of recipients to correspond with names on the bank accounts and send them to various P.O. boxes. Mainly to Patterson, NJ, and Orlando, FL.

"But why would they have him do that?" Sinsel asked.

"Yeah, Al Qeada usually hands stuff off in person why would they trust the mail?" Jackmann asked.

"I don't know but Alban completed his part of the mission, but at the time he had no idea what it was for but El Barwan knew. KSM, the orchestrator of the first World Trade Center bombing in NYC in 1993, had a secret operation going and Alban's task was a part of this mission we all know now as 9/11."

"El Barwan then communicated to the group he was sent to Europe to meet up with a guy named Binalshibh. Al Qeada's money man.

"Binalshibh was on his way back to Germany from a meeting in Spain with Mohammad Atta—the so-called mastermind of the 9/11 attacks in the US. El Barwan was slotted to become part of the 9/11 plot and that's why he was in Europe.

"Over the next week el Barwan tried to get into the US via Germany but he was continually denied an exit visa. Atta would have to do with only 19 hijackers.

"Binalshibh and el Barwan called KSM the third week in July 2001 from the Kreuzberg Pub just outside Berlin to let him know the el Barwan was still in Germany and not with Atta in the US. KSM ordered el Barwan back to Al Farooq for further instructions.

"When he arrived, Khalid Sheikh Mohammed, Alnahban, and Derwish told el Barwan the mission would go on without him and KSM had something else planned for him. The Six would become an important second wave piggy backing on the chaos and destruction created by the hit on the Twin Towers and the Pentagon."

Sinsel was growing impatient. Putting his head in his hands as if in defeat, he simply and blurted out, "For Christ's sake cut to the chase."

"El Barwan was supposed to be 'muscle' on the planes that hit New York. He missed out on the largest attack ever against the US," I said.

"He was supposed to be the 20th hijacker?" Lymes asked surprised.

I just nodded my head 'yes.'

The agents and Lymes chimed in. "Well that's an interesting new fact, but that really doesn't help us now does it?"

Jackmann, "Yeah, what was the piggy back mission?"

"The Six's mission was to black out the entire Northeastern US and Canada right after the attacks on the World Trade Center and the Pentagon."

"Well that's definitely something new. Tell us more," Lymes muttered almost knowing it already.

"Yeah, you never told me that part Marcus. Why?" Baynard barked.

"Sorry, buddy. I thought if I gave you too much info you might get into trouble."

"A little late for that," Baynard said.

"So this is what I left of the story the Six's plan—it was to hit the Niagara Falls Power Plant and incapacitate all of the turbines at the power plant at once. Their plan was to dive the reservoir and deposit an Improvised Explosive Device (IED) by hand into each of the 13 intake tubes for the plant, thereby shutting down the plant and sending the Northeast US and Canada back to the Dark Ages.

"That's a suicide mission. They would have been sucked directly into the turbines," Jackmann stated.

"They knew this. But they were up for it anyway. They became familiar with the power plant by taking the guided tours the plant offered.

"Yeah but that's the inside of the plant, that would haven't been sufficient for their needs," Jackmann said.

"You're right. So they got themselves the schematics to the plant and access to the security cameras."

"I understand they could get the power schematics, but how'd they get into the security cameras?" Lymes asked.

"They found out the entire security system was web based. So they downloaded the manual to the system and put in a back door so they could access it right form their phones," I replied.

"So what was their plan? Break into the reservoir and leave their equipment?, 'Cause that's what I'd done," Sinsel added.

I immediately thought it was the first intelligent thing he said all day. Maybe he wasn't as dumb as I thought.

"Exactly," I replied.

"El Barwan became a hard taskmaster, drilling in to the Six procedures such as meeting times and back up plans, manufacturing the IED's, and what to do following the hit. This was about the end of August of 2001."

Chapter 48

"Then on September 10th the Six was activated via a phone call from Derwish. El Barwan told him everything was in place, their gear and the IED's were at the reservoir, and they were ready to become martyrs and hit the intakes at the Niagara Falls Power Plant.

"At 8:46 on September 11, 2001, Tihir's wife, an America girl, ran into the bedroom to tell him the news of the attacks. Instead of being concerned he acted as if nothing of importance had happened. He said his prayers kissed his wife and child goodbye. He knew the next couple of hours would be his last.

"Tihir left his house headed to the pre-arranged meeting place. He ducked between the dilapidated row houses in his neighborhood to avoid the FBI surveillance.

"He told me at one point he thought he had been seen but as luck would have it, a school bus came between where he was hiding and his car. The slow moving obstacle gave Tihir enough time to get his car and drive away undetected."

"He's lucky. I was in Buffalo at that time and the place was in total lock down," Jackmann added.

"When he arrived at the reservoir, only Mohammad and el Barwan were there. Everyone was needed to complete their mission, el Barwan was livid.

"So let me understand this. It was supposed to be the Buffalo cell that hit the power plant and not the terrorists from Canada?" Sinsel asked.

I thought maybe I had given Sinsel too much credit moments before.

"Later that day the cell met in the basement of their mosque. El Barwan questioned Alban, Gallad, and Goya as to why they all failed to make it to the power plant. After the yelling and arguing subsided, the fact remained that they had failed to execute their mission.

"Oh ok it was given to the Canadian cell because who failed," Sinsel stated in a moment of epiphany. "El Barwan just didn't figure on the fact that half his crew would disappoint him."

Just a page or two behind I thought.

"Exactly. Now he focused on getting in touch with Derwish. He needed to know what KSM and bin Laden wanted him to do.

"Goya called Derwish's satellite phone the afternoon of September 11th but he didn't pick up. Who had no idea if Derwish had been captured or had placed himself on one of the planes to take el Barwan's spot. The Six watched the aftermath of 9/11 unfold on the T.V. with the rest of America.

Baynard added, "I remember the news quickly pinned Osama bin Laden as the mastermind. Kinda quick I thought."

"The cell panicked when a US criminal prosecutor came on the news networks spoke about the US criminal code that would be used against anyone who was caught after the fact and who had any part in the planning and execution of the attacks or anyone associated with Osama bin Laden."

Lymes' assistant handed me the section of the Anti-Terrorist and Effective Death Penalty Act of 1996 and it read as follows:

"Section 2339A of title 18, United States Code, is amended to read as follows:

Sec. 2339A. Providing material support to terrorists (a) OFFENSE- Whoever, within the United States, provides material _support or resources or conceals or disguises the nature, location, _source, or ownership of material support or resources, knowing or _intending that they are to be used in preparation for, or in carrying _out, a violation of section 32, 37, 81, 175, 351,831, 842 (m) or (n), _844 (f) or (i), 956, 1114, 1116, 1203, 1361,1362, 1363, 1366, 1751, _2155, 2156, 2280, 2281, 2332, 2332a,

2332b, or 2340A of this title or _section 46502 of title 49, or in preparation for, or in carrying out, _the concealment from the commission of any such violation, shall be _fined under this title, imprisoned not more than 10 years, or both. (b) DEFINI-TION- In this section, the term `material support or resources' means currency or other financial securities, financial services, lodging, training, safe houses, false documentation _or identifi-cation, communications equipment, facilities, weapons, lethal substances, explosives, personnel, transportation, and other physical assets, except medicine or religious materials."

"They finally got word from Derwish a week after 9/11. KSM specifically told Derwish to tell the Buffalo Cell to stand down and wait for further instructions."

Lymes asked, "How did Derwish contact them?"

"The Six didn't call him. We were on'em. We had wire taps and all the Local Usage Details (LUD's) of all cell phone calls made and received from their phones," Jackmann added.

"Yeah but not Derwish's SAT phone in the Middle East," I told them.

"So, the Buffalo cell was deactivated and sent into sleeper mode by KSM and bin Laden?" Lymes underlined my point.

"Yes," I said.

"Why?" Jackmann asked.

"It was because of you, the FBI," I said.

Jackmann replied, "What do you mean?"

"After 9/11, the FBI came into Buffalo with guns a blazing. You weren't any better at surveilling them then you were of me. If you would have done it right you wouldn't have freaked out el Barwan."

"What do you mean by that?" Jackmann asked curmudgeonly.

"He wouldn't have contacted Derwish, and maybe he would have tried to complete the cell's mission later on. You could have caught the Six in the act."

"We just couldn't take the chance. The country was in chaos," was Jackmann's reply.

"Well I avoided the FBI for three years back in college selling fake I.D.'s. I could pick out your FBI surveillance in my sleep."

"Well thank God you're not the terrorist's Marcus," Jackmann stated implying their dumb nature allowed them to be caught.

"Yeah and you're lucky I'm not," I stated.

"What the Hell is that supposed to mean?" Sinsel asked.

"I mean when you were on me, you questioned my neighbors and sat in your standard FBI vehicle, a blue Chevy Suburban. The fact that you were black didn't help either."

"Why is that?" Jackmann replied with a tone of pride.

"'Cause there aren't any black people in my neighborhood. You stuck out like a sore thumb.

"You know, not everyone is afraid of the FBI," Baynard said. He threw it right in their face.

"Yeah, he's right. I knew you were watching me, I was only a stockbroker. Why would you think the Six would be scared of you if I wasn't?"

"So what you are telling us, Marcus, is el Barwan was supposed to be the 20th hijacker and the Buffalo Six knew about the attacks of 9/11 before they occurred?" Jackmann asked.

I nodded my head in approval at his ponderous insight.

"Do you have proof of this?" queried Lymes.

"What do you think?" I replied.

"Just tell us," Sinsel barked.

"It's all in the legal documents I stole from el Barwan's lawyer, Patrick Mallory, while I was at the Erie County.

"El Barwan exploited and used his attorney/client privilege. They just didn't count on me stealing his legal documents."

"Maybe el Barwan was trying to use the information to get a deal by, but Mallory never used it," Baynard added.

"I'm not sure why, but maybe he decided that it would only hurt his case."

Chapter 49

"Mallory knew the government's case against el Barwan was pretty much circumstantial," I said.

"How can you say that? They all went to a terrorist's training camp," Sinsel stated.

"The government's case was preemptive justice. There was no actual proof the cell in Buffalo was involved with murderous activities, but they were arrested based on the fact that they might have been.

"You're all twisted up Marcus," Jackmann said.

"Am I? Not until right now did you actually know of anything the Buffalo cell was going to do," I stated.

"The men from Buffalo were used to scare others," Baynard interjected.

"Yea, maybe that was the writing on the wall Patrick Mallory saw."

Lymes asked, "All of this information can be verified from your files from Butler?"

"Yes. Your big break into 9/11 is sitting in a locker that's probably been rummaged through by criminals," I said.

"Why would you say that?" Lymes asked.

"You don't know much about jail do you?"

"No I guess not? I'm not a criminal," Jackmann stated proudly.

"By now the guards that saw me leave with you have already told at least one inmate."

Christopher Prior

"C.O.'s are the worst gossipers. They're like fucking school girls," Baynard underlined my point.

"The information about me leaving with you probably got to my dorm an hour after we left. My locker was ripe for the picking—my locker is filled with tons of goodies. And I just got a package from my father a couple of weeks ago so. You just better hope they take my clothes and food and leave the files."

This statement worried all of them, especially Lymes who now understood the ramifications, but there was nothing they could do about it now.

"Question though," interrupted Jackmann. "Why didn't you share this with Baynard when you told him the story at FCI Loretto? The fact that you stole the files."

"Yeah I would like to know that too?" Baynard said.

I said, "It's one thing to tell a story in jail to a buddy, it's another thing to say you have first-hand knowledge of the 9/11 attacks."

"I can understand that," Lymes stated.

"I didn't know if Baynard hated the Government as much as I did. I couldn't take the chance so I made sure not to directly implicate myself.

"Maybe if you weren't so busy trying to lock my ass up you guys would have had more men on the Six. The clues were there. I know for a fact Alban contacted the FBI in Buffalo the very day of the attacks and offered his help."

"How do you know that?" Jackmann asked in a pissed way.

"Come on, really? That was just one of many times he contacted you but the Buffalo office you never took him up on his offer or did they?"

"What's that supposed to mean?" Jackmann questioned.

"Oh nothing," I shot Jackmann a look of 'ok you can stop towing the FBI line.'

"Alban was the last person to be chosen to go to al Farooq. In fact, I don't think Derwish wanted him there, but Alnahban fought for his inclusion. You guys didn't think it was suspicious Alban contacted your offices in Buffalo?"

Neither Jackmann, Sinsel nor Lymes reacted to my question. This trio of silence made me nervous. Did they know what I knew about Alban?

"If I hadn't gotten myself locked up, you wouldn't have any of this. It's funny how things work out, huh?

"By moving into Buffalo after 9/11, you guys gave the cell all the time it needed. El Barwan, thinking you had been clued into their plan, had Goya call Derwish a third time. Derwish told el Barwan he was sending Dosari back to Buffalo to give them information on KSM's new plan for them.

"But why did he send Dosari? Why just not use the mail again?" Jackmann asked.

"Probably because he knew we were listening now and he didn't want to take the chance the message wouldn't get though," Lymes stated.

Baynard just looked pissed as Jackmann spoke. Probably because he understood just how dumb these guys really were. And they were just like the ones from the DEA that nabbed the good doctor. I just lifted up my shoulders and turned over and opened up the palms of my hands, indicating I echoed his point. I think Lymes was coming around to our side.

"Exactly, so Dosari showed up in Buffalo bearing news and El Barwan was pissed," I said.

"I would have thought he would've been happy. I don't get it," Jackmann stated.

"Dosari came to Buffalo to take the Six's mission from them and to transfer it to the Hamilton cell that was finishing up training at al Farooq.

"Again el Barwan had been passed over. The hit on the Niagara Falls power plant would go to the Hamilton cell.

"Dosari knew the Six were frustrated. They wanted a mission, especially el Barwan."

"They were just itching to die huh?" They should have called me I would've gladly shot some lead into those towelheads," Sinsel added.

Sinsel, gung ho through and through.

"A week later, Dosari headed back to the Middle East with a parting promise to pass on their concerns to KSM in Afghanistan. By January 2002, Dosari had failed to keep his promise the Six were ordered to meet the freshly trained Hamilton cell.

"El Barwan met Abdul Ghafoor, Mudar Mueen, and Sa'dan Ruhi—at a Niagara Falls strip club called the Pump 'n Dump. It was in these less than salubrious surroundings el Barwan handed over the schematics of the power plant, security codes, the location of the IED's and gear at the reservoir.

"A few days later an e-mail from KSM arrived stating to el Barwan he was to travel to Bahrain and the rest of the cell was to practice drift drives while he was gone.

Lymes seemed confused, "Drift driving?" he asked.

"Drift diving is where the diver is transported by the currents in a river," I told them all.

"I remember this he said his sudden departure was to meet a potential wife," Jackmann stated.

"This was a cover story concocted by Derwish, KSM and Dosari," I stated.

"The Six had to assume el Barwan was being summoned to Bahrain to receive their new mission," Lymes said.

"They were probably excited again. Another opportunity for martyrdom and all those lovely virgins," Baynard said.

"Yeah but you know the funny thing is that they never stipulated whether or not they were male or female?"

"Very funny, but a good point," Jackmann stated.

"El Barwan told the cell to sell as much weed, coke, and heroin as they could," I said.

"Why would he do that? If they got caught slinging dope or anything they'd be locked up and he would've had no one to help him," Jackmann asked.

"He probably wanted to make sure they would be properly funded upon his return for their mission," Baynard added.

"And he's now funding his own cells mission. I tell you this is the reason why we can't win over there. These guys are crazy," Sinsel said.

"By April 2002, el Barwan was back in the Middle East. He traveled to a camp outside Bahrain to meet with KSM and bin Laden. A month later he traveled to South East Asia to an Al Qeada training camp," I said.

"Why would he go to south east Asia? What there weren't enough camps in the Middle East?" Sinsel asked.

"'Cause 30 percent of all Muslims live there," Baynard added.

Lymes nodded in agreement and said, "Plus, it's a lot easier to hide a camp in the jungle then it is in the desert."

"On May 18, 2002, the FBI intercepted the now infamous e-mail that CNN, MSNBC and the like ran with about the Big Meal which if I had to paraphrase it went as follows:

'How are you all beloved? God willing you are fine. I would like to remind you of obeying God and keeping him in your heart because the next meal will be very huge. No one will be able to withstand it except those with faith. There are people here who had visions and their visions were explained that this thing will be very strong. No one will be able to bare it.'"

"The Six now had their mission. In effect, they had their Happy Meal. And if you remember I told you bin Laden said something similar to Alban when he met with him."

Lymes interrupted, "Very clever, Mr. Declan but do you know what their new mission was? What was the target?"

Jesus Christ, I thought, "No. El Barwan was supposed to bring it back from Bahrain, but after the e-mail the fate of the Buffalo cell was sealed. You had them."

Lymes said, "Yes, two months later the CIA had el Barwan picked up by the Bahraini police."

"That's when the house called in the marker on the Six. For the third time the cell failed and you got your break into Al Qeada. I guess the third time was not the charm for the Six."

"What do you mean we got our break?" Jackmann asked.

"El Barwan told you everything you needed to know once he was in custody. I don't know what you did to him to make him give up everyone, but it must have been pretty bad."

I knew damn well what they did. Perhaps a little water boarding or a car battery to the cahonies for good measure. Whatever the method it worked.

Lymes said nothing but a smiled crept out of Jackmann.

"Why did you bust el Barwan on the anniversary of 9/11? A little melodramatic don't you think?"

Jackmann responded, "The President wanted to put on a big show. That was all him."

I asked, "I still don't get it, though. Why wouldn't you just follow him back to the US to see if you could uncover the next plot? They had already transferred a mission once."

Jackmann said, "Yeah, but we didn't know about the power plant at the time."

I went on, "Listen, you guys only found out what el Barwan wanted you to know. So now you had el Barwan singing like a bird, he gave you all the information you needed or should I say what he wanted you to know. He gave up the Five back in Buffalo, Tihir, Mohammad, Gallad, Goya and the guy that had called the FBI numerous times to offer help, Alban. He gave up Alnahban and Derwish. He gave you the camp that they went to, Al Farooq and who he met there, Binalshibh, KSM, and bin Laden. Finally, he gave you Dosari, the guy that recruited them all in the first place at the request of KSM. He gave up the whole crew. El Barwan was your Sammy the Bull.

"You guys picked them off one by one. I remember watching the news there was a missile strike in Yemen. The news said you guys were tracking the mastermind of the USS Cole bombing, Abu Ali. With the missile strike you guys got a two-fer."

This got Lymes's attention.

"I bet after you guys picked up the Buffalo Six you got Derwish's SAT phone number from either Goya or el Barwan. Then, it was just a matter of tracking the signal and sending the missile to it. So were you really going after Abu Ali or were you after Derwish?"

Lymes's face said it all.

Turning to Lymes, I said, "Now I know you were after Derwish, and I'm sure Abu Ali too, so it was the CIA who ordered the assassination?" I asked Lymes.

"I ordered the missile strike. The President had given orders to me he wanted everyone involved eliminated with extreme prejudice."

This statement vindicated my suspicions of Lymes. He was a player and a huge one at that.

How many people had he executed? Were Baynard and I next? Hell, he might even set his sights on Jackmann and Sinsel, which would've proved no personal loss to me. But how far was he willing to take all of this? Had our government become what we all feared, the self-styled police of the world? If so, who polices the police? Who has the power to stand up to them? The realization hit me right then. Maybe that's what the cell from Buffalo and Al Qeada were fighting against. Was it the good fight? The right fight? It was too early to tell. Those kinds of questions are answered only by history. Everyone on the plane was frozen by Lymes' admission. I pushed through those thoughts as the pilot announced we would be landing soon.

Jackmann stated the obvious, "Story time is over."

I thought to myself, 'Why would Jackmann say story time?' Asshole. Maybe he didn't believe my own lovingly crafted tale of shock and awe? I didn't give a shit. I had talked for what seemed like hours and I needed another drink. Anyway, there were a multitude of facts I had left out intentionally. Those bombshells I planned on saving for the Pentagon. I was gonna rock the establishment to its foundations.

Chapter 50

As we circled to make our approach, I looked out the window at the Potomac River below. It hit me. We were landing at Andrews Air Force base—the President's own personal landing strip. Did I deserve to be on par with the President? The mere thought scared me. Lymes had mentioned the President's involvement on the plane. Was this with whom I was to meet? Maybe I had truly gotten myself in too deep this time.

My thoughts again turned to escape but even if I some how got away it only would have delayed the inevitable. I was going to the Pentagon. I could either go quietly or kicking and screaming. In jail the squeaky wheel got the grease in the form of a beat down and a stay in the hole. I could only hope for a beat down once we landed because the hole Lymes could put me in reached to China.

Andrews was a familiar place. A friend, Jason Babcock, had brought Teek and I there on several occasions to play golf at one of the three courses located on the base. Jason renamed, Trout a decade ago be me, used to be one of the major players in my fake I.D. business. He set up deals for me while he attended the Naval Academy at Annapolis but the lofty ranks of naval intelligence beckoned after he graduated in '96. I guess his quick thinking and time involved with shady dealings with me and Teek had served him well.

Now on the ground I asked, "So what's the deal anyway? Are we headed directly to the Pentagon?"

Lymes replied, "No, we have you scheduled for the morning, at O'eight hundred."

With more than a hint of foolhardiness, I asked, "So what are Baynard and I supposed to do until then? You better not put us back into a cell?"

Baynard clearly wanted to know the answer to this question as well.

Lymes enjoyed letting us all hang on his well-prepared decision. "Boys, I'm going to let you have a night in DC."

"Seriously?" I asked.

The agents were shocked.

"Yes. Go visit your buddy, Teek," Lymes said going against all known accepted protocols.

I thought to myself that must be the difference between the FBI and the CIA.

"So I can just go see Teek? Alone?" I asked.

He answered, looking at Jackmann and Sinsel. "Don't get too far ahead of yourself, Mr. Declan. I wouldn't say you're going to be alone. Someone will be around keeping tabs on you.

"As for Baynard, that's up to him. He can either go with you or maybe the doctor wouldn't mind catching up on some ol' times with me?" turning to Baynard, Lymes offered, "How's about a steak from Smith & Wollensky?"

Baynard nodded. In fact I swear I saw him lick his lips at the thought of what this Faustian pact would produce in the coming hours. Jackmann and Sinsel, however, were furious about their latest in a long line of babysitting assignments.

As we exited the plane I had one last question for Lymes.

"How do you know that I'm not going to run? I just told you Jackmann's surveillance was sub-par. I could lose them easily."

Jackmann didn't appreciate the jab.

Lymes simply said, "You won't run Declan. In fact, I think you can see your opportunity here. Also, I'm pretty confident you're aware of what will happen if you do attempt to run."

His response solidified my healthy of fear of Lymes and Vincent Price movies.

Chapter 51

It was late but I knew Teek would still be working at the job site in downtown Arlington, VA, just a couple blocks away from the last TVD Construction or (Teek Van Dine Construction) project—a 33 story high-rise which became the headquarters of the mattress business I set up before I went to jail.

I decided a little detour to see what my money had bought me was a sure-fire way to clear my head of the day's events. A chance to reallocate my mind if nothing else. It was late afternoon and it felt good to be free, albeit with metaphysical handcuffs.

When we were younger Teek and I had built many things together, decks, garages and two additions. We always fantasized about what we would build if we had the money. The problem was that I had all the money and no time. But that changed the moment I went to jail. I had no money and a lot of time.

So I secretly sent plans to Teek via my lawyer. Since I could remember, I had read books on design and architecture. But just because I could design a building didn't mean I had a clue about construction. I left that up to Teek. It had become his purpose in life and I was glad to let him revel in his hard hat life.

The building was beautiful. It was exactly how I designed it. Lymes had organized a driver for my night on the town, and as my silent companion pulled up to the entrance, I looked up through the moon roof of the limo to the top floor, the thirty-third floor to be exact. I had chosen 33 because it was my numerology number, same as Jesus, Hitler, Winston Churchill, and Gandhi to name a few. Throughout history, builders have worked significant numbers into their construction projects and this one was no different.

An example is The Great Pyramids in Egypt. The pyramid bases are equal to the sum of ℗ [pi] or 3.14159265. This attention or reverence to numbers gave the building a life of its own.

The doorman of the building opened the limo door for me, a nice touch by Teek, very NYC. I asked the doorman what floor the offices were on. He told me they were located on the 18th floor, Teek's old lacrosse number.

I made my way to the elevator and pressed 18. The elevator doors opened and I exited into a double floor atrium that housed the main offices. I couldn't believe this was the company I had started only 18 months ago—Teek had really run with the idea.

The receptionist, to my disbelief, already knew who I was. She told me that both Karen, Teek's sister and Teek Van Dyne had said that I might show up unannounced. They knew me too well. I was impressed.

She asked me to follow her to Karen's office. We caught Karen talking on the phone. When she saw me she immediately came over to give me a hug. It had been a long time since I had felt the touch of a woman. Her embrace felt like home.

Karen asked all the obvious questions. I tried to answer as many as I could, given the situation. She told me that Teek was still on the job site. She wanted to call him but I told her I wanted to make it a surprise. She motioned for me to follow her.

As I entered a private elevator and she pressed floor 33. When the elevator doors parted, she silently, with a gesture of her immaculate hand, motioned for me to walk inside. The floor was filled with brand new everything; furniture, computers, desks, and even some artwork on the walls Matisse, Salvador Dali, Pablo Picasso, Vincent Van Gogh, Georgia O'Keefe, Frida Kahlo just to name a few. 'Christ,' I thought. 'This collection would make the MOMA's Ann Temkin blush with envy.

In the distance I could see a card standing up-right on a conference room desk. I turned to look for Karen but she had disappeared.

I made my way to the card. It read, "Welcome back Buddy! We all missed you. I hope you like what I've done with the place. It's all for you Buddy! I know, with all that free time you've had, you must have some incredible ideas marinating in that head of yours and I didn't want you to have to wait to get started."

It was signed, "Your best friend, Teek."

Barely holding back the tears, no-one was around to hear my reply. "Yes, you are, man. Yes you are."

I stood there for a moment and walked towards the large set of windows in my new office. The building stood at the corner of North Fenwick Street and Arlington Boulevard in the distance I could see the Pentagon. Just for a moment, I wished Teek had built our gleaming citadel elsewhere.

I looked down to the street to see Jackmann and Sinsel being hassled by the building's security guards. As I smiled at the absurdity of the scene playing out far below, I made my way back down to the lobby.

Chapter 52

I rubbed my eyes and composed myself. On my way out I stopped by Karen's office and grabbed the address of the job site.

As I exited the building I saw Jackmann and Sinsel leaning against their Suburban. I walked over to them before getting in the limo to say, "Listen, do you guys have to follow me so close? I thought I've earned a little trust here."

Sinsel replied, "We don't trust you, don't get it twisted that was all Lymes."

"Little cranky huh?" I replied.

"So what's this building?" Agent Sinsel was back to being his usual dick self.

"That's for me to know and you to find out," I replied sarcastically.

Maybe Sinsel was pissed we hadn't finished our 'discussion' from the plane. No matter, he didn't look froggy, so I kept the boys holstered.

Jackmann sensed the tension and said, "Listen, you just do what you want to do and we'll do what we have to do."

I replied, "All I'm going to say is this, if you guys don't fade into the background my buddy is gonna to pick you out. So if this secret is going to be kept like it's supposed to, you need to hang back. I'm not going anywhere." I could only hope they would take my advice. It was like they had taken the short bus to surveillance school.

I handed the driver the Post-It note Karen wrote the address on. As we drove I noticed it was a boom time in the nation's capitol. Whole neighborhoods were being transformed from ghettos to high-rises with retail store fronts. I guess the former murder capitol was movin' on up.

We crossed the Marriott Key Bridge into Georgetown and headed to a construction site near the future home of the Redskins. Most of the buildings around the stadium were at two to three stories.

But there was one tall building taking shape. As the limo turned, I saw a banner proudly proclaiming, TVD Construction, a P.T. Barnum rip off if I ever saw one.

We pulled up to the job site and I found the project manager's trailer. I went to the door and knocked. Inside were a couple of engineers and a building foreman. You can always tell who they are because they're never dirty like the guys that do the 'real' work. I asked them where I could find Mr. Van Dyne. The foreman said, "He's up there. In fact, that's where his desk is." I laughed. Teek couldn't just have a regular office. It had to be a dangerous office.

The foreman handed me a hard hat and said, "Follow me I'm going that way." We made small talk as we rose into the air. I didn't care for heights without a parachute. As the elevator came to a stop the foreman pointed in the direction of Teek. I made my way over to my buddy.

I yelled over the hum of the construction, "Hey, I'm looking for the tough guy running this project?"

Teek turned towards the sound of my voice. I don't think he recognized me right away because the last time he saw me I was about 120 pounds heavier. As I moved closer his expression changed from confusion to elation.

Teek traversed a couple of naked beams of steel like a water nymph—he always had great balance. He grabbed and hugged me with an embrace that took the wind out of me. Teek wasn't my brother by blood but by sweat.

We left the open steel floor and headed back down to ground level. On the elevator we talked or shall I say Teek pummeled me with questions. I had to watch what I said. I didn't want him to become another oarsman on my boat of self-destruction. I felt I was lying to a priest, but it was necessary to protect Teek.

"So how the fuck did you get out?" Teek asked.

I quickly came up with, "I won a Habeas Corpus motion and got out earlier today."

Teek said, "That's fucking awesome man, but I thought you still had at least two years to go?"

'Marcus, my boy,' I thought. 'Better keep up the pretense.'

"Apparently they screwed up on my case from New York and bam, they had to let me go. I only had to wait seven days until the judge rendered his decision."

I don't think he believed me, but he was so happy to see me I don't think it registered.

"What about parole, piss tests, and curfew?" Teek asked.

"Nope, I don't have any of that shit now, I'm a free man," I answered.

Now at ground level Teek said, "Just let me duck in here'n tell the foreman I'm leaving and we're outta here buddy."

Teek's quick exodus to the trailer gave me a chance to scan for Jackmann and Sinsel—I didn't see them. The 'short bus' had left the depot without Jackmann and Sinsel on it.

Chapter 53

We jumped into Teek's yellow Hummer and left the construction site. He immediately reached into his center console and out came a bat-box filled with marijuana with a one hitter.

"Man I haven't seen one of these since college," I said.

Teek handed it to me and told me to me to pack the one hitter, but I really didn't want to smoke pot right now. However, a refusal would have literally sent up smoke signals and made Teek suspicious.

So I pulled a Clinton as we weaved through the rush hour to our destination—Teek's house. We pulled into the driveway and I noticed there were two other houses on the street on either side of his house. We exited the Hummer and entered his house I asked him, "Who lives in the other houses?"

Teek replied with, "Karen has one and the other is for you."

"Are you serious dude?" I asked.

"Business has been good...you know. What can I say? I got you bro," Teek proudly said.

Stunned at the generosity and the foresight of my partner in crime, I barely reached the front door upright. "I never in thought you could've done so much in such a short time," I said.

"Well, the mattress business took off about three months into it, right after we partnered up with three of the top national bedding retailers. The rest is history, it basically runs itself. Just like you set it up, bro.

"I'm just glad to have you back motherfucker," Teek said.

I replied, "It's great to be back. And now I can see every day I spent behind those fuckin' walls was fucking worth it."

Teek motioned with his head he understood exactly what I was saying and asked, "So, what do you want to do?"

"It's your town. What the Hell's goin' on in our nation's capitol tonight?" I asked.

"Well I, I mean, we, have a suite at the Capitol Center and there's a hockey game tonight. And you're never gonna guess whose playing?" Teek stated.

"Don't even tell me the Cap's are playing the Sabres," I said.

"Damn right! I was already planning on going before you showed up. You up for that? Or do you want to do something else?" Teek asked.

I answered, "Naw. I fuckin hate hockey."

At first he wasn't sure if I was serious. Uncertain if jail could turn a man against a game woven into the very center of his soul. The look on my face provided the answer.

"Ok smart ass," he said. "A Sabre puck fest it is. It'll be Falcon, Trout, you, and me, OK?"

I knew Trout, but I didn't know Falcon which kinda concerned me. I guess he was a new friend of Teek's but that was the least of my problems right now.

I asked, "What about some poonanny?" Teek knew exactly what I meant—we had been using that name for pussy since high school.

Teek said, "Let me call Falcon."

As Teek dialed I went to the fridge and grabbed two beers. I half listened to their conversation out of habit. It was something I learned to do while I was behind bars. As soon as I realized I was ear hustling his conversation, I stopped myself. There was no need to do it here. I was safe with my best friend.

Teek laughed into the phone as I handed a beer to him and asked, "So what's up?"

Teek pulled the phone away from his face and said, "Oh just Falcon being Falcon. It's like the guy has ESP. I told him you were out and immediately asked, 'So are we gettin' hookers tonight or what?' It's like he knew what was on our minds. Or maybe he just has pussy on the brain 24/7.

"So," he asked in a suitably Alex Trebeck style, "How do you like your pizza?"

I guess my time inside must have dealt a severe body blow to my bullshit radar as this seemed a perfectly normal question.

"I don't know man, hot I suppose."

"I suppose? Well, me too. Hot and delivered, right?"

By now my friend's behavior was turning weird. He went from hookers to pizza. "What the fuck are you talking about Teek?"

"Falcon's ordering up some escorts, that's what. They'll be hot and definitely delivered."

Laughing my ass off I said, "Niccceee. I think I like this Falcon dude already."

Teek suggested we shit, shower, and shave because everyone would arrive shortly. As the water hit my face I realized I had temporarily forgotten the real reason I was in DC. I grabbed my precariously perched beer on the inside towel rack and finished it. Then I stuck my head completely under the water. Surface dirt and grime was easy to wash off but my past was a far more stubborn a stain to get rid of.

Chapter 54

After my shower as I dried off I looked down onto the cul-de-sac below only to see Jackmann and Sinsel in a Crown Victoria a quick reminder of my predicament. I heard Teek make his way downstairs so I quickly dressed and followed the sound of his foot steps.

As I entered the kitchen, Teek handed me another beer. He told me as he looked at his BlackBerry, the girls, Trout, and Falcon would be here in 10 minutes.

It was a little past seven o'clock and the game started at eight. I really wanted to confide in Teek but 10 minutes was not enough time to reveal the truth as to why I was in DC. He seemed so happy to have me back—I don't think he had stopped smiling since I saw him on the job site.

I hadn't eaten all day, so the beer was playing rope-a-dope with my brain, helping to create a buzz of well-being I hadn't experienced in a long time. Only the clanging of Teek's less-than-subtle door bell shattered my happy psycho-cocktail.

I thought, 'Why would Falcon or Trout bother ringing the doorbell? Teek never locked door.'

As the door opened, Teek's sister, Karen and her young son, Finnegan walked in. The last time I saw little Finn was just before I got locked up. He had grown so much. He was about one or so when I left on 'vacation' and now he was about to turn five.

Karen apologized for the doorbell and said that Finnegan wanted to ring it. I reintroduced myself to Finn. It felt weird at first he

Christopher Prior

didn't know what to make of me, but then Karen said as she crouched down to the level of her son, "Don't be shy Finnegan, that's your Uncle Marcus."

He looked up at Karen for some reassurance and then ran over to give me a big hug. I had never been called anyone's uncle before. The importance of my adoptive family hit home hard.

Teek told his sister our plans for the night, obviously leaving out the part about the hookers. Karen said she and Finn were sleeping at their parent's house in Chevy Chase, MD because tomorrow was grandpa's birthday which made little Finn smile.

"So don't go too crazy tonight you two or dad will be pissed," Karen added as little Finn wondered why his mother's voce changed.

Teek and I look at each other and said, "Who us?"

She shot us a stern look and I said, "Don't worry about it. I defiantly don't want to get on your dad's bad side after only being out of jail for 24 hours." It was funny I had made it through jail but Teek's father still scared me. I guess when you're a SEAL they do something to your personality that makes everything you say law.

Little Finn, still smiling, had one request though. He begged Teek to call him up to wish him goodnight. Of course Teek said, 'yes.' Kisses and hugs were exchanged all around and Teek promised Finn he would call one last time.

Waiting for the limo in Teek's office, I scanned the cul-de-sac for my re-named Jackmann and Sinsel through the bay window. My 'Agents Provocateur' were no-where to be seen.

Soon Falcon had arrived in a limo with the girls and yelled, "You guys ready or what?" as Trout shouted from the sunroof flanked by two girls.

Now parked, I introduced myself to Falcon and then embraced Trout. Fucker had barely changed. As we exchanged introductions the girls poured out of the limo like maple syrup forming a chorus line of beauty.

Falcon said, "Well since this is your night Marcus, you get to choose," as he extended his hand like the 'Barker's Babes' showcasing a product.

There were four of us, but there were five women, two blondes, one brunette, one Asian, and a redhead. Falcon must have sensed my confusion and butted in, "Teek told me you had a thing for redheads so she is definitely for you, and since you have been on 'vacation' for a while, and I took it upon myself to pick you up extra som'thing som'thing."

From that moment on I knew I would like Falcon. I picked the redhead and the blonde with the short hair. I almost went with the Asian chic but I knew Teek had a thing for them. We all clambered into the limo and headed for the arena.

Chapter 55

The Washington Capitals were playing my home town team the Buffalo Sabres. It's a funny thing about people from Buffalo. We still love our old town even though we left it for dead years ago. If I had 30 friends in high school 29 of them left and never moved back. We all look back at the place we grew up as a safe haven, a fond memory. Especially Teek and I. We played 20 years of hockey together in that town.

The limo pulled up to the arena and we were escorted up to our box. Teek had invited a couple of business associates who were already there. Introductions were made and we took our seats to watch the game. The box was fully equipped with food, drinks and a pair of waiters at our beck and call.

I felt weird being in an arena surrounded by so many people. Teek jumped right into mingling with our hired entertainment. The girls were students at a local university, not the usual fare. I always wondered about prostitutes, assessing their needs, reasons and pervious lives. Throughout history their services have been used by paupers and kings alike and tonight I felt like both.

By the end of the first period the Sabres were down by a goal which, through my years of torment, I knew only too typical for the Sabres. Teek, now unencumbered by his other guests, sat beside me to root our team on. In the second period the match was tied up and the third, with two minutes to go, the Sabres got the go ahead goal. We were high fiving and spilling our beers everywhere.

As the air horn blew to signal the end of the game, we began discussing our plans for the night. Pretty soon, we were headed to Chadwick's in Georgetown.

In the limo I decided to follow Falcon and Trout's lead from earlier by standing out of one the sunroofs. The redhead and Teek joined me. The other sunroof was soon occupied by Trout and Falcon. We screamed and yelled at the passersby. It was such a relief. The tension of the day had finally disappeared for a brief moment.

I scoped the surrounding vehicles for Jackmann and Sinsel, but I didn't see them. Teek sensed something was wrong, but he would have had to have been a Svengali to know what I was looking for. We passed all of the great monuments and buildings of Washington on our way to Old Town filling me with a momentary sense of patriotism.

Maybe I should have come forward with what I knew? I thought about my decision to keep my mouth shut. Had prison changed me? Did I really have the power to give the US the upper hand in the war on terrorism with the information I had locked in my head. How many American lives could I have saved by revealing what I knew? I looked at Trout. What would he think if he knew about the information I withheld? These questions loomed large as the night continued.

Teek sensed my distance as we pulled up to Chadwick's and entered. He asked me if everything was okay.

I paused and said, "You wouldn't mind if I went back to the house would you?"

Teek replied, "No man, whatever you want to do is cool with me. We have plenty of time to party. So if you're not up to it, whatcha wanna do?"

The group minus Teek hemmed and hawed over my reluctance to celebrate my freedom but I stuck to my guns and said, "I think I'm gonna just take the limo home and send it back for you guys, ok?"

Teek shot one finger in the air to say 'wait a minute.' As my hand hit the cross bar to the exit door I heard Teek from behind me say, "You didn't think I was going to let you go back by yourself did you?"

I said, "Thanks, man. It's all just a little too much for my first couple of hours of freedom. You can't imagine what I have been through over these past four years."

Teek replied, "I can't even attempt to put myself in your shoes, bro. We'll go back and just chill."

Chapter 56

The ride back to Teek's was quiet. I had run out of energy. In jail I had decided I would no longer live a life of lies but I had, by unseen forces, been forced back into the life I no longer wanted to lead. The weather had turned down right wintery small flakes hit the glass melting immediately on impact.

I asked the driver to pull over at a convenience store so I could get caffeine and nicotine. In jail I had become addicted to both, much to Teek's surprise.

I rolled down the window, lit up a smoke, and took a sip of coffee. After about 10 minutes the caffeine kicked in and I felt less lethargic. We pulled into Teek's driveway where we saw the lights on in the house. Teek mumbled, "That's weird." My immediate thought was Jackmann and Sinsel had been inside.

It was weird to be home early. I used to have a reputation as partier and at one point I think I knew all the words to 'Closing Time.' I worked hard and I played even harder and for me to give up a night of drinking and carousing was out of character.

Teek and I made our way to his office to play some pool. He grabbed a couple of beers from the bar and we shot a couple of games before we went out to the back deck to talk. Our conversations were that of a priest and sinner, confidential and at times full of reverence. But as we sat there, I couldn't tell who the priest was and who the sinner was. Who was I fooling? We were both sinners.

Stepping out on the deck I expected to give my confession but Teek made an abrupt left turn. I asked him, "Where are you going?"

Teek replied, "I thought you might want to see your new house and something else."

As we walked the lawns between the houses, Teek pointed to a long rope swing hanging from a tree. "Look familiar?" It's just like the one I had at my fraternity house. Damn I miss those days."

As his mind continued to lurch from one drunken frat boy memory to another, I saw Jackmann and Sinsel's Crown Vic. I quickly snapped Teek back to the present and guided him to latest in a long line of Declan abodes.

Now, we were walking through the back yard of the house but the back looked like a front. It was embellished with picturesque windows, tiers of decks and a full manicured garden slowly dying off into the changing of the seasons not to mention a long boat dock that headed toward the Chesapeake Bay.

Entering the house through one of the many sliding glass doors on the deck, we walked into the first floor kitchen, then my office, nearly an entire wing to itself, and finally the great room. Which was at least 2,000 square feet itself. Teek led me up to the second floor which had nine bedrooms. This was a pimp shack for real. All it needed was a pole in the corner for strippers. Lastly, we headed down to the basement. Each floor, including the basement, was connected by a huge centralized marble staircase with wrought iron embellishments. I applauded his attention to detail. I asked, "How'd you remember all the shit I wanted in my dream house man?

Teek simply said, "I wanted you to have what you wanted. But that's not all I have for you."

We walked over to a large copy of 'Starry Night' by Vincent Van Gogh. Teek touched the right side of the print to revel a secret walk way. We entered past the now sideways print to a descending spiral staircase. It was like being in a 007 movie.

"Where does this go Dr. Evil?" I asked.

Teek answered, "You'll see."

Once down the staircase, we entered into an underground room that had been decked out with all the goodies. We had talked about having something this crazy, but I never thought I would see the day it actually came to pass. There was a huge bar, a dance floor, a bank of flat screen TV that rivaled NASA command, walk in humidor, and a wine cell renascent of a castle in France. Teek was proud of himself and rightfully so. He had turned our lives into a huge playground. We made our way back to the ground floor and walk down a flight of stairs to a tunnel connecting to my place to Teek's and to Karen's. This was one embellishment too far, I thought, but I was in no position to be to second guess his craziness when he has endured so much of mine.

As the night passed, I told Teek war stories from jail; stabbings, fights and other things I witnessed. He was amazed I had made it out of there alive. I had to agree with his assessment. Beer after beer we sat and shot the shit by catching up on old times and talking about the future. But it was all bullshit. If Teek knew what was really going on, that his and his sister's house were being watched by a pair FBI agents I'd be face down in a pool of quick drying cement. As I drained my last beer, thoughts of betrayal and the consequences mingled like a fucked-up Glee club.

It was 'round midnight and my meeting at the Pentagon was only hours away. I finished my beer, placed the empty bottle on the glass table and sat there looking out over the Chesapeake Bay. The water against the deck and the hull of Teek's boat reminded me of simpler times growing up in Buffalo. I spent summers with my cousin Brad and Joe Kotor on Lake Erie. Brad's father worked for a local marina and always seemed to have a boat on hand. We would fish, sail, and water ski all day long. These were simple pleasures I hoped, after all this, I could return to.

"Yo dude, we're out of beer! Let's go grab some more," Teek yelled as he walked back onto the deck. "But first, I got one more surprise for you."

How many more surprises could he possibly have?

Chapter 57

We entered Teek's garage and he flicked on the lights. In the last bay there was what appeared to be a sports car covered with a canvas tarp. This was obviously the "surprise".

I played along. "What's under the tarp?" I asked.

Teek's smile was from ear to ear, and he said "Wait for it, wait for it."

We grabbed the left-hand side edge of the tarp and with a, "one, two, three", the car was unveiled. It was a Bugatti Veyron, black on black.

"No way! No you didn't? Holy shit. Teek this thing costs like a million and a half dollars," I said.

"Yeah, I know," he said, "'Cause that's what I paid for it."

Throwing me the keys, he said, "It's for you."

"Are you serious?"

"Yes. The car gets squirrely quick though. So give me back those keys and I'll drive tonight and tomorrow you can have your fun."

Teek started the 'Bugat' up and hit the gas. The whole garage shook. I have never heard or felt a car like this before. "How much horsepower does this thing have?" I asked.

He answered, "987, and it can go zero to 60 in 2.4 seconds. The top speed is like 250."

Climbing in, I uttered, "These seats feel like butter."

"Yeah, I know. Buckle up, baby."

The car had a five-point seatbelt system and when Teek tells you to buckle up you'd better. He opened the garage door and put the car into reverse. Teek backed the car out slowly revving the engine again. I was getting nervous. The fastest vehicle I had been in the past two years was a prison transport bus.

In high school, Teek and I would go on these things called, 'Hell Rides' in preparation for lacrosse games. A friend of ours had this little shit box of a car, a Datsun 210. We would take turns driving through a local cemetery and scaring the crap out of one another. The look on Teek's face said this was about to become a 'Hell Ride.' I figured if he killed us at least I wouldn't have to go to the Pentagon.

As we crept down the driveway Teek's demeanor turned serious and he said, "What's really going on man? There's clearly something up. I've known you my since we were five years old and I know when something is bothering you. I don't get it. Something doesn't add up. Yesterday you were in jail and today you're here with me. Did you bust out or something?"

"Naw man, like I told you, they screwed up on my New York State case and they had to let me go because of the motion I filed for Habeas Corpus."

"So why didn't you tell me you had a chance to get out? You know I would have dropped everything to come and get you."

"Yeah, I know, Teek. I just didn't want you to get your hopes up if shit got all fuck'd up you know?" I replied.

"Okay, man, if that's the story you're sticking with...," and he lifted his foot off the brake. As he pulled out the Bugatti's headlights squarely lit up Jackmann and Sinsel's Crown Vic but the agents appeared to be elsewhere. 'Lazy fuckers,' I thought.

Teek revved the engine, looked at me one more time and asked, "So there's nothing you want to tell me?"

It was like the car was preventing Teek from releasing his anger.

I replied, "Naw man."

Teek let the clutch go and hit the gas.

Teek and I closed in the Ford with incredible speed. I thought to myself, there is no way they could ever catch up to us. Then Teek did something I couldn't even fathom. He rammed the Crown Vic on the driver side door. The last thing I remember seeing was the car's light shinning on Jackmann's eyeballs. They were inside. My last thought was, 'Why didn't we take the Hummer?'

Chapter 58

At first I didn't know what happened. The throbbing of my head caused me to reach for my forehead. I felt wetness so I pulled my hand back and it was covered in blood. I looked over to the driver's seat see if Teek was injured but he was gone.

The blood was now running into my eyes. I looked out the car's front window to see Teek standing outside the Crown Vic. He was pulling at the crushed doorjamb to get it open. Now my bad dream had catapulted into a full-blown nightmare. I unbuckled myself, pushed the door open, and fell out into the fresh now bloody snow.

Teek's little stunt had jettisoned Jackmann and Sinsel's car off the road into a side gully. I pushed myself up off the pavement and saw him with a Glock 45 GAP in his hand, yelling at Jackmann and Sinsel who were on their knees with their hands behind their backs. Teek threw me two pairs of handcuffs, which I missed completely.

"What the hell are you doing man?" I asked.

Teek asked, "Who are these guys?"

"You don't want to know," I answered.

By now Teek was pissed and bordering on the psychotic. I knew I couldn't reveal the agent's true identities or why they were following me. I also knew I was betraying my best friend, but I couldn't bring him into my personal dilemma. Between Teek screaming at the agents and me with increasing murderous intent, the only thing I could say was, "I can't tell you who they are. Believe me you don't want to know, bro. Really, you don't!"

"Fuck that, Marcus. What do you mean you can't tell me? That doesn't make any sense. I want to know who the fuck these guys are. They've been following us all day. Shit, you broke out of jail didn't you?"

"No, Teek, I didn't break out of jail. Listen man, you can't shoot these guys."

"Why not? Are these guys Mob? Fuck'em! We'll kill them and be on the next plane to Costa Rica," Teek yelled.

At this point, it was an idea I was willing to entertain. Just disappear and take my chances. But the look of growing concern on the agent's faces, plus the thought of Lymes taking great pleasure in screwing with my father's life brought me back to my senses.

"No man, they aren't Mob. Does he look like he is in the Mob? He's fucking black!" I said pointing to Jackmann.

Teek replied, "Well, if you're not going to tell me I'm gonna have to get it out of them. Cuff 'em. We're gonna take this shit outta the street and move it to the house."

I was on my own to conjure up a plan. He was dead serious, to use a terrible pun, about killing them. Teek was in full on protection mode and that Glock was looking nice and cozy in his hand. I could only hope that Jackmann and Sinsel had some kind of back up arriving soon. At least for their sake.

Chapter 59

Teek forced Jackmann and Sinsel back towards the house and up his driveway. He had a crazed look about him. I only hoped I could persuade my best friend to let them go. I glanced back at the tangled mess of cars.

As we got to within 10 feet of the garage door, Teek opened the Hummer driver's side door and reached in to hit the opener and barked, "OK, everybody inside. Marcus, you grab a couple chairs from the dining room and put them in the middle of the floor.

As the garage door closed behind us, all I thought of was 'What in the Hell does he have planned?' I quickly grabbed the chairs and carried them to the garage. I had a terrible feeling I was about to witness an execution. Two to be exact.

While Teek threw me a roll of duct tape, he ordered the agents to sit in the chairs.

As I taped the agents down, Sinsel mouthed a menacing, "Fuck you, asshole."

They looked helpless. Now they knew how I felt. I asked Teek a question, "So what's your plan and where did you get the gun?"

"It's the black dude's gun. I grabbed it while they were both dazed. Oh and here's a burner for you," Teek said as he tossed me a gun.

"And this one?" I asked.

"Christ, Marcus, where'd ya think? It's the white dude's gun."

If Teek only knew who they were. A fleeting thought crossed my mind to turn the gun on Teek to force him to free Jackmann and Sinsel but my friendship was too valuable.

"So are you going to tell me who these guys are or do I have to get it out of them myself? Why are these guys after you? Is it because of your case? They look like hit men to me," Teek asked.

"They're not hit men, dude," I said.

"Ok, then why have they been following you all day?" Teek asked.

The questions went around and around for 30 minutes. I tried my best to dodge his questions, but as the tension escalated, Teek said, "I guess I'm gonna have to shoot one, and then the other will talk."

Teek placed the gun to Jackmann's head, looked back towards me, and said, "You are obviously in trouble, and you won't or can't tell me."

Keeping his eyes on the agents, Teek took me aside and said just loud enough for the agents to here bits and pieces, "Listen man, if you're in trouble, I'm in trouble. I've hid millions in offshore accounts. I'll just pop'em both and we're off to wherever. We could live like kings."

I spoke to Jackmann, "Listen, I have to tell him who you guys are or he's gonna kill the both of you. For real."

My tone confused Teek. I think he was surprised I cared at all. But I did.

"Listen, Teek can hold water," I said, "Once he knows, we can end this standoff and Lymes doesn't have to know shit. Do we have a deal?"

Jackmann and Sinsel looked at each other and nodded their heads in agreement.

Jackmann then said, "Your friend is doing you a solid right now Teek. You should take his advice and let us go. He is trying to protect you, but if you have to know and want to share his burden then I guess we have no choice."

Teek turned towards me confused. I said, "He's right bro. I have been trying to keep you out of my shit since I arrived. I was just hoping you wouldn't notice their surveillance, but I should have known better."

I turned to Jackmann and Sinsel, "I fucking warned you two at the office to back the fuck off. You really fucking suck at surveillance. Screw it, I'm tell'em everything."

Teek's unexpected involvement complicated an already complex situation. "So what do you want me to do with these two?" I asked.

"I say we leave them taped up and hop the next plane outta here," Teek answered.

I laughed and said, "I would love to do that but I can't. I have a chance to do the right thing here, and get out from underneath all the bad shit I've done. It's what your dad would expect. I might be greedy but I'm still an American, bro."

Teek lowered the gun and handed it to me. I immediately took out the clip, popped all the bullets into my hands and put them in my pocket. I set the guns at the agent's feet, took a deep breath and told Teek why I was let out, who Jackmann and Sinsel were and what I was in DC to do.

"We've gotta cut'em loose now. Where's a knife?" I said.

Teek's cell trilled into life. It was Falcon announcing his imminent arrival as he pointed to a closed locker. I calmly told Teek there was no way anyone else could be let in.

"So what are we going to do now? There are two smashed up cars outside, and the garage floor is covered in blood," I asked.

Jackmann and Sinsel, now free, focused on the impending arrival of the limo party.

Jackmann immediately got on his phone and walked into the kitchen. I offered Sinsel a wash rag and pointed him in the direction of the bathroom inside. Jackmann hung up, returned, and asked, "Where are they now?"

"Who?" I replied.

"The people in the limo," Jackmann said.

Teek said, "They're just leaving Old Town from a bar called Murphy's. They'll be here in about 20 minutes."

Jackmann said, "Okay, give me the cell number of the guy who just called you."

Teek handed over his phone so Jackmann could get Falcon's number. Jackmann immediately got back on his phone.

Chapter 60

To this day I can't fathom why Teek and I decided to get all domestic with each other by trying to clean the blood from the garage floor. But we did, anyway. Finding us on our hands and knees, smearing coagulated red liquid around in circles, Jackmann said, "Don't bother with any of that, I've called in a cleanup crew."

I whispered to Teek, "What did he call, Stanley Steamer? Merry Maids? I don't think they do crime scenes."

Sinsel turned to see us laughing and said, "What's so fucking funny? You two have jeopardized everything."

I composed myself realizing this was no time to laugh and asked, "So what do we do?"

Sinsel answered sternly, "Don't DO anything. Nothing. Just go in the house, we'll take it from here."

Teek and I sat in the living room, both of us trying to grab hold of personal conclusions from the previous hour's chaos. It was useless though. The only consolation was Teek's sister had left for the night.

Within five minutes, nine Crown Vic's pulled into the cul-de-sac followed by two flat bed trailers, a medical unit, a bus, and a semi with a pay loader that had forks instead of a bucket. You had to admire the way the FBI takes care of business.

There was an army of Fed pigs outside. The pay loader was quickly decanted from the semi and they began loading up the smashed cars. The agents were huddled around Jackmann getting a debriefing on the situation. Sinsel made his way to the medical unit as the rest of the agents on site began to sweep up little pieces of car that littered the road.

As the surreal scene unfolded a huge stretched Chevy Suburban Jackmann immediately approached it. I could only assume this was Jackmann's boss.

The back door swung open and a six and a half foot tall man emerged with a temper to match his stature taking the tone of an irate parent, Jackmann's boss proceeded to give the agent the worst ass chewing I had ever witnessed.

Finally, a large group of agents walked through the front door, three making their way to Teek and I. Most were carrying and pulling various objects, but our trio were medical staff.

The other agent maids began to clean up the blood. They had all types of gear, even a black light which they used to locate even the smallest specks of blood.

All patched up by the FBI medical crew, I decided to go outside with Teek. Jackmann saw us and immediately yelled, "I thought I told you two assholes to stay in the house."

"Yeah, I know, but the limo will be here soon," I told him.

Jackmann said, "Listen, I got that situation under control too. Why do you think I asked for that phone number? The local police have had the limo stopped on the Arlington Bridge. You can go back inside. It will be a while before they get here."

I guess Jackmann was better at damage control then he was at surveillance. If I had a gold star sticker I would have placed it on the bloody lapel of his jacket and gave him an 'attaboy".

Teek and I stood on the front porch just taking in what was going on. It was all quite extraordinary. The FBI cleaned up the entire site in less than 40 minutes.

The smashed up cars were on the flatbeds and the pay loader was being put back on the semi. The cul-de-sac was clear of any indication any of this ever happened. Everyone returned to their cars and began to leave. Jackmann, now joined by Sinsel with his arm in a sling, walked up to the house.

"Are we good? Everything cool?" I asked.

"Yeah we're good," Jackmann said, "You better be worth all this. By the way, the limo is on the way."

Pretty soon we heard screaming in the distance and the roar of the limo's engines being gunned too hard. As Teek's driveway filled with coked-up, drunken sorority girls turned prostitutes I laughed at the absurdity of the scene in front of me.

"So what should I tell them about my head?" I asked Teek.

He replied, "Tell them you hit it on the tree swing because the snow made the rope slippery."

It was definitely going to be a long night.

Chapter 61

Trout and Falcon ran into the house tracking in particles of the freshly fallen snow into Teek's house.

"How did they get so wasted? We only left them two hours ago," I asked Teek.

He replied, "Trout's buddy bartends at Murphy's and you know that it don't take that long to get that fuck'd up."

The limo driver popped the trunk and started unloading the beer onto the front porch and apologized about the delay.

By now the limo passengers had decided to get down to their skivvies. The Asian girl in her thong and bra approached Teek and started to undress him. The redhead in a pair of sexy boy shorts and the blonde made a sandwich out of me.

When I woke up 24 hours ago I was in a jail cell surrounded by a bunch of mooks, and now I was dancing half-naked with two hookers in a DC living room. What a difference a day makes.

We danced, drank beers and did shots of tequila for about an hour before Trout noticed the cut on my head. I gave him the swing story and made my way to the hot tub with everyone else. That was, except for Trout. He mumbled, "I've got an early morning. My boss just called an 'emergency' meeting and so this lady and I are going to retire for the evening." He shot us a salute as he left.

I thought who in the Hell says, 'retire' anymore? Trout's polite Midwestern sensibilities made me laugh.

Then I noticed Teek looking directly at me raising his eye brows. But I didn't understand what he was getting at, so Teek motioned with his head in the direction of the exiting Trout. Then it hit me like the smell of garbage on a hot, rancid day, 'shit', I thought, 'What now?' Trout works at the Pentagon.

I looked to Teek for a moment. His reply to my desperation was a shrug of his shoulders.

Falcon was next to make his exit. He was far less politically correct with his intentions. "Let's play hide and go anal!" he screamed. His date seemed less than amused as she coyly slapped him on the shoulder as if to be offended by the remark and said, "So you're a Family Guy fan huh? So should I just call you Quagmire from now on or what?"

"Giggity," was Falcon's only response as he helped her out of the water.

I sat there with my arm stretched over the edge of the tub with a beer in one hand and a smoke in the other. My dynamic duo were rubbing me like a greased pig and the Asian chick was straddling Teek.

I had something more pressing on my mind bending my head around the blonde, "So do you know where Trout works in the building?"

"No idea, man. But I do know that his security clearance is high. Hell, his boss is the head of naval intelligence," Teek stated.

I guess the only thing I could do was hope for the best, "Fuck it. It's the largest office building in the world what's the chances I'm gonna run into him?"

"Exactly," Teek said. It wasn't a solution but at this moment it was the best I could hope for.

The redhead, whose green eyes emanated an irresistible innocence, stood over me placing her breasts into my mouth. The water and the cold air pulled her skin tight and made her nipples erect. The blonde submerged herself between my legs, which prompted Teek to say, "Look out beloooow." As soon as the blonde resurfaced the redhead went down.

"You're really packin'," the blonde cooed, while Red soon echoed her assessment.

I asked them if they knew what Black Irish was, but they were oblivious.

Teek got out first and headed upstairs. I followed with my companions. He made a right into his bedroom and pointed down the hall to the other bedrooms and said, "Just pick one."

Standing in the hallway naked with two beautiful hookers I went to open the first door. Inside Trout was fast asleep with his arms around the brunette, a gentleman to the end.

The next door we tried was across the hall. I opened it to see Falcon hanging from the canopy of the bed being sucked.

The next bedroom was empty...

Chapter 62

I ran and jumped on the bed, twisting mid-air and landing spread eagle. I was about to end the longest dry spell in my life. I was given a show and my approval was involuntary and self-evident.

With the show over, each of them slowly slid up my leg with their tongues they felt like hot stones in the sand. Their warmth tensed every capillary in my body. The next two hours were a blur of positions, standing up, stacking the girls atop one another, double reverse cowgirl, and so on and so forth. I couldn't get that line from a Prince song out of my head, "23 positions in a one night stand." Yeah, that was what I was aiming for.

We would intermittently make small talk while resting between sessions. I learned the blonde was studying to be a doctor and the redhead a stockbroker. I told them the circumstances that led to my incarceration.

The fact I had been in jail didn't seem to faze them even though they told me they were new to the 'profession'. I thought maybe they just told us want we wanted to hear. No one wants to be told that they are going where many men have gone before. But this these girls wanted more. Hired help usually quits after the deed is done. Maybe they felt for my situation or maybe Falcon paid them extra. No matter their reasons for the extra effort, I took full advantage of their generosity.

Eventually the blonde passed out leaving the redhead and me alone. She positioned herself between my legs pulling off the used condom with her teeth. I was completely flaccid until she began. She treated what she referred to now as, the 'Boa', so gently that I went into a state of meditation. The rush of endorphins, and the varying degrees of veracity in which she pleasured sent me to another place.

Suddenly she stopped and said, "I want you inside of me."

I went to reach for a condom, she then said, "I have to tell you something. This is the first time I've done this type of thing."

She pointed to the blonde and said, "She brought me with her tonight; this is her third time."

There seemed an innocence awaiting me within these girls. Maybe I was getting played or maybe it was the impending day I had. But mostly it was the sincerity in which she asked that prompted me to go without a jimmy hat.

I wondered if her request was genuine and pulled her up to my chest. Her breasts were warm against my body. The look of anticipation in her eyes was enormous. I rolled her over onto her back, and looked directly into her eyes as I slid in slow. The warmth of being inside her sent a shiver down my back.

The next hour was full of tight embraces as we figured out each other's sexual peccadilloes. When all was done I laid there in a sea of flesh and sweat cuddled on one side by Amber, the redhead, and on the other side, Marie, the blonde. It felt fantastic to have their arms draped across me. Unfortunately, there was too much on my mind to enjoy it for very long.

I laid there wide awake. My thoughts hovered between whether or not Jackmann and Sinsel would rat me out and what would Lymes do if he discovered the evening's near disaster. I thought about what I would say later that morning. Was I going to actually tell them everything this time and not the amended version I told on the plane? Would I truly be a free man if I didn't?

I looked at the clock and it was just after 4 AM. I got out of bed, staggered out of the bedroom, and headed downstairs.

Chapter 63

Desperate actions of a desperate man is all I could think of as I weighed my loyalties as an American posed against that of self-preservation. Thoughts raced through my head as I made it to the bottom of the stairs and turned into Teek's office. I had the power to give my government and country something they desperately needed—a way to infiltrate Al Qeada.

But despite the assurances I had received, I realized when all was said and done at the Pentagon, betrayal was a possibility. I couldn't let that happen. There was too much at stake now.

I proceeded to start the task at hand—saving my and Teek's ass. I began searching the internet for what I needed—an encryption program to protect what I was about to record. I found it, the Department of Defense (DOD) 1024bit algorithm. I was halfway there, but I needed a friend to complete the task.

Geoff Sondon was not only my favorite professor during my years at Butler University. He was also a computer genius and conveniently an insomniac. I sent him an e-mail.

I could only hope that Geoff was not in the hospital. He would go in to receive medically induced sleep treatment. Because when you go without sleep for two or three weeks or more as Geoff did his body would begin to shut down. I wondered, as I waited, if the Feds were monitoring the connection. Finally, a response from Geoff. I sent back a response to verify that it was truly him. His response sent

Christopher Prior

a warm shiver through my body like a shot of whiskey. It was him. I flung out my hand for help. Would he be able to reach it?

"Geoff, I don't have time to explain right now but I need a program that will break up an encrypted video file into 33 different parts with a public and a private key. The private key has to disassemble or kill the virus just in case I want to stop it from being released across the entire internet. I have the DOD-1024 256 bit encryption program, but what virus can I use to disseminate, split, and reassemble the video along with having the option to stop it if I want?

"Oh, and if that's not difficult enough, I also need to give the virus an automatic execution or release date of 72 hours.

"Can u help?"

I pressed 'send' and hoped for the best.

Chapter 64

Geoff had received these types of requests from me before.

I recalled how he helped me automate the fake I.D. business. When I was a broker, Geoff designed a program to track market maker's buy and sell orders. The program would automatically buy and sell orders for stocks. It made intraday trading easy. The program simply allowed me to piggy-back on the largest traders in the market without their knowledge. That, coupled with the inside information I received, made me and my clients rich.

He was the one guy who everyone wished they had in their corner. In the past I had given Geoff ample time to help me, few could resist his genial intelligence but I wasn't in a position to afford him that luxury this morning.

I received a link to a website from Geoff. The page displayed two boxes, one for a username and one for a password. I typed in my old password from the trading program, no luck. He knew that I had gotten busted for fraudulent sale of securities. I bet he figured that the Feds had access to that username and password, so he removed it.

I tried the old username and password from the fake I.D. days and I was in. There was a link to a Virtual Private Network (VPN). I clicked on the link and was immediately connected to a web-based web cam conference with my computer guru.

"So, who are we trying to keep from this?" Geoff asked getting right to the point.

"The FBI and the CIA," I replied.

"Okay," Geoff said casually and leaned over out of sight.

"Well, we have about three minutes until they break the encryption. I sent you a packet sniffer which will inspect every bit of data for anything out of the ordinary and line verification," Geoff said. He didn't have to tell me what to do with either. The packet sniffer tracked and checked all the packets from one computer to another making sure they were not intercepted. The line test verified the connection was working properly with no variance of impedance electrically because if there was that meant the line was tapped. All was good I told him.

The VPN allowed Geoff control of the computer in front of me. I watched as he prepared everything. It looked like a psychedelic screen saver because of how fast he closed and opened everything. Two minutes later he was finished. Teek's desktop showed two icons in the middle of the screen.

The first desktop item was a configured encryption program linked to a digital recorder and the second, a virus to send it out into the net.

Geoff was never one for small talk and finished up our VPN session by typing, "You're good to go. Call me if you get out of what you're into this time. Good luck!"

Then he was gone.

I exited the VPN and then ran the packet sniffer and line check again. They were clean. Maybe the FBI and CIA hadn't thought of this, and I was a step ahead of them again. I booted up the program, positioned the web cam, and began to speak.

"If you're seeing this it means I was betrayed by the US government. I have successfully done what many governments in the world have unsuccessfully tried to do since 9/11. I have infiltrated Al Qeada.

"The government in the form of two asshole FBI agents, Jackmann and Sinsel approached me while I was in Butler Correctional State prison. They assured me that if I provided them with the information I had concerning Al Qeada, my sentence would be vacated and I would be set free.

"If this video has made its way on to the internet it can only mean that they fucked me over and didn't hold up their end of the bargain, and I'm afraid I am either dead or imprisoned in a non-sanctioned prison far away from any legal representation.

"I am not an enemy combatant, I am an American. No matter how the government spins this in the press, decide for yourself, listen to the tape, and listen to what I have uncovered. I know who was supposed to be the 20th hijacker on 9/11, I know the players still in the Middle East, and I know Al Qeada's next target.

"Either way, this recording is my last hope. If you are an American and you see this confession of what I uncovered living and speaking with the members of the only Al Qeada terror cell arrested in the US, know that your government has turned its sights on the American people and you could be next. Get my story out."

"I spent the next hour retelling into the video the events over the past two years. Including how I met the Buffalo Six, how I socially engineered them into tell me everything they knew about Al Qeada.

It was now 6 AM, only about two hours before my meeting at the Pentagon. I had assembled the video within the virus and all I had to do now was press send to launch my life preserver into the viral world.

The virus would quickly turn every computer it came across into one of its drones, exponentially replicating itself. There was no way to stop it once it was released. The internet is the ultimate equalizer.

Chapter 65

I felt like I was in a movie. The camera came in 'tight', first on my face, and then cut to a shot of my index finger plunging down towards the Enter key. I depressed the key and my encrypted video was gone.

Jackmann and Sinsel would arrive shortly to escort me to the Pentagon. There were still secondary agents outside Teek's house now keeping an eye on me.

As I mustered up enough energy to get ready I peered out to see the surveillance team animated out of their car. One agent pointed at the house while talking on his cell phone both he and his partner made their way towards the front door. Initially the agents did a fast walk and then changed gear into a frenzied gallop. What was going on now?

Suddenly the power in the house went out. I turned to the computer, it was still on. "You magnificent bastard Teek," I said aloud.

The system was on battery backup. The virus continued to send itself out. The agents kicked Teek's front door off its hinges and were now in hot pursuit of the office. I locked the doors and slid a lacrosse stick in between the handles to keep the agents at bay—if only for a few seconds.

"Open the fucking doors Mr. Declan," one of the agents yelled.

"Fuck you," I yelled back. I just wanted to give the computer as long as I could before they tried to stop it.

"We know what you're doing Marcus," the same agent yelled

"Oh yeah what's that?" I asked coyly.

"You're sending something out on the computer," the other agent said calmly, "Why do you think we're here?"

I looked towards the computer and figured it had at least sent it out a 1,000 times and that was good enough. I opened the doors to find them breathless and ready for a rumble.

I casually asked, "What happened to the power?"

One of the agents answered, "We shut it off to stop whatever you were doing."

I replied, "So what am I doing with the computer?"

I stood between the two agents and the computer screen. They probably figured that cutting the power had stopped it. The longer I could stall them the better. Plus I set the screen saver to one minute and to black so when it went on it would look like it was off.

Suddenly one of their phones rang. I could hear the voice on the other side screaming, "It's still being sent out!"

The agent pushed me aside. I'm sure I heard the voice rise to hysteria, "Stop it, now!"

The agent's attempts to cancel the program were clumsy. Finally, in defeat he pleaded into phone, "What are we supposed to do now? I can't shut the fucker down."

The other agent replied as only Neanderthals can—he pulled out his service revolver, pulled the trigger and shot the screen.

The virus had propagated itself enough so I said, "You know that only works in the movies right? It's just the screen. It's not the actual computer," pointing to the computer tower.

The Neanderthal shot that, too.

I said, "Nice shot dumb ass. Why didn't you just pull out the power cord?"

He went to hit me with the side of his gun, but I quickly ducked out of his aim.

Teek then burst through the office doorway with a shotgun and said, "Let me guess, more agents?"

Again Teek had gotten the drop on FBI and for the second time in a matter of hours I was reluctantly holding an FBI agent's service revolver.

Outside, the sound of screeching car tires signaled the arrival of Jackmann and Sinsel. Desperate to avoid another tongue lashing by their superiors, the agents took in the surreal scene.

"What the fuck is going on here?" Sinsel asked.

"Same shit, different day," Teek said.

The computer's assassin tried to explain. "Declan was sending out an encrypted file from that computer."

Jackmann replied, "Yeah we know, we were monitoring the network traffic. Where's the computer?" Jackmann looked at the destroyed computer tower and said, "How are we supposed to find out what he was sending out?" Surveying the damage, he placed it on the desk, slid off the side panel, and said, "You shot the hard drive. I can't believe this shit."

Jackmann turned to me. "What were you sending out?"

I answered, "My insurance policy."

Sinsel asked, "What insurance policy?"

I told Teek to lower the shot gun and said, "Listen, I need to take a shower. There's coffee in the kitchen. I'll be done in 10 minutes and then we can go. You know it's my big day." As I left the office I primped my nonexistent bow tie.

Jackmann ripped out the hard drive and examined it with a grimace. Sometimes it's better to be lucky than good.

Chapter 66

I toweled off and dressed. Back in the suit I bought yesterday, I assured myself in the mirror that everything would go as planned.

I walked down the stairs my desperate tone from earlier had disappeared replaced by confidence. It might have been self-delusional but I would take it. I had to act as if I was the one holding all the cards.

Heading on to the Beltway in the morning light made everything seem serene. After a 20 minute drive we pulled into an underground parking garage at the Pentagon. Two armed guards walked towards us but, did nothing more than that. One twisted his head and spoke loudly into the air.

"They're here, sir."

His yell produced a higher ranking officer who walked towards us and simply said, "Follow me."

Pat downs and checkpoints were negotiated before an elevator took us to a hallway on the ground floor. I expected to see pictures of generals, presidents or at least Colonel George Armstrong Custer, the patron saint of military lost causes. Would this be my last stand?

As we turned a corner I couldn't believe my eyes. It was Trout less than 50 yards from us. From the angle I entered the hallway, he couldn't see us. I noticed he was talking to an attractive officer, so his attention was devoted to her. The distance between Trout had become less than 10 feet when he turned his back to me.

Now right beside him I did my best Carnac the Magnificent and mentally projected to him—'Don't turn around'.

My peripheral vision kept me aware of Trout's precarious situation. Then, out of an adjacent side hallway came Lymes' assistant. He directed the three of us to follow him. If Lymes' assistant said my name the gig was up. Thankfully he didn't. A few twists and turns and we were in the foyer of Lymes' office waiting. Baynard exited the office and gave me a look that meant 'heads up'. The assistant motioned for us to enter.

Lymes was sitting behind a desk going over some papers. He motioned for us to sit.

He placed the papers to the side, sat back in his chair, and said, "So you had a little fun last night, Mr. Declan? Yes?"

Uncertain as how to respond to what I perceived as a blatantly misconstrued rhetorical question, I merely sat mute beside Jackmann and Sinsel.

Lymes regained his composure and continued. "I would like some kind of fucking explanation for what I can only call your assaulting these agents last night. Am I to believe it was just a colossal fuck up by these two over here? I thought we had come to an understanding yesterday Mr. Declan?"

I calmly took a deep breath and let Lymes have it, "I don't owe you jack shit. I don't work for you. If you want answers ask these two fucking retards. I told them earlier in the day to back the fuck off and they didn't. So they got what was coming to 'em. We're all here now. I'm not here to help me, I'm here to help you and don't you fucking forget it."

I went from 0 mph to 100 mph so fast no one knew what to make of it.

Lymes replied with, "But do you really understand your predicament? That's what I really want to know. But don't answer right away. Please, take a few seconds to consider."

I paused and said, "Definitely my freedom and probably my life."

Lymes got up from his desk, stood directly in front of me, and said, "Is that all that you can think about? Yourself? There are bigger things in play here Mr. Declan. I think that you need to reevaluate why you're here."

He stood there staring directly into my eyes. It felt like he was performing some kind of Jedi mind trick. What he didn't know was the harder they squeezed the stronger I became.

I was sick of being bullied. I was going to state my position. I leaned to within inches of Lymes' face and said, "Listen, I'm not scared of you. I just spent the last two years surrounded by killers just like you. The only difference is you get paid to do it. I'm a dangerous man, very dangerous to you. You think you have me painted into corner. Well, you don't. You're the one who needs to evaluate your position. Did you think I wouldn't have a backup plan? When these two [pointing to Jackmann and Sinsel] showed up this morning, I wasn't sure that you would keep up your end of the bargain. So, if I go down, so do you."

My Tough Tony talk caught Lymes off guard. He stepped back and leaned against the front of his desk. I hadn't taken my eyes off his. It was a game of chicken and he flinched first and took his eyes off the road.

"Perhaps I underestimated you, Mr. Declan," Lymes said. He turned and barked an order to his assistant. "Take these gentlemen to the conference area, I'll be there shortly."

Chapter 67

As we made our exit, Lymes said one last thing, "You better be worth it. We've bent a lot of rules for you Mr. Declan."

I replied, "You didn't do it for me. You did it for yourself."

Lymes' assistant, Jackmann, Sinsel, Baynard and I made our way to an elevator which took us on a descent into the unknown—at least for me. The others could have kept on going south and found themselves with their good friend Satan as far as I was concerned. The doors finally opened to reveal a squeaky clean subterranean corridor that resembled a throw back to Perry Como, Ascots and foul-smelling pipe tobacco, in other words, the Fifties. There were no pictures on the walls to indicate time or place, but there was various colored lines inlaid into the floor as well as symbols inlaid into the lovingly polished marble floor.

The inhabitants of this secret level wore uniforms emblazoned with patches I was certain bore no resemblance to any recognizable military unit.

We entered the room and I noticed the same symbol. This time, on the inside of the door jamb, the plaque was worn like a wood railing from hands constantly rubbing it like a good luck symbol.

Lymes' assistant directed Baynard and I to a desk in front of the conference room. I sat atop the desk and Baynard grabbed a chair. Jackmann and Sinsel made their way to the peanut galley to sit for the show. Slowly, an alphabet soup of agents trickled into the conference room with credentials shown, NSA, CIA, FBI, DEA, you name it, they were all there.

Baynard noticed that each person touched the plaque upon entering the room. "They're saying something to it," he said, "I just can't make out what they're saying."

To me, this Masonic-like ritual was akin to Notre Dame Football players slapping the famous, 'Play Like a Champion Today', sign. Not for the last time that day, as we would discover, Baynard and I shared an eerie sense of foreboding.

Chapter 68

The conference room was soon filled with about 50 people. They all seemed to congregate in departmental groups. As they readied themselves I noticed there weren't any Navy people represented in the conference room yet, but just as the thought crossed my mind, the sailor boys entered all Spic n' Span in their dress whites. Trout was with them. This time I was in plain sight and there was no way I could hide. Plus it was nice to have a secret friend in the room.

I took a moment to honor Trout's achievement up the military ranks. I never knew he was so high up in the Navy, 'cause if he was here today that meant he was a somebody.

When Trout realized he was here to see me, but was startled back to reality by his boss, Philip Stoddard, the Director of Naval Intelligence, he walked to the various silos of power and exchanged paperwork.

The ringmaster Lymes entered accompanied by a Four Star General and a Brigadier General. Lymes walked up to our desk, much to the surprise of those in the room, and said, "Dr. Baynard, this is General Middlehouse, someone I believe you should remember."

Baynard got up, extended his hand to the General, and said, "Casper Middlehouse, I haven't seen you in 30 years."

General Middlehouse would have given Stonewall Jackson a good run for his money. "Yes. Africa," was all he said.

Baynard had never previously mentioned the rescue in Rhodesia but an army officer came up to Baynard and introduced himself. I strained to hear the conversation but the gist was this officer was the CIA helicopter pilot that saved him. I read his name off his uniform -Middlehouse. This meeting of the minds was becoming an incestuous 'family affair' for Baynard and hazardous for me.

By now the crowd had doubled in size. I was beginning to feel like a lab rat. The members of each group were huddled and staring at me while they talked in hushed tones.

I canvassed the room and noticed that Jackmann and Sinsel were speaking with the gentleman that showed up at Teek's house earlier and lambasted Jackmann. I could tell by Jackmann's demeanor he was being asked some hard, searching questions. Body language was the key here because I couldn't trust the words coming out of anyone's mouth. I examined my own posture. I was, in my own assessment, looking very comfortable. I had taken a position of power by sitting on top of the desk. My carefree attitude represented by my swinging legs suggested that I was like a child in a park on a sunny day.

A second desk with a computer was positioned next to Baynard. We were about to begin. I readied myself. They were going to come at me hard. I reflected back to lessons learned in jail. When confronted by someone, you need to make the first strike because you might not be able to get in a second one. I needed to let them know straight away I was swinging 500 and I wasn't going to take any shit. The sharks were circling and they smelled blood.

Chapter 69

All eyes of the congregation were on Lymes as he addressed the crowd, "Everyone please take your seat."

He paused, waiting for everyone to comply, "You are all here today for this briefing for one reason, to assess what I believe to be the largest break in the war on terror. Mr. Declan has accomplished something we've all been trying to do since 9/11—infiltrate Al Qeada. Mr. Declan has accomplished this by developing an asset and pressing that asset for information by use of social engineering. He has made it clear to me that he has no love for the people that are in this room right now. He sees you, as we all see Al Qeada, very much as the enemy. Mr. Declan has spent the last two years locked behind bars. His road has certainly been the road less traveled, but it is that road that has afforded Mr. Declan the insight and information about Al Qeada. I think that after you hear him speak, you will agree with me that Mr. Declan's journey is going to be an invaluable asset to the intelligence community. And, for that reason, I don't believe we are in a position to judge Mr. Declan. This is not a perfect world and we all have taken many paths to get here today. I have done things that were questionable morally, but I believe in my heart of hearts it was for the greater good. We are all Americans here and we are fighting now for our freedom against an enemy that has no country. This is the new world order, and I believe Mr. Declan is about to tip the scales in our favor."

Christopher Prior

The crowd remained impassive. Lymes turned to me and said, "I believe the floor is now yours Mr. Declan,"

Lymes took a seat and tapped his cane on the floor as a not so subtle hint for me to begin. My future rested with how I performed in this briefing today. Baynard looked scared. I took a deep breath and hopped off the desk.

Chapter 70

I walked the room to the front of the desk and began, "As you all know I'm a convicted felon and for the record I don't trust a single one of you in this room. You are all a part of the same government that sent me to prison. It goes against the very fiber of my being to become an informer. But there is something in this for me and that is one of the reasons why I am here. Mr. Lymes has made sure to let me know he was the one responsible for tracking down and executing the USS Cole bombing perpetrators. You and I know what he is capable of. He has offered me a deal, which I expect him to keep in exchange for me being here today."

I looked over to Lymes and he nodded in agreement. I went on, "I have taken certain precautionary measures which I will get to later, if necessary, to make sure this promise is kept."

I paused and looked around to make sure I was completely understood and then went on.

"I want you all to know that I am an American and I choose to remain one. I allowed myself to be arrested by agents Jackmann and Sinsel because I didn't want to live my life on the run. I had planned to live the rest of my life as an expatriate until my father intervened. Faced with imprisonment or leaving, I chose imprisonment. As it turns out, my time in jail was definitely not wasted. I spent the last two years locked up with killers, murders, and general lifetime losers and made it out alive. I have done what you all could not. I'm sure most of you think my motives here are self-serving. I can't deny this,

Christopher Prior

but I felt it was my duty to come here today. You may not respect what I did to become incarcerated, but you must respect the effort and planning it took to extract what I am about to tell you."

I paused and realized that nobody in the room actually cared about my story, who I was or what I had been through. They we were growing impatient to hear what I hoped would be my lifeline to free-dom.

Chapter 71

"Enough with the speeches Mr. Declan. Can we please get to the reason we are all here today," General Middlehouse said.

His arrogance and impatience gave me a chance to draw a line in the sand. I said, "Listen, Middlehouse, this isn't the Six O'clock news, I don't do sound bites."

I stood there waiting for a response. He said, "It's Brigadier General to you."

I replied, "I don't care how many stripes or medals you've accrued, I got my stripes Upstate, in prison."

The Four Star placed his hand on the Middlehouse's shoulder to calm him down. "Please continue Mr. Declan," the Four Star said.

I went on. "I'd like to start by finding out who is represented here today. I would ask the most senior man for each agency to state who you are and the organization you represent."

No one in the conference room expected this. Their pause and indecision prompted me to speak again, "I think it would be helpful, especially to me, if one of you took the lead."

I focused my attention on the Brigadier General, "General Middlehouse, would you be so kind as to stand and tell us who you are and what you represent."

I knew full well he wasn't the most senior man. He began to stand but Four Star pulled him back down. I figured he was going to tell me to eat shit and just continue with my presentation, but the exact opposite happened.

The Four Star stood and said, "I am the Chairman of the Joint Chiefs of Staff, which makes me the highest ranking military officer of the United States armed forces, and the reason I am here is to put the muscle behind any action that will come of what you say here today, Mr. Declan"

"Thank you, and please all of you call me Marcus," I said.

He replied, "Since you believe we're on a first name basis you may call me General Jensen."

This pried some laughter out of the room.

Next a guy with a very similar suit to Greene stood up and said, "I am, Todd Sherrington, the Director of the NSA. I was the first to be contacted about this information uncovered by the DEA and in turn I contacted the CIA. The head of the DEA contacted me to ascertain the identity of the person speaking with Dr. Baynard."

The head of the CIA was next. "I am, Bill Tunney, the Director of the CIA, and I assigned Charles Lymes to ascertain the identity of Mr. Declan and to verify the validity of the conversation recorded by the DEA agents doing surveillance on Dr. Baynard. The Director of the NSA informed me that there were creditable attributes mentioned in the recorded conversation. I charged Operative Lymes to see if what you, Mr. Declan, had was of any value to us. Apparently because you are here, you have convinced Charles Lymes that information is of value to us. I think the question on everyone's mind here, is can you convince all of us?"

Next up was an imposing man, dressed in a black suit with a white shirt and black tie. I thought really? Men in Black? A little much. It was like he was playing the role of his job.

"I am Director Bryan Greene of the FBI; I was contacted by Lymes because it was our domain to gather intelligence on American soil. As you all have read in the report compiled for this meeting, Agents Jackmann and Sinsel headed up the investigation and uncovered the unknown person, who was, you, Mr. Declan."

One by one each branch of the military and other agencies continued to stand and identify themselves. Trout's boss, the Head of Naval Intelligence was next. He was followed by the Air Force, the Joint Task Force on Terrorism, and finally the Head of Homeland Security. They all echoed the remarks of Greene. They wanted to know how they could use the information to further their agency's fight on the war on terrorism.

They were all just chomping at the bit to ask questions but I needed them to holster their inquisitiveness for a moment longer so I could ask a question which was, "Now that I know who all of you are, what do you know about the Buffalo Six?"

Chapter 72

I had expected Lymes to be the one to start. He just sat there. I walked to my files from Butler Correctional Facility. The very files I feared may have been pilfered after my quick exodus a day ago. I pulled out a hand written timeline I had made. I moved to a huge white board and grabbed a marker.

The room sat silent.

"Well alrighty then...I guess I'll start," I said.

I wrote on the board, referencing the timeline, "Buffalo NY is the stage; here are the major players, Mukhtar el Barwan, Sahim Alban, Jahbri Alnahban, Faysal Gallad, Yahya Goya, Shafal Mohammad, and Yasein Tihir."

"What's that you have in your hand?"

I answered, "It's a timeline."

"Of what?" Lymes questioned.

"Of what you believe to be true and what I know to be true," I answered.

Lymes, Jackmann, and Sinsel were pissed. I had failed to mention this on the plane.

I wrote the rest of the players on the board, "Derwish, Alnahban, Dosari, bin Laden, al Zawahiri, KSM, Abu Ali, Osama bin Laden's son, Saad, Tafiq bin Atash, also known as Khallad, Mohammad Atta, and Binalshibh.

I waited for someone to comment. Trout's boss, Philip Stoddard, spoke, "I know how some of these men are linked to the Buffalo Six. What I can tell you all for sure is the reasons the Six took the trip to Al Farooq. It was because of Kamal Derwish in 2001 and his influence at the religious discussions."

I spoke as I wrote this on the board, "That's close. It really started in 1999, but please continue."

Greene began, "The Six would meet in Derwish's apartment to listen to his preaching. His sermons were enough to convince the six men from Buffalo and one other—Mukhtar el Barwan, Sahim Alban, Yasein Tihir, Faysal Gallad, Yahya Goya, Shafal Mohammad, and Jahbri Alnahban to leave for jihad training in Afghanistan. In preparation for the trip, the Six and Derwish developed a cover story to keep the trip's real purpose a secret. To all those who asked, they were going to Pakistan to study with the Islamic Evangelical group Tablighi Jamaat as part of the search for a deeper understanding into their Islamic faith."

I wrote on the white board, 'Dosari arrives and Derwish leaves for Afghanistan.'

Greene continued, "Juma al Dosari was a Muslim combatant and a friend who fought alongside Derwish in Bosnia they were close friends. Dosari moved from Indiana to Buffalo to take over control of the group in Buffalo. When he arrived in Buffalo, the charismatic al Dosari gave sermons railing against Arab governments who do nothing while Muslims die on a daily basis at the hands of the West. Al Dosari's militant tone didn't sit well with the Muslim community in Buffalo, but resonated with the Six. With Dosari now as the leader of the small group, sometime between April and May 2001 the Buffalo men left for Al Farooq. Dosari split the men in two groups."

I wrote on the board, Group 1 and Group 2, while Greene continued to fill in the blanks. "Group 1 was Yasein Tihir, Faysal Gallad and Shafal Mohammad who left in late April. They flew to Pakistan on or around April 29th then continued on to Al Farooq, near Kandahar, Afghanistan, a few days later. Group 2 was Sahim Alban, Jahbri Alnahban, Mukhtar el Barwan, and Yahya Goya. They took a flight on May 14th out of Toronto to Pakistan. When Group 2 arrived in Pakistan they were met by Derwish. Derwish further split up the second group sending el Barwan and Goya straight to Al Farooq and directed Alban and Alnahban to an Al Qeada guesthouse in Kandahar."

I marked a small asterisk next to this statement. I didn't want to stop Greene in full flow, but he was treating some facts with a cavalier approach which didn't' sit well with me.

Greene continued, "There, Alban and Alnahban were visited by Osama bin Laden. During the meeting with bin Laden he told the two men that Al Qeada needed brothers who were willing to carry their souls in their hands. Bin Laden hinted at an impending conflict with the US."

Next I wrote, 'Al Farooq', on the white board.

"At the camp, the eight men were trained in the use of weapons, rocket-propelled grenade launchers, and explosives. A few days into their training, bin Laden made an appearance at the camp with Ayman al-Zawahiri, the leader of Egyptian Islamic Jihad. Bin Laden and Ayman al-Zawahiri announced the merger of their two organizations."

I placed an asterisk next to bin Laden's appearance.

"In the spring of 2001 the Buffalo FBI Field Office received an anonymous letter about the Six. The letter said that the group had traveled to meet bin Laden and stayed in his camp for training. The letter was forwarded to my office in Washington. Based on this letter, I ordered each of the men, upon their return, to be interviewed. Alban was the first to return but stuck to the group's cover story."

I wrote, 'Alban returns', on the board and circled it, while Lymes took a very deliberate and nuanced sip of water.

The morning's de facto dictator rumbled on, "Alban completed only 10 days of the six-week training. He faked an ankle injury to get out early and asked Derwish to help him leave. Derwish agreed. Securing Alban a ride to Kandahar. Once there, while staying at the Al Qeada version of the Underground Railroad, waiting for a ride back to Pakistan, Alban was summoned to a personal meeting with Osama bin Laden. Bin Laden asked him why he wanted to leave and Alban replied that he was more or less homesick. Bin Laden was not satisfied with his answer and asked about the status of Muslims in America and what they thought of martyrdom operations. Bin Laden granted Alban's departure but not without a caveat. Bin Laden ordered Alban, before leaving Afghanistan to deliver two videotapes. One to a contact in Pakistan at a safe house and the other he was to bring home to the US. Alban agreed and delivered the tapes.

"Next, Gallad, Tihir, and Mohammad left the training camp."

I wrote, 'the first Group is home'.

"Near the end of June, four of the six men had returned to the US, but Goya and el Barwan stayed to finish their training and then returned home in August 2001. We questioned them both but they, too, stuck to the cover story. Kamal, Derwish, and Alnahban remained in the Middle East. The Buffalo Field Office had no evidence of anything illegal at the time and had no real reason to believe they were lying."

I wrote, 'Second Group', circled this, and underlined el Barwan's name three times.

"Two weeks after September 11th, Juma al Dosari left Buffalo to fight with the Taliban in Afghanistan and Bosnia. The Buffalo FBI office continued to investigate the Buffalo Six to uncover if they were involved in terrorist activities but they looked 'clean'."

They still didn't have any idea of their plans. I wrote on the board, 'Buffalo Six's mission is scrapped by KSM', and said, "We need to backtrack. You skipped nearly a month."

Middlehouse jumped into the conversation. "What mission is scrapped? What do you mean we missed a month?"

I replied, "This is what you all missed. This is what I have to offer. The difference from your official story and the story I was told by the terrorists. From the moment of their return, the Buffalo Six were trained by Dosari for a mission. When the Buffalo Six were ready he left."

Suddenly animated, Charles Lymes added to Greene's soliloquy.

"We nabbed Dosari in the fall of 2001. During my interrogation of Dosari, I extracted the same intelligence on Dosari, Derwish, and the group from Buffalo. After my interrogation I sent him to Gitmo. Dosari confirmed that the Buffalo suspects were members of Al Qeada. I had what I needed, something I never shared with anyone until now. That's why I know Mr. Declan was telling the truth."

I wrote on the board, 'First lead, Dosari gives up Buffalo Six'.

The FBI Director gave a disapproving stare at Lymes and said, "So, in the spring of 2002 we received, I guess, the same information from Dosari at Gitmo. So I forwarded it to the Buffalo Field Office on May 17th. Our assessment was the Buffalo group was a sleeper cell. I gave the President daily briefings on the status of the Buffalo suspects. I assembled a counter terrorism team of agents from around the country. We were granted dozens of wiretaps to conduct round-the-clock surveillance by the FISA court (Foreign Intelligence Surveillance Act)."

The Director of the NSA then added his two cents with, "From an electronic intercept the NSA picked up what 'we' described as assessment calls between Derwish and two of the Buffalo suspects. We know one was Goya, but the other has yet to be identified. I informed Director Greene of the intercept and told him we feared Derwish and Dosari might be activating the recruits from Buffalo."

Back to the board, 'Mission transferred' I wrote.

Greene quickly reasserted his authority. "Despite the round-the-clock surveillance, there was no evidence suggesting the Buffalo group was engaged in anything other than their normal daily routine. For the next year we closely monitored the Six including Mukhtar el Barwan trip to Bahrain for his marriage. Everything seemed legit until the NSA again informed me they had a creditable intercept suggesting the sleeper cell was less than a benign group of friends. In late spring of 2002, a series of e-mails from Mukhtar el Barwan were forwarded to me by the Director of the NSA. The group of e-mails discussed el Barwan's wedding."

I wrote on the board, 'El Barwan travels for new mission'.

"The use of the word 'wedding' made our analysts nervous it had been known as code for an impending attack. It was the same term used by the planners of the USS Cole bombing," Sherrington of the NSA threw in.

Greene nodded and continued, "Another e-mail sent by el Barwan was equally suspicious. The e-mail was titled 'Big Meal'. A decision was made to try and persuade the President and the Justice Department to classify the Buffalo Six as enemy combatants."

Then Sherrington added, "One year to the day, September 11th, 2002, I had Mukhtar el Barwan detained by Bahraini police per the request of the President. During the interrogation el Barwan admitted to attending the Al Farooq camp and gave up the cell members names. I forwarded this information to Director Greene."

Greene then added, "On September 12th and 13th the task force picked up the remaining members of the cell in Buffalo and charged them with providing material support to a terrorist organization. On November 3rd, 2002, Charlie Lymes called me to have Kamal Derwish's name removed from the indictment and labeled, Uncharged Co-conspirator A."

"I had a line on his whereabouts and didn't want the indictment to alert him. I had gathered the intelligence by tracking Derwish's cell phone. I informed the President that he was traveling through the Middle East by car with Abu Ali, the planner of the USS Cole bombing. The President signed an addendum authorizing the CIA to use extreme measures. A Predator drone was ordered and sent in to kill Abu Ali and Derwish," Charles Lymes then explained

Greene then added, "That's what we know. So what do you know Mr. Declan?"

Chapter 73

"Everything I'm about to tell you came from two sources. The first is obvious. The papers contained within the bag over there are the direct correspondence between el Barwan and his lawyer, John Mallory. Mallory also just so happened to be my lawyer and like most lawyers, he would visit two clients on the same day at prison. This meant Mallory would have the information when I scheduled a meeting with him, and thus I was able to gain access and copy el Barwan's files."

Middlehouse asked, "How did you do that?"

"I staged a prison fight which led to a lockdown. It was during this time I was able to sneak the documents down to the library and make copies. I managed this because I grew up in Buffalo and I had many family members and friends from Buffalo that worked at Erie County jail. They had no idea what I was up to other then I wanted access to Mallory's files.

"Now, armed with inside information, I went to work. The documents gave the basic logistics, but missing were the dynamics of the group and detailed goals. From this I formulated a plan to fill in the blanks. At first I targeted all six members. They all seemed equally involved at the start, but under further examination of el Barwan's documents and through talking with them, I surmised el Barwan was the leader of the Six and Goya was second-in-command. Tihir seemed to be everybody's best friend and confidant while it appeared Mohammad and Gallad were more or less along for the ride. Alban was the black sheep and a late addition to Al Farooq, but Derwish pleaded with Dosari to allow Alban to travel with them.

"I worked the Six on a daily basis, first in Erie County, then INS Detention in Batavia, NY, MDC Brooklyn, USP Lewisburg, and then finally at FCI Loretto. At first my questions were ignored, but eventually I gained their trust by keeping my word of not revealing their identities to the other inmates, and by saving el Barwan and Tihir's life at Loretto. It took a year for me to finally break one of them and that person was Tihir. He finally told me everything."

"That's impressive work Mr. Declan. But I have just one question, why did you do it?" Four Star asked.

"In all honestly? Simply because I was bored."

The Brigadier yelled out incredulously. "Bored? You expect us to believe that?"

I replied, "Jail is day after day of nothing. A project helped pass the time. Also, I just had to know. If the stock market hadn't crashed, I doubt I would have been incarcerated at all. So essentially, I wanted to know why? Why the stock market plunged? Why I had to go to jail? Who set all this in motion? Why did they want to kill Americans? I sniffed around and discovered, unfortunately, much more than I wanted."

Chapter 74

The conference room sat silent. Even Trout was surprised by my answer. I wondered if I was I too curt. I realized it didn't matter. They didn't have to like me or my methods. What mattered was the information I had to share.

I continued, "The first thing I want to explain is the beginning of the timeline. Director Greene stated that all of this began in 2001, but it really began in 1999 when Derwish returned to Buffalo. He was born at Mercy Hospital in South Buffalo. He used these ties to start the Buffalo cell. Derwish used the stories of fighting with his Muslim brothers and his beliefs in Wasabism to influence the newly formed cell."

"Don't you mean Wahhabism?" Greene corrected.

I replied "Yes. Don't think the cell was influenced by a Japanese spice."

The room echoed with laughter.

"It was these two main factors that allowed Derwish to influence the Six—his connection to Buffalo and his knowledge of Wahhabism. Tihir said these two things are what lead to the Six's final leap to join their Muslim brothers in the fight against the West. I know Greene mentioned this, but I have one thing to add. The press, the public, and even the government believed the trip to Al Farooq stemmed directly out of Derwish's influence. But what I learned from el Barwan's documents and from Tihir himself was this, the Six had been traveling to the Middle East a lot more than you guys think."

"What do you mean?" Four Star asked.

"1999 and 2001 are the only years the Six allowed themselves to pop up on the radar for you to see. I can confirm that for all of you. For at least 10 years, five of the six men from Buffalo had been traveling to the Middle East. They were groomed for the better part of a decade by Al Qeada to become terrorists."

Lymes threw his opinion into the mix, "So, who was the member that didn't travel with the rest of the group?"

"I'll get to that individual," I answered. "The better question would be who was doing the grooming?"

"Who then?" the Brigadier asked.

I was beginning to enjoy the banter. "Good question but I'm afraid I don't know the answer. The one aspect of that question I can tell you is that both Tihir and el Barwan told me that it was a family member. This person arranged the trips to the Middle East and provided fake passports and I.D.'s. This is why the Six's travels never popped up during the investigation into the Buffalo Six. Everyone you captured kept the early beginnings of the Six and the mysterious family member a secret. If you can find out who the mystery man is, then you will find bin Laden."

"That sounds a little far fetched Mr. Declan. You don't give us enough credit. You don't think we would have found this out by ourselves?" Greene questioned.

I replied, "No, and that's my point. You'd have nothing credible without me. You were spoon fed a concocted story and you ate it up. You don't have to take my word on this anyway. However, I do have the aliases they traveled under."

I moved over to the computer, sat down, and asked, "Do I need a password to get in?"

Greene replied, "It's a Pentagon computer what do you think?"

I said, "Well then, either give me the password or have someone come down and log in so I can prove to you the depths to which you all failed the American public and the staggering ineptitude of thousands of people charged with the task of keeping us all safe. Maybe you just don't want to know the extent of your incompetence."

Four Star then turned to the Director of Naval Intelligence, Philip Stoddard, who, in turn, looked to select a member of his team to fulfill my request. Was he going to call on Trout? Thankfully the female assistant next to Trout stood up and walked towards the computer. She sat down in that starched way military personnel possess after years of being fucked in the ass by their supposed superiors.

She asked me for the names and proceeded to run them through the database. "They flew out of YYZ, Toronto International airport," I told her.

One by one each of the names popped up from the database. I had given them 10 years of travel records for the aliases.

"Is that proof enough?" I boldly questioned.

Nobody answered.

Chapter 75

I went on, "The 'mysterious family member' who we will call 'the candy man' from here on out faded into the background as more major players emerged. The soldiers were ready and now it was time for the top brass of Al Qeada to deploy them.

The first of the players to emerge from the database was Alnahban. He had taken to speaking at the local Masjid Alhuda Guidance Mosque in the first ward of Buffalo during Dars. Every Friday night Alnahban rallied and pushed the men to join their Muslim brothers in the fight against the West. The Muslim population in Buffalo felt uncomfortable with such radical talk in the community. So, fearing the Six might be swayed, Alnahban moved them to his apartment, isolating the men, thus preserving his influence.

During this time, Derwish was brought in to help Alnahban. Now, held up in the apartment away from the watchful eye of the elders, the team of Derwish and Alnahban went to work on the unsuspecting young men. Tihir told me that they felt guilty for not taking up the challenge before them. Derwish watered the planted seeds with hate of the West. He also provided them with a chance to wash away their drug dealing pasts and start anew.

"Like any good speaker Derwish controlled the conversation. He asked only things he knew the answers to. Eventually, Derwish hit a wall with them. They needed one final push to turn them into Jihadists and Derwish knew just the man who could perform the task Juma al Dosari. Dosari agreed to come to Buffalo to speak on the call

Christopher Prior

to all Muslims for Jihad but before Dosari arrived in Buffalo, Derwish returned to Afghanistan to continue his fight with the Taliban.

"The time lapse between Derwish leaving and Dosari's arrival gave Alnahban time to prime the pump. Derwish left them with many unanswered questions forcing them to stew. Always leave your audience begging for more.

"Finally, Dosari showed up and in short order closed the deal. Dosari, Alnahban, Derwish, and 'the candy man' had assembled a team. These four individuals had successfully manipulated Tihir, Mohammad, Goya, Gallad, Alban, and el Barwan into going to Al Farooq in April of 2001. This is what you all missed and the reason why I'm here.

Chapter 76

"So, are we all in agreement that's how the Buffalo Six arrived at Al Farooq," I said, "Minus the fact you knew nothing of the 'the candy man'?"

"Yes, please continue Mr. Declan," Four Star confirmed.

Tihir also told me Derwish unexpectedly pulled Alnahban aside for a secret conversation. It was not until six of the men from Buffalo returned to Buffalo the details of that private meeting emerged.

"With the second group now split, Derwish sent el Barwan and Goya directly to Al Farooq, and Alban went with Alnahban to a safe house in Kandahar, Pakistan."

I underlined each of the two groups again on the board, highlighting again the fact the men were specifically split into those two groups.

"While in Pakistan, Alban headed to the safe house with Alnahban. Alban assumed they were taking a different route to throw off any suspicions. However, this could not have been further from the truth. Alban was to meet bin Laden but that was not the only surprise. When he arrived he also met someone else."

"And who was that?" Greene asked.

"He met Binalshibh, the person responsible for funding 9/11. Binalshibh was the go between for Mohammad Atta, KSM, and bin Laden.

I paused for effect and continued. "At the safe house, Alban had no idea he was to become a key player in 9/11 and was quickly given a choice: join Al Qeada or be murdered. For those of us gathered here today, moral valor pitted against the promise of an inglorious demise is anathema. But we're not dealing with rational minds here. We all know why he made the choice he made.

"At the safe house Alban was told by bin Laden and Binalshibh that he needed to quickly return to the US. The problem was that if Alban didn't return to the camp the rest of the Six would become suspicious. As we know, Alban stayed at Al Farooq for about one more week. Alban's fake injury story, thanks to Derwish, gained traction. It was a perfect cover for Alban's true mission."

"And what exactly was that?" Middlehouse asked.

I answered, "Bin Laden wanted Alban to deliver two tapes to the safe house in Kandahar, but that is only half true."

"What do you mean by that?" Four Star asked.

I replied, "Under questioning, Alban said that both tapes contained Al Qeada propaganda specifically highlighting the bombing of the USS Cole. The fact is that one of the tapes had that information on it and the other tape had something very different."

"What was on the second tape Mr. Declan?" Middlehouse questioned.

"At this point 9/11 was only months away and Alban's special mission and separation was only part of the Buffalo Six's involvement in 9/11. Al Qeada still needed one more person from the Buffalo group to step up to the plate. This is where Derwish's split of the second group becomes so crucial. El Barwan and Goya had been chosen for the Double Jeopardy round."

Chapter 77

"Alban and Alnahban finally arrived and told none of the other men about the secret meeting with bin Laden in Kandahar. Reunited, the Six went to work but Tihir sensed he and the other five were being singled out.

"This feeling was heightened when the group witnessed the merger of the Egyptian Islamic jihad and Al Qeada. The Six, along with others at the camp, felt like something big was about to happen. Alban was to be a huge player in that 'something big.'

"So, what was his role Mr. Declan?" Greene asked.

I replied, "Alban later left the training camp early to complete a part of the mission KSM and Binalshibh were running. Alban's role was laid out on the second tape for him. It was a recorded video explanation with numbered bank accounts, instructions to manufacture fraudulent identification for the individuals, who subsequently ended up on the planes of 9/11, and to transfer funds to both New Jersey and to Florida. I don't know who was in New Jersey but I know that Mohammad Atta was in Orlando, Florida.

"Alban did as he was instructed and wired the monies to both places along with the I.D.'s. Alban completed his part of the 9/11 mission, but he had no idea what he was a part of until he saw the pictures of the suspected hijackers on the news."

Greene looked uncomfortable after I told them all this and said, "So you're saying without Alban's help, the terrorists would not

Christopher Prior

have been funded and therefore probably could not have completed the attacks on 9/11?"

I answered, "I would assume as much, though I'm pretty sure it would have merely delayed the mission, not stopped it."

Greene nodded and I went on, "Now that you all understand Alban's true role, there's still one more player that stepped out of the group from Buffalo."

"Who?" Four Star shouted out.

I answered, "The 'First group', Tihir, Mohammad, and Gallad came home early too. The official story was they were not interested in what was going on there, but we all know now that's not true. Tihir never gave me a reason for why they were sent back early, but I think I figured it out. Let me break it down. Out of the eight men from Buffalo, Derwish and Alnahban were promoted and Alban already had his part to play. This left KSM, Binalshibh, and bin Laden to choose from the remaining five. Tihir, Mohammad, and Gallad were weeded out as less than committed to Al Qeada's goals. That left only two, el Barwan and Goya. Al Qeada knew where the Buffalo Six stood before they touched down the Middle East. This is why Derwish's decision to separate the 'Second group' into two smaller groups becomes so important."

"How so?" Greene asked.

"The second group was split into Alban, Alnahban, el Barwan, and Goya. I just told you the real reason why Alban traveled with Alnahban—to receive his mission. That left Derwish to lead el Barwan and Goya to Al Farooq personally. To el Barwan and Goya it probably seemed to be a non-issue but it was actually a calculated move. They were separated so Derwish could feel them out. Goya lived with Alnahban in Buffalo eating up all the radical talk, but el Barwan must have shown Derwish a whole hearted commitment either in Buffalo or Pakistan because he was the one chosen to stay. Goya was sent back to the safe house in Kandahar to wait for el Barwan.

"Al Qeada was only dealing out information on a need to know basis and Goya didn't need to know, so he left."

"Know what?" Four Star asked.

254

"That El Barwan now was the last candidate up for Al Qeada's grandest mission to date. He was chosen to become the 20th hijacker."

"Where's your proof?" Four Star demanded.

"It's all here in Mallory's notes," I countered.

I shuffled through the papers, placing the proof on the under digital projector. It was like a solar eclipse. They looked at it from every angle and tried to shield it from themselves but it still hurt their eyes to see it.

"How do we know these notes are what you say? You could have manufactured all this yourself," Stoddard stated.

I explained, "I didn't. But if you want proof you're gonna have to wait to see the Wizard at the end of the road just like everyone else, sir. We don't have time for your forensic hand writing experts to verify that these notes were written by Patrick Mallory."

"Please, continue Mr. Declan. But let's keep the grandstanding to a minimum," Greene replied.

"Simultaneously, Binalshibh was meeting with Mohammad Atta in Cambrils at the Hotel Monica as Derwish was selecting his candidate. You all know what that meeting was about. Binalshibh, the money man for 9/11 and the leader of the attacks were having their last pow-wow but were interrupted by good news from Al Farooq. KSM told Binalshibh to inform Atta he would have the last person he needed for the mission; el Barwan was arriving in a week. Atta left Spain and headed to Orlando, and Binalshibh returned to Germany to meet el Barwan."

"Now in Germany, Binalshibh and el Barwan immediately flew to Malaysia to an Al Qeada training camp. Following training there, el Barwan was to fly out of Malaysia directly to Orlando to meet up with Atta. El Barwan told Mallory that he tried to get a visa from Malaysia to the US but he couldn't. So el Barwan and Binalshibh returned to Germany. Once there, they made a second attempt to get el Barwan a visa. Again, they failed.

This unexpected hiccup forced Binalshibh to call Atta and tell him there was no way for him or el Barwan to get to Florida in time. Atta, who was livid, told Binalshibh to contact KSM at Al Farooq. El

Barwan watched his chances of becoming a martyr crumble before his eyes during these conversations. The end result was el Barwan was ordered back to Al Farooq by KSM.

Tihir told me el Barwan was beside himself over his failure to obtain a visa that would, of course, allow him to join his Muslim brothers in their fight against the West. Until..."

"Until what?" Four Star asked.

Chapter 78

With Whitey alongside him, Zimmy raised his hand high into the air to signal the guard running the gate. Suddenly Marcus's father heard the buzz then a pop. He walked out the door and turned to Zim and said, "What the Hell do you think I should do?"

"Whitey, this is way above my pay grade. I've never seen what I just saw back there in the Warden's office. I wish I could tell you how this was gonna end, but I really don't know."

Walking back to his car, suddenly burdened with doubt beyond his comprehension, William Declan found himself at an impasse. How was he going to find out where his son had been taken? As he cranked the ignition of his car he thought of all of his connections, but he couldn't think of one he knew in the FBI. He sat there thinking, hoping for a spark of gut instinct to kick in, maybe a piece of Divine Intervention. He laughed at this final thought. 'This shit is so fucked up, I wouldn't want to even burden Him.' And with that, he drove away and discovered nothing but road.

As he headed for Interstate 90 that runs across NY State, his focus was half on the road and half on the cell he had cradled in his hand. He thought about who he could call? Who could he call? Again and again. Over and over.

Then an idea popped into his head to call Marcus' lawyer, Patrick Mallory. He scrolled through his phone's address book and clicked Mallory's cell number. Whitey put it up to his ear as the phone dialed out, only to hear Mallory's nasal voicemail message.

"God damn it," Whitey screamed, "You have to be fist fucking me right now." He was prompted to leave a message so he collected himself and as calmly as he could said, "Patrick I just drove up to Butler to surprise Marcus but the warden told me Marcus was taken by the FBI. They picked him up this yesterday morning. Please call me ASAP."

Whitey held the phone in his hand spinning it around and decided to try Mallory's office. The secretary picked up on the third ring.

"Mallory, Schinderman and Floyd, this is Linda speaking how can I help you?"

"Hi Linda, it's William Declan, Marcus' father, I was wondering if you could tell me where Pat is? I tried his cell but no luck." Whitey asked.

"Sorry Mr. Declan, but Mr. Mallory is in court all morning but I think he may want to talk to you as soon as he returns.

With an attitude of calm insouciance, Whitey replied, "Oh, really? Why's that?"

Linda had always liked Whitey, but she liked his son more and was willing to indulge in a little cat and mouse game to enrich her amorous intentions despite the flagrant abuse of protocol.

"Because we got a fax this morning from Butler that is related to Marcus."

"Really? What does it say?"

"I don't think that I can tell you Mr. Declan. It's Marcus' confidential information and I can't tell you anything over the phone."

"Why not? He's my son," Whitey told her.

Determined not to disappoint or indulge the old man too much, she adopted a conspiratorial tone while retaining a facade of professionalism. "Mr. Declan I could lose my job and this isn't something that you want to hear over the phone. Mr. Mallory should be back later on this morning. Why don't you come here?"

With his resilience already on a fragile plane, Whitey pleaded with her, "I just need to know what's happened to my son. Please, I need you to tell me right now."

Linda finally admitted she had read the fax. "I can't tell you the specifics, Mr. Declan, but I can assure you Marcus is doing something very good for himself right now. Really good. So don't panic. Just take my word on this OK?"

"Ok Linda, I trust you. Tell Patrick to wait for me, OK? I'm on Route 14 almost to Interstate 90. I should be in the office within two hours."

"Fine, Mr. Declan. In the meantime, is there anything else I can help you with?

Whitey dismissed the pleasantry and headed for some answers.

Chapter 79

Whitey made good time getting back to Buffalo. As he pulled into the car park next to Mallory's office, he noticed Patrick's car, a black SEL Mercedes.

With no words exchanged, Linda directed Whitey to Mallory's half open door. Foregoing the usual fake, but nevertheless comforting chit chat the legal profession are so inclined to indulge in, Mallory presented a very concerned man with what he hoped would be good news.

"Listen, I have only been on this for 45 minutes and I've made a couple of calls so I don't have much right now, but here's what I have."

Patrick slid across the desk a fax his office received dated the previous morning from the Office of the Governor. As Whitey began to read it, Mallory said, "What you're looking at is, for lack of a better term, a pardon for Marcus with some caveats."

Whitey tossed the fax back on the desk and asked, "What? A pardon? How in the Hell did Marcus get a pardon? Is this something you and he were working on?"

Throwing up his hands in mock horror, Mallory went on the defensive. "Absolutely not. I certainly wasn't aware of Marcus meddling with his case and I have no idea how this pardon came to light but, I can assure you this was no motion he submitted to the court. This came directly from the Governor himself."

"Well then how did he get a pardon?" Whitey demanded.

Although he knew Whitey would never do anything rash, Mallory still felt his long-standing golf partner would require very little encouragement at this moment to swing a seven iron around his Mercedes. Full transparency was the road to travel right now.

"Like I said," Mallory replied. "I've only been working on this for less then an hour. Give me some time and I'll get to the bottom of this."

As he stood to leave, Whitey had one more question. "If it's not a motion Marcus submitted to the court then how did the Governor of the state of New York get involved? Does Marcus know him or something?"

"I'm not sure Whitey. He might, but this looks like it was drafted up by the US District Attorney and not the NY State Attorney," Patrick explained.

Shooting his eyes towards heaven, Whitey was now close to exasperation. "Well, what does that mean? Listen, Pat, I've had a pretty bad morning so far. Just give me an answer in black and white. No more legal bullshit," Whitey pleaded.

"It means whatever Marcus did to get this deal it's Federal and not State. And the fact that it was the FBI that grabbed him yesterday morning adds weight to my theory," Mallory said.

William Declan stood bewildered for a second. Neither the victor nor the vanquished at this point, he could barely summon the energy to shake Mallory's hand or fully trust the attorney's parting words. "I will find out where Marcus is. Don't worry."

As he left the office, Whitey muttered, 'Never believe a lawyer when he says not to worry, because that's when you should worry the most.'

Chapter 80

Now back at home, Whitey sat in an easy chair in the living room trying to think of something he could do to find his son. He flipped on the TV and thumbed through the channels before settling for ESPN. Lazily watching a re-play of a college lacrosse final between Syracuse University and United States Naval Academy at M&T Bank Stadium in Baltimore. Whitey was transported back to his own son's lacrosse matches. All of a sudden an idea occurred to him.

Walking into his kitchen, he found his cell and scrolled to Teek's cell number. "Fucked if I'm not calling in a few personal favors," was all Whitey required for a reason to click 'call'.

The phone rang three times before Teek picked up, "Hey Mr. Declan. What's up?"

"Hi Teek. Sorry to call you but I have a question I need to ask you?"

"That's OK. Is something wrong 'cause you sound upset, like something's happened," Teek replied playing it cool.

"Something did happen, Teek. Marcus is missing and I've been told he was snatched up by the FBI yesterday morning from Butler Correctional. No one knows where he is, but I think you might."

Considered a more than competent chess player, Teek's impeccable sense of strategy suddenly left him. Because of his doubts and fears for his own safety, Van Dyne found himself unwilling to reveal anything other than half truths and inconsequential words of support.

"Well Mr. Declan......" Teek said drawing his response out. Prompting William Declan to say, "Please Teek if you know something please tell me."

"Listen, I don't know what I can or what I can't tell you Mr. Declan. But what I can tell you is that, Marcus was in DC yesterday but I don't know where he is now. All I know is that he was released into FBI custody and...." Teek paused to think.

"And what? Tell me the rest Teek," William asked his son's best friend, "I'm sorry Mr. Declan. I wish I could help."

"I guess that how it's gonna have to be," William sighed and hung up.

As the line went silent, Teek wondered exactly what his best friend was involved in and what, if anything, he could do to help answer a father's understandable desire to find his son. Lacking coherent options was a new sensation for Van Dyne and he didn't appreciate this opportunity of self discovery. "Fuck this shit," he said, suddenly remembering his friend in naval intelligence.

Teek anxiously waited for Trout to answer but after seven rings his call went straight to voice mail. "Listen buddy I just got a call from Marcus's father and he's worried about his son. I can't go into details, but I can tell you Marcus was picked up by the FBI yesterday from NY and brought to DC for a meeting at the Pentagon. I know you work there, so can you find out where he is?"

For 20 minutes Teek heard nothing until he received a phone call from the 716 area code he didn't recognize.

"This is Teek Van Dyne."

"Mr. Van Dyne, this is Patrick Mallory, Marcus' lawyer. I just got off the phone with his dad. He told me you saw Marcus and he's in DC with you. Is that true?"

"Yes Mr. Mallory. Marcus is here in DC but he's not with me now."

"Well then where is he?"

"I'm sorry, sir, I can't tell you. I'm sure Mr. Declan already told you that when you talked to him."

"Yes, that's exactly what he told me but this doesn't make any sense at all. I'm Marcus's lawyer. Why can't I know where my client is? Listen, I know the FBI picked him up and so it's the Feds telling you to keep your mouth shut. I can help you and Marcus please tell me."

Just then Teek's cell phone beeped. "Listen Mr. Mallory I have to deal with this text," and Mallory was abruptly dismissed.

It was from Trout—"You're not gonna believe this, but Marcus is standing right in front of me. I can't explain now but I'll call you later on."

Chapter 81

The mood is the room was palatable. I couldn't believe they didn't know all this already and I said, "El Barwan returned to Al Farooq after leaving Binalshibh in Germany to meet up with KSM. El Barwan assumed he'd head back to Buffalo empty handed. Upon arrival at Al Farooq, el Barwan, who was upset, was told that his mission would go on without him. KSM further explained Alban's role in the mission he had missed out on. KSM stated without Alban's help, none of the sleeper cells would have been funded or able to complete their ultimate mission.

"Seeing how distraught el Barwan was, KSM told him 'the candy man' had been sent a package and it contained their new mission. The Six now had their goody bag of evil."

"What was the mission?" Middlehouse replied.

I thought to myself as he shot me a 'what the fuck' look, this guy is a real dick.

I could understand where Middlehouse and the others were coming from, I had what they needed. But I was always taught you attract more bees with honey than salt. I didn't like Middlehouse, he was pushy and arrogant.

"The details are what are important here. KSM explained to el Barwan he was only one of a handful of people who knew of the upcoming 9/11 attacks. El Barwan's sole purpose now was to reveal the mission to his cell when he returned to the US. He was specifically ordered not to mention the goody bag to Goya when he met up with him at the safe house in Kandahar.

"El Barwan wanted to know why he was to wait until Buffalo, KSM said 'the candy man' had called to inform him that Tihir, Mohammad, and Gallad were all interrogated at JFK by the FBI when they returned. Also, Alban had been questioned by phone. Something had tipped off the authorities so stick to the cover story of traveling to the Middle East for religious reasons. KSM stressed the importance of el Barwan's mission. El Barwan met back up with Goya at the safe house and they left for the US.

"Both el Barwan and Goya were consequently questioned at JFK but they too stuck to the cover story and were released by the FBI. Upon their return to Buffalo, el Barwan and Goya were faced with a confused group of men. They had been handed building blueprints by 'the candy man' but, had no idea what they were. Alban, Tihir, Mohammad and Gallad were told they needed to obtain diving gear. The blueprints were of the Niagara Falls Power Plant in Lewiston, NY. The Six's mission was to blow up the plant on 9/11, tossing the entire Northeast into a blackout and further chaos after the planes hit New York City and Washington, DC.

"Tihir told me el Barwan explained everything upon his arrival, including the reason for Alban's early departure. El Barwan mentioned that he made two separate trips. One to Malaysia and the other was Germany to meet Binalshibh, money man for 9/11. He told them that he had been given an opportunity to participate in Al Qeada's big strike to date but he couldn't obtain a visa in either place to travel back to the US. He returned to the US with a new mission for the Buffalo cell.

"Tihir said Goya was pissed el Barwan never mentioned any of this on their way back to the US. El Barwan simply explained that he was instructed not to by KSM, Derwish and Alnahban. El Barwan said it was probably a good thing too, because they were questioned at JFK and Goya looked as though he was going to crack.

"From then on out El Barwan took total control of the cell. They only had three weeks to get everything in place. They had to learn to SCUBA dive and to manufacture the bomb IED's was the first part of the plan. Then part two was placing the explosives at the power plants reservoir, all the while staying under the radar of the FBI. Tihir told me that el Barwan purchased 20 prepaid phones and told the cell to stop any other illegal activities. El Barwan couldn't afford to have any of them popped on a drug beef.

"Tihir and el Barwan were the ones who delivered the explosives to the reservoir because of their familiarity with the Indian Reservation where the power plants' reservoir was located. The familiarity with the Reservation was a result of the time they spent there purchasing products from their drug dealer.

"The Six's plan was to dive the reservoir and place the bombs into the intakes of the power plant. This would therefore destroy the plants ability to provide power and cause a surge. The power surge would trip the multiple breakers attached to the national grid. Now all they had to do was wait for the call from Derwish."

Four Star interrupted, "This seems all pretty unbelievable, Mr. Declan, especially because the Six never bombed anything before we arrested them. The Northeast power outage stemmed from a Canadian power plant and it wasn't a terrorist attack.

"Are you certain of that General? I asked. I looked to Lymes, "So he's in the dark too?"

"Ok, then why don't you enlighten us, Mr. Declan? Tell us about this so called terrorist attack. Tell us how they caused the Northeast power outage," Four Star demanded.

"That's a good question General? How did they do it?"

"They transferred the mission and I'll tell you why. Early in the morning of 9/11 Tihir received a call and was told that he and the rest of the group were to meet at the mosque in Buffalo. El Barwan told them that 'the candy man' had received communiqué from KSM that today was the day. They were to wait until the planes hit Manhattan and the Pentagon and then make their way to the Niagara Falls Power Plant reservoir and complete the mission.

"Tihir told me as they left the mosque he had never been so scared in his whole life but he did what he was ordered to do and waited for news of the attacks. At 8:32 AM the first plane hit. Tihir got in his car and drove to the reservoir. He and el Barwan got there first so they waited for the rest of the crew to arrive. Forty minutes later the remaining members of the cell had still not arrived. El Barwan was livid. There was no way they could dive the reservoir and place the bombs on their own el Barwan scrapped the mission.

"Back in Buffalo, Mohammad, Alban, Gallad and Goya had their excuses ready. To sum it up there were just too many FBI agents around and Gallad and Goya told el Barwan their car wouldn't start. Their excuse's sent el Barwan through the roof starting a fist fight among the members of the cell. When the dust settled, Tihir asked el Barwan what they were to do now. His reply was to contact Derwish through 'the candy man'. This, Tihir said, was weird because the cell members thought he was speaking directly with KSM. They didn't know Derwish was the intermediary.

"'The candy man' came back with word to cease any attempt to finish the mission and to go into sleeper mode. Derwish told him that someone would be sent to Buffalo, so the Six waited."

"Who were they sending?" Middlehouse asked.

"On 9/12, Alban called the FBI agent who previously posed as an insurance agent and asked the Agent if he could help in any way. Alban and the rest of the Six knew they were going to be on the radar screen because they had been stopped at JFK. The group felt that it was better for one of them to call the FBI then to have the FBI call them.

"The Six knew they were the targets, so the Six turned to 'the candy man'.

"He told the members of the cell to hang tight and KSM was sending Dosari to Buffalo. Dosari, to eliminate suspicion, headed to Detroit first. I came across a newspaper article in the USA Today mapping out the largest population of Muslims in North America was in Canada between Detroit and Buffalo. The article showed all the Mosques which dotted the map like landscape. It looked like a little slice of Muslim heaven. Or should I say haven."

I placed the article face down on the projector. There was no disputing its truth.

I went on, "Dosari showed up a couple days after 9/11 and informed the Buffalo cell their mission to black out the Northeast was going to be transferred to a new group of recruits training at Al Farooq. El Barwan tried to plead his case to Dosari that he and his men were ready to go, but Dosari insisted that the Six stand down.

"El Barwan was ordered to hand over the mission to the cell from Hamilton, Ontario. Dosari told el Barwan and crew that the Hamilton group had a couple of weeks remaining in their training. When they were finished, they would return to Canada and el Barwan was to meet with them.

"El Barwan was pissed. This was the second time in a month a mission had slipped through is fingers.

"A week later 'the candy man' was contacted by Derwish and el Barwan was ordered to set up a meeting with the new Canadian cell. He chose a strip club called Temptations in Niagara Falls to make the exchange. El Barwan, Tihir, and Goya delivered the goods.

"Now left with nothing Dosari tried to reconcile with el Barwan and explain that it wasn't their fault, but it was to no avail. El Barwan wanted a mission. Dosari said he would speak with KSM about another mission as soon as he got to Afghanistan. A week later Dosari left for the Middle East and the Buffalo Six were left with nothing."

"A month passed and the cell began to lose their motivation. Finally they got word from Dosari. 'The candy man' told the Six Dosari would soon hand down a mission for them."

"It wasn't soon enough for el Barwan, though. 'The candy man' pulled el Barwan aside and told him Dosari wanted to speak with him directly. El Barwan called Dosari's satellite phone."

"During the call Dosari handed the SAT phone to Alnahban. Alnahban told el Barwan that he, Derwish, and Dosari had a meeting with KSM. Derwish and Dosari explained that Al Qeada was about to lose six important members of the cause if the Six did not receive a mission soon. A day later KSM brought bin Laden to meet with Alnahban, Dosari, and Derwish. Tihir said Alnahban told el Barwan, 'It's never good when the boss wants to talk to you.' However, Alnahban would soon learn he was wrong.

"KSM and bin Laden charged Alnahban to supply the Buffalo cell with a new mission and funding. Alnahban relayed this to el Barwan. El Barwan in turn informed the rest of the cell.

"Dosari told Alnahban of the noticeable FBI presence. There were out of state Crown Vic's and navy blue Suburban's everywhere. Alnahban now worried the 'the candy man' cover could be blown. That's why Derwish wanted to speak directly to el Barwan instead of going through 'the candy man' as they had done for over a decade.

"El Barwan understood, but questioned how he would be able to get his orders for their new mission. Alnahban told el Barwan he was working on it, and he needed the cell to lay low for awhile. He didn't want to see anyone from the Six arrested before they could complete their jihad. Alnahban said he would be in contact as soon as he figured out how to safely provide the Six with the details of the new target.

"By now it was December. Alnahban decided to inform him his cover story was complete: an arranged marriage was ready for him in Bahrain. El Barwan now had his cover story. Once he landed in Bahrain, Alnahban told el Barwan Derwish would reveal on the real plans.

"It's important to note here why they chose Bahrain. It is the only island state in the Arab world. That meant easy access to ships.

"So, over the next six months, el Barwan told no one of his conversation with Alnahban. He began to lay the tracks down for his trip by telling everyone he had been looking for a wife from the Middle East. "Finally, Alnahban called el Barwan and he left for Bahrain. The local FBI office knew of his search for a wife. So when el Barwan left in May of 2002, it was as a legit trip.

"This period of time is important to the government too. This is when you guys got your first break in the war against terrorism, right Chuck?"

Chapter 82

I noticed Lymes' demeanor. He was the kid in class caught looking out the window. His attention was elsewhere. He already knew what I had been explaining but now I needed his full attention. I was about to fill him in on what I held back on the plane.

Lymes said, "This is the same time period when Dosari was snatched in a raid in Afghanistan. He was moved to a black site and I went to work."

Greene asked, "What do you mean you 'went to work'?"

"Dosari was considered an enemy combatant. So we did what we do to enemy combatants."

"What does that mean exactly?" Greene asked.

Lymes wasn't going to answer that question. He had been a crypt keeper of dirty little secrets for nearly 30 years. The conference room was silent. All eyes were on Lymes waiting for him to speak.

He finally answered, "We interrogated Dosari in an undisclosed location, got what we needed, and then handed him over to the military. As you all know he was moved to Guantanamo Bay. That's all I'm at liberty to say."

"I guess that leaves the rest of the story up to you," I said to Four Star, "You have command of Gitmo, right?"

The Four Star answered, "Our interrogators learned from Dosari that the Six had been to Al Farooq, along with Derwish and Al-nahban. Dosari admitted to recruiting them."

I replied, "Sir, I know there's more. Lymes do you have anything to add?"

Unwilling to add anything, it took a withering look from the Four Star for Lymes to eventually splutter into revelatory mode again and hesitantly began like a child busted in a lie.

"Our interrogation of Dosari netted some other previously unknown facts. He told us that el Barwan was to be the 20th hijacker and revealed that the Buffalo cell was to black out the Northeast on 9/11 by destroying the power plant in Niagara Falls."

Now this is getting interesting, I thought.

"Those are two pretty important details Mr. Lymes, but that should have been shared. It proves what Mr. Declan has been telling us for the last hour is true. To what advantage was it to keep this from all of us? I don't understand you assholes at the CIA," Greene hissed angrily.

Lymes replied, "This is exactly why Mr. Declan is here today. Dosari revealed to us that the explosives were hidden at the reservoir. A team was sent in to investigate, and just like Dosari told us, the explosives were there. We dismantled the bombs and left them there disarmed as a trap, but no one returned."

I pushed harder. "So Dosari did give you the Buffalo cell's mission? I wondered about that, but what Dosari didn't tell you was that the Six handed over the mission to the sleeper cell in Canada. Also, I'm almost certain, there was one more piece of information Dosari gave up to you during that interrogation. I think he gave you Derwish's cell phone and we all know what you did with that."

"What difference does it make if Dosari gave up Derwish's cell phone number? And what are you implying?" The Four Star questioned.

There was only one person who knew the answer to that.

I rephrased his question but this time shot it directly at Lymes. "So, why is it important? Why don't you tell us what you did with that extra little piece of information Mr. Lymes?"

Chapter 83

It was obvious Lymes had his own agenda. He wasn't a man swayed by the tides.

"I believe Mr. Lymes was thinking one terrorist at a time. The tragedy in NYC and Washington had just happened but Lymes understood 9/11 was the squeakiest right now but there were other wheels in need of greasing too.

"Mr. Lymes focused on the solid intel he had. He wasn't just chasing after who was responsible for 9/11—he had previous debts to settle. He did it smart. The entire US wanted the government to re-act quickly. You can shake a tree and some apples will fall off, but if you want them all you get a ladder and pluck them one by one."

"So, if you did know all about the Buffalo Six's involvement why didn't you share this?" Greene questioned.

Lymes was pissed I don't think he thought I had figured it out.

"I had my reasons. There were more players than the Buffalo Six and I wanted to know who else was involved. I was after bigger Al Qeada fish. I knew the interrogators would eventually break Dosari at Guantanamo, and the FBI would have tried to use the information immediately to arrest the Buffalo cell, which is exactly what they did. I needed the time."

"We're not pointing fingers here today, Director Greene. Please continue Mr. Declan," Four Star requested.

I went on, "Six months later Alnahban called el Barwan and he immediately hopped on a plane to Bahrain."

Greene answered, "And that's where we lost him. We knew he was meeting up with Alnahban and Derwish."

I replied, "The reason you lost him was because you assumed that if he left Bahrain he would fly and Al Qeada knew that. That's why Alnahban chose Bahrain. It has seaports which allowed the three of them to escape from your so-called surveillance undetected. That's how el Barwan gave you the slip. They were headed to Malaysia by boat. I'll show you Mallory's notes will confirm this."

I placed the note on the overhead projector.

"El Barwan told Mallory that he, Alnahban, and Derwish went to Malaysia to prepare for another mission, which included scuba diving, welding, and learning the knowledge needed to manipulate ballasts."

"Why Malaysia? Why not the Middle East?" Middlehouse asked.

I said, "If the block is hot then you move to the next corner. You don't post up."

Greene said, "It makes sense. After 9/11 they needed some place that was off the intelligence community radar."

I continued, "Apparently, it worked because el Barwan didn't pop back up on your radar until he sent the infamous e-mail."

"El Barwan was spotted in Bahrain in May. He did some traveling around the Middle East, and then July 18 he sent the e-mail. That was two months after he first touched down in Bahrain. So now we know where he was for those two months. So, Mr. Declan do you know what Alnahban, Derwish and el Barwan were up to?" Greene supplied.

I replied, "No...They never told me. But if you recall the e-mail's content—that the meal will be so big that you will not be able to withstand it -I'm guessing they were about to be involved in something devastating, something to rival 9/11."

Lymes jumped in, "After the e-mail was sent, the NSA and the CIA watched el Barwan for two months. They tracked his movements through Derwish's cell phone but nothing seemed out of the ordinary. That is, except the e-mail. Everything pointed to them preparing for el Barwan's wedding. I personally asked the NSA to keep el Barwan's e-mail a secret as long as they could. I knew as soon the e-mail saw the light of day, it would skyrocket through the chain of command, eventually reaching the President's desk. I needed a bargaining chip for what I knew was coming next. The President, I suspected, would order us to pick up el Barwan, but we were ordered to wait until 9/11 of 2002. The Bahraini police arrested el Barwan one year to the day of the attacks. It was a political stunt that probably cost us our best chance to catch bin Laden and even though we didn't know el Barwan was getting a new mission we probably could have uncovered that too."

Greene followed that little gem. "On the 12th of September, upon a request from the President, I had the local FBI in Buffalo arrest the remaining Buffalo cell members."

Lymes explained. "With the indictment of the Buffalo Six about to emerge, I felt it would ruin my last lead. The court documents named everyone, Tihir, Mohammad, Gallad, Goya, Alban, el Barwan, and Derwish. I played my hand. I headed straight to the White House. I explained to the President that I understood his reasons for having the cell picked up, but I needed a favor. I told him I had the mastermind of the USS Cole bombing located, Abu Ali, through Derwish's cell phone. I told him I needed Derwish's name taken off the indictment. The President agreed and called the US Attorney's office and had Derwish's name changed to 'Unknown Conspirator A'. The President asked what I planned on doing about the Abu Ali situation and I told him. "Sir, I respectfully request Presidential decree.

The decree specifically allowed the use extreme measures against anyone linked to the war on terror. The President declaration was signed, sealed, and delivered to yours truly.

I was beginning to like Lymes talent for the dramatic.

"The President gave me the name of United States Central Command (USCENTCOM) General in the Middle East where Derwish was currently being tracked and said to contact him if I needed any assistance.

"While I took my commander-in-chief at his word, about a month after our meeting, I requested the attack. I provided the

CENTCOM Commander with Derwish's SAT phone number and ordered the dose of medicine they deserved. Within minutes Abu Ali and Derwish were, to be blunt, extinguished."

Lyme's juice with the President shocked everyone in the room. There were a hundred people in the conference room but I don't think anyone of them could be granted such favors form the President.

"The Buffalo Six minus el Barwan were all in US custody by September 12th 2002. I, on the other hand, was not arrested until May 19th 2003, which was right in the middle of the prosecution of the Buffalo Six. I watched as Gallad was the first to go down in January. Next to arrive was Goya and Mohammad in March, followed by Alban in April. Tihir was sentenced in the same month I was arrested. This is when I first met the members of the cell. I spent a month with the other cell members before el Barwan was brought to the Holding Center in June.

"Mallory, my lawyer, always seemed more preoccupied with el Barwan's case. It was far more important to Mallory's career than mine—I was just another greedy stockbroker. I voiced my concerns but he convinced me he was fully committed to me and my case. I foolishly believed him.

"I worked in the law library at the Holding Center. Jail life was tough but was tolerable because I had family members and friends who worked there. They would bring 'outside food' in, such as pizza, subs, hamburgers and fries and allowed me special privileges. The most important item they smuggled in was a cell phone. Everything I have talked about here today became possible because of my family and friends' faith in me.

"In jail, until el Barwan's arrival, Tihir, Mohammad, Gallad, Goya, and Alban were all very talkative. But as soon as el Barwan showed up the talking was over. This sudden change prompted me to dig deeper. With my connections, I staged a fight that allowed me to obtain the evidence against el Barwan from Mallory's notes on his case. These terrorists were part of the reason I was in jail. If it weren't for 9/11 and Al Qeada, who knows if I would have done what I did."

There was one thing I had yet to tell anyone until this very moment and I was about to come clean. "You all know I socially engineered the members of the Buffalo Six, using the information I stole from Mallory. But, nothing I have given you up until this point will help you in the fight against Al Qeada. Once I tell you what I'm about to tell you, everything will change.

"The one person never brought into any of this was the 'the candy man'. He was the man pulling the strings."

"So? Who is this masked man?" Apparently sarcasm was not one of Middlehouse's better traits.

I replied, "I'm getting to that."

Middlehouse interrupted, "So what then. What can you give us?"

"Simply this—I let the members of the Six use my smuggled cell."

The room fell silent.

Then Greene spoke, "You let the first group of terrorists arrested after 9/11 use an illegal untraceable cell phone?"

"Yep!" I said glibly.

My remark and my tone did not go over well. Even Lymes, a man devoid of emotions, looked upset. I scanned the room and all I saw were angry faces. Even Trout was upset. I just stood there smiling.

"What the fuck are you smiling about?" Middlehouse asked.

"All of you," I said laughing hard.

"Why?" Greene questioned.

Truly I had them all. My nights of terror in the cells fighting off the creeps and their atavistic nomenclatures had paid off. These assholes sat there looking like a bunch of doe eyed first graders on pop quiz day.

Chapter 84

"Mr. Declan, I think I speak for everyone here when I ask that you explain yourself," Four Star said.

I answered, "Simply put, I have the number and with that number you'll be able to look up the records of every call made from that phone. One of those numbers belongs to the anonymous 'the candy man'."

The girl running the computer leaned over to the edge of the desk and asked, "What's the number please?"

I gave her the number and 60 seconds later there on the screen lay every call made from my phone. I pointed out which calls were mine and which were made by someone from the Six. There were dozens of international calls. I stood there in my morning glory until Greene tried to piss in my Cheerios.

He said, "These numbers are two years old. How do we even know if they are still operable? We need the conversations that took place to those phones. That's we need."

I looked directly at him and said, "You're a glass half empty kind of guy, aren't you? Do you honestly think given everything I have told you here today that I would miss an opportunity?"

"I think the only opportunity here was for you to waste all of our time and get out of prison," Greene said and continued, "Agents, I think we have heard enough from Mr. Declan. Take this fake patriot out of here."

As Jackmann and Sinsel approached me, I stood relaxed against the desk and awaited my escort back to jail. They were happy as Hell that I was going back. But just as Jackmann and Sinsel took a hold of me, the girl running the computer alerted the rest of the conference room she had found something very strange.

She said, "Wait. Wait. Wait a second. There's something here but it doesn't make sense. There is a second ECN number attached to this phone."

"So what does that mean? Four Star asked as I was pulled off of the desk.

"The phone has been cloned and is still active," she informed them.

She looked to me and I smiled. She knew what I did. "Go ahead and tell them," I said as I tugged my arms out from Jackmann and Sinsel's grip.

She answered, "It looks as though Mr. Declan cloned the cell phone he had in jail and hooked it a Private Branch Exchange (PBX). The second signal is located in Virginia and is in passive mode. It only turns on when the phone is in use. There's something else, too. Anytime the phone was accessed, a virus was passed along to the recipient's phone."

Only half the room immediately understood the significance.

I said, "She's right. The phone is hooked up to a computer running a recording program hooked into the national cell phone grid. It's a modified PBX which sends out a virus that attaches itself to every phone it has had contact with and records the conversation that takes place."

"So you've recorded all of the conversations that took place from that cell phone? Okay, I understand that but what's the virus for?" Four Star asked.

The computer assistant attempted to explain. "If I'm correct, it's a way to track down every phone that was ever called and every other phone that was secondarily called and so on. It's like a huge pyramid. It started with the phone from jail and just continues to grow because of the virus. It's like a mini-telephone company running on a computer. All we have to do is grab the hard drive to retrieve what was recorded."

I said, "Right again. But I can save you the trip to Virginia?" I stuck out my thumb and motioned that I needed her to get up. I needed access to the computer terminal for my coup de gras.

She looked to the General and with a nod of his head I was in the driver's seat. I logged into the computer running the virus and recovery program and it was all there. 'Thank you very much', Geoff Sondon I whispered to myself.

"To the left of the screen of the digital projector you see every phone conversation that was recorded between my drop cell phone and the phones that were called. Just click on any of the recordings to hear them.

As for the virus, it's true; it does attach itself to each phone that is subsequently called. So every person who was called from my phone has the virus, as well as any other phones that were called by those phones."

Everyone was thunderstruck by my sneakiness. I had one up'd 'Big Brother' big time.

The Director of the NSA asked, "Where did you get this program?"

I replied, "I can't tell you that, but everything you need is here. All the conversations recorded are time and date stamped."

I pressed play to listen to one of the recordings. The conversations were in Arabic. I asked, "Can anyone translate?"

Chapter 85

America the brave suddenly displayed the demeanor of kids on Christmas which came early for the US powers that be. I even witnessed Four Star crack a smile as we listened to six of the recordings. One by one the conversations were translated by a NSA operative. It became obvious the conversations were definitely meant to sound innocuous but there were certainly were less than innocent. We needed to break the code.

Meanwhile, another NSA agent worked on locating all the phones that had the virus. One by one every phone number gave us another unknown phone. Each phone found lit up a map on the front screen in the conference room. I had given them something they could use. A few people actually came up to me to shake my hand and thank me.

It seemed like everyone was calling someone else. I just sat there and watched the ant hill grow. Soon other people started to arrive in the conference room. Lymes and Greene approached me.

Lymes spoke, "Well Mr. Declan, you really delivered the goods for us. I don't see any reason for us not to live up to our end of the bargain."

"Thank you, but there's still more I can offer," I replied.

"More?" Greene questioned.

"I know who 'the candy man' is," I said.

Everyone peered in my direction.

Christopher Prior

"It's someone you've already questioned," I said, "Do you remember the guy who runs the candy store in Lackawanna? The guy you questioned over transferring the money? It's him. He's the only member of the cell the US doesn't have in custody. It's Alnahban's uncle, Elnahban."

Greene said, "We questioned Elnahban over some suspicious money transfers to the Middle East. His claim was he was sending the funds to family members, but it was millions of dollars. His story seemed unlikely but we never found any proof to the contrary."

I replied, "Elnahban was the man behind the scenes. He was the one who invited the Six as young men to the Middle East and it was his family that Alnahban lived with in Saudi Arabia. That's the connection you all missed and how the man who ran the candy store end up in Buffalo. The two of them, from what I learned, were extremists and deeply committed Muslim and when Al Qeada emerged they saw it as their chance to strike. As for the money, it came from selling drugs and I doubt that it was truly for family members in the Middle East like he said. It was more like his Al Qeada family members."

Chapter 86

I said, "I remember a conversation I overheard when I let Alban use my phone while in the Holding Center. Alban spoke primarily in Arabic but then in the middle of the conversation he spoke in English reciting a series of numbers. They were bank accounts and international routing numbers."

"How do you know that?" Greene asked.

I replied, "I was a stockbroker. I used those types of accounts all the time.

"Alban was the money man for the Six but with him in jail, there was no way for him to move the funds. His phone call was to give someone else the account numbers to extract the money for other Al Qeada missions."

I handed my notes with the account numbers to Greene. He immediately turned to his support staff in the conference room to investigate this information. I overheard Greene directing them to find out whether or not any of the accounts matched Elnahban's. He returned and informed us that they were legit. Now they had the proof that what I was telling them was true.

One of the NSA translators stood and said, "Gentlemen, I think you need to hear this." We moved towards the computer to listen. The NSA operator replayed the section of one of the MP3 recordings and paraphrased the conversation that was taking place.

"So what do you have for us?" Lymes asked.

The NSA operator nervously began, "The two men on the phone are speaking about the funds Alban had control of and they sound worried. The man with the deeper voice—I've nicknamed him Deep Throat—is telling the younger man he has a safe way to get hold of Alban without alerting the authorities. Deep Throat is explaining he will get the account numbers from Alban and transfer the money as soon as possible so they can start the next mission. The younger man is relived to hear this. Deep Throat is now reassuring the younger man he will deliver the funds in time. The younger man is now informing the other that the recruits are only two weeks from completing their training.

"I think this verifies what Mr. Declan has been telling us, Sir," the NSA operator stated to our group.

Greene asked, "Do you think el Barwan's mission from Bahrain was transferred to another sleeper cell?"

"Why don't you ask your informant Director Greene? He seems to be reliable," I said.

"What do you mean by that?" the Director said as he turned into Oscar the Grouch.

I replied, "I can't be the only one aware that you had someone on the inside of the Buffalo Six. Lymes had his ace in the hole and so did you. So are you going to tell them or should I?"

The whole group looked toward Greene as he disappeared under the bus.

"I guess I'll do it then," I said.

"Alban was your boy. The FBI busted him selling drugs, which is how you got your hooks into him, but he was never charged with anything so I know you guys cut him a deal. It's probably the reason why Alban was a last minute add on to the trip to Al Farooq. The guys from Buffalo didn't fully trust him until the group reassembled in Buffalo and he explained his real reason for returning to the US—to fund 9/11."

"How do you know that?" Greene asked.

"I spent three years in jail, I can smell a snitch from a mile away. It's just something you pick up in jail. I have a master's degree in deception," I declared.

I caught Greene off guard. It was nice to know I wasn't the only one keeping things back from this supposed open conversation. It was like the chess matches Teek and I used to play, but this time it was the Grand Masters who were being toppled.

Greene said, "Yes. Alban was working for us. That's how we became aware of the Buffalo Six's trip to al Farooq."

I said, "So it wasn't that bullshit anonymous letter from the Yemenis community that led you to the Six? Even Mallory's notes hinted he thought the letter was a lie."

Greene explained, "That's correct. There was no letter. The FBI provided that cover story to the press so we could keep Alban's identity a secret. He was too valuable an asset."

I said, "Well, he couldn't have been that valuable considering you guys never really pulled anything useful out of him."

"I don't follow Mr. Declan," Greene said

I replied, "The whole time Alban was supposedly working for you as an informant he was really playing you. He fed you bull shit info and you ate it up. He's an Al Qeada's double agent and you invited him in.

"First off he didn't tell you about transferring the money to Atta for 9/11 to Florida and New Jersey. He didn't tell you el Barwan traveled to Europe to become the 20th hijacker. He didn't tell you about el Barwan's travels to Malaysia or Europe with other Al Qeada members. He didn't tell you about the Six's mission to black out the Northeast on 9/11. He didn't tell the power plant attack mission was transferred to a cell in Canada. He didn't tell you he used my drop cell phone in jail to contact Elnahban to transfer the remaining funds to the new recruits coming out of Al Farooq. Lastly, he never mentioned anything about the mission el Barwan received in Bahrain. He didn't tell you shit."

Greene, with his face painted red, "Well you seem to be the one with all the answers Mr. Declan. What was el Barwan's mission?"

I replied, "El Barwan never fulfilled his mission because the CIA picked him up. Maybe you should ask Lymes. He's the one who kept Derwish's cell phone number from everyone except the President. Listen, I think both you guys have skeletons and maybe, just maybe, if you told each other the truth you might be further along in your war on terror."

"You didn't answer the question Mr. Declan. And it's not just our war it's your war too," Greene retorted.

I said, "All I know is the Six were planning to use diving gear and explosives to cripple the power plant in Niagara Falls. So, if I was running the sleeper cell, I think I would use the skills I knew the group possessed. Given that, what would be the most likely target?"

The Four Star replied, "Enough with the games Mr. Declan, just answer the question and stop lecturing us like 5th graders. Do you want more Americans to be killed? We now know from your phone taps that el Barwan's mission was transferred. It could be going down today, tomorrow, who knows. Do you want that on your conscience knowing you could have prevented it?" Four Star asked.

"This is your problem. None of the agencies want to figure it out for themselves. You just want me to spoon feed you. You are supposed to be the best of the best. I'm just an ex stockbroker who spent time in jail."

"So what are you saying?" Greene questioned.

"You have to think like a criminal to catch a criminal," I said.

Lymes said, "He's right. Is everything out on the table now Mr. Declan?"

I replied, "Yes, everything you need is up there on that board. Just step back from it. Think about it as if you were the Six. Put yourself in their shoes. There's really only one target and that target is Manhattan."

I watched and listened for a reaction. They were still thinking like bureaucrats. They were using their square block mentality to solve a round hole problem. So I offered them a clue, "Think diving suits, think New York."

"What's underwater in New York?" Four Star asked.

"Piers?" Middlehouse questioned.

"The naval ships docked in Brooklyn," Greene added.

"The bridges, that makes the most sense," Lymes commented.

I jumped in, "No, but you're getting close. The terrorists already knew you would be covering all of the bridges and piers and the naval ship yards have no value. Think about what the Six was training for."

"They would hit something that would cause more chaos," Lymes explained.

"If it's not the bridges into New York, what else is there?" Middlehouse questioned.

"That just leaves the tunnels," Four Star stated.

"Exactly," I said.

Greene replied, "We have that covered. We monitor all the traffic in and out of the Lincoln and Holland tunnels."

I said, "They know that. So now add the under water diving part to the equation. If the targets are the Lincoln, Queens-Midtown, Brooklyn Battery and Holland tunnels, how are they going to achieve their ambitions of striking New York City again?"

"They're going to dive the East River and place the bombs on top of the tunnels," Lymes explained, suddenly wishing he hadn't.

I said, "Exactly. If I were the terrorists, that's what I would do. I would wait until rush hour and implode them. The implosions would kill thousands, probably even more people than the World Trade Center and Pentagon attacks combined. Also, New York traffic would be crippled for years to come."

"So that's your guess?" Lymes questioned.

"I don't have to guess, I know."

Chapter 87

An NSA agent spoke, "Sir, we've located a cell phone with the virus in Hamilton, Ontario. We traced it back from two phones, one coming from Yemen and one from Malaysia."

Weary eyes turned to the screen that had accessed the server in Virginia. The sheer number of phones that began to populate the screen surprised all of us. Most of the phones were concentrated in the Middle East, Malaysia, and Europe, but as we watched more and more were right in our own backyard.

I always assumed there had to be other cells, just not so many.

"What do you mean when you say you don't have to guess?" Lymes asked.

"When the Six and I were moved by the US Marshalls to MDC Brooklyn, two things happened. The first one disturbed me the most. We landed in Newark and we were loaded onto a bus to go into the city. On the seat in front of me somebody had scribbled, 'Osama will save us' and then something in Arabic. I requested Tihir to translate. He said that it meant 'Muslim brothers unite'. Now completely freaked out I pleaded with Tihir to tell me if there was anything I needed to know at that very moment. He said 'no', and we made our way into the city without incident, but something about that graffiti on the seat bothered me."

"Why was that?" Lymes questioned.

Christopher Prior

"How did someone get a black magic marker on a prison transport bus? I knew guys who hid stuff up their ass but it was usually drugs not magic markers. It was just weird."

"And the second source of your confusion?" Lymes asked.

I said, "We were all moved to the 14th floor which really wasn't big a deal until I looked outside. MDC Brooklyn sits within view of Manhattan and Ellis Island. I witnessed the Six huddled out against the metal grate of the yard pointing down to NYC and the Statue of Liberty. At the time I thought they were just sightseeing from jail, but I later found out from Tihir it was actually a discussion of the Buffalo Six's mission el Barwan brought back from Bahrain.

"To my knowledge this was the first time it was discussed with the rest of the men. El Barwan informed them that Alnahban, Dosari, and he had planned to hit NYC again. El Barwan told his crew they were to have dived the East River and place bombs atop the tunnels and implode them."

"So you knew this all along?" Lymes questioned.

Finally Lymes and co. realized the weight of the information that had been my burden to bear. The weight was now theirs. Actionable intelligence is what every person in this room was waiting to hear, and I just delivered it.

Greene immediately broke away. He requested divers be sent down to verify my story. Lymes, the Four Star, and the head of Naval Intelligence huddled together.

My work was done. I walked to the other side of the room, grabbed a bottle of water, and went to talk to Baynard.

Chapter 88

"So do you really think they're going to let us go?" Baynard asked.

"They better or they'll regret it."

"Why?" Baynard questioned.

"Let's just say I got us covered, Doc."

Baynard and I sat there watching the conference at work. I watched Lymes in particular. He was just staring at the screen of infected cell phones. The blips now encompassed the whole world. I bet Lymes was wishing he could send a Predator attack drone to each and every one of those blips.

Two hours had passed and I was getting hungry. I asked one of the Navy personal if there was somewhere I could get some food. He directed me out of the conference room doors and to make a left down the hallway. Baynard and I got up and walked towards the exit unnoticed until Greene stopped us, "Where do you two think you are going?"

"We're going to get something to eat. Do you have a problem with that? We've been here all morning with nothing," I said.

Baynard and I left and walked down the hall and arrived at a bunch of vending machines. I turned to Baynard, "I don't have any money do you?"

"Nope."

I looked around and all I saw was a bucket and a mop. I grabbed the mop and unscrewed the handle.

Baynard asked, "What are you gonna do with that?"

"Get us some lunch."

I hit the glass. Nothing broke.

"Are you fucking crazy?" Baynard hissed.

I hit it again and said, "Why, what more could they possibly do to us?"

Baynard, pausing for a moment to ponder this truism, asked for the mop handle, swung it like an MLB pro and shattered the vending machine window. "On the chow," he exclaimed.

Picking through the glass to grab our treats, two officers rolled up on us and demanded and explanation, "What do you two think you're doing?"

"Getting lunch," I said with a smile.

As the guards escorted Baynard and I back to the conference room, I couldn't help but wonder if I'd made a mistake. Not about smashing the vending machines, but leaving the conference room. What were these bastards plotting about my future? I mentally kicked myself for my error in judgment as I walked back into what I had now come to consider a den of inequity.

Chapter 89

As I reached my hand into my bag of Cool Ranch Doritos I said, "You guys are lousy hosts. I was hungry and had no money. Where's the complaint box?"

Baynard nearly pissed his pants. Even Lymes smiled as he directed us to sit down. For dessert, I decided to split a pack of Hostess Cupcakes with Baynard.

"You can taste the difference right?" I said.

"Fuck Little Debbie, Hostess makes a good cake."

Our little picnic was interrupted when Lymes came over. "I can't believe you did all of this by yourself."

The compliment made me wary. So I asked Lymes the $64 million question, "When can we leave? I don't have anything else to tell you and if I did I don't think you could handle it. Your plate runneth over. Look at the screen up there. There are hundreds of people for you to kill."

Lymes's hesitation said it all. I turned to Baynard and said, "I knew we shouldn't have left. We should have ordered Papa Johns'. Do they deliver to secret bunkers?"

"Listen Marcus there's been some talk...," Lymes said.

"What kind of talk?"

"You'll just have to wait and see," Lymes smiled as he replied.

Despite his assurances I really began to worry. Baynard hit me in my arm as the group began to speak again, saying with his eyes, 'keep cool'.

Christopher Prior

I calmed down after I realized I still had my trump card. I looked to the clock on the wall. The computer virus had been running for six hours, 42 more hours until the rest of the world would know exactly what was said in this room.

I fought the urge to walk around. It would have made me look nervous, but Baynard didn't have the same fortitude. He repeatedly stretched his legs.

The Four Star marched over to us. "You must have something else? I give it to you Mr. Declan, you got balls. Only a man on solid ground doesn't fear the quicksand all around him."

I just smiled and replied, "Let's just hope you never have to find out what that something else is."

There was no longer any reason to keep me there unless they had something else planned for Baynard and myself. I wasn't going to sit around and wait to find out. It was time to force the action. I got up to leave and told Baynard to follow.

"Where do you think you're going this time?" Lymes asked.

"As per our arrangement, I'm leaving. You guys have everything I know. There's no need to keep me here any longer. I hope you intend to honor our deal. So is there anything else?"

My question was answered in the affirmative.

Chapter 90

"Listen Lymes, there's gonna be consequences if you don't live up to your end of the bargain. Severe ones!" I said.

"Is that some kind of threat? You're not in any position to be making threats Mr. Declan," Greene bellowed from across the room.

I replied, "It is not a threat, it's a promise. My position surpasses anything you can think of. So if you think your gonna fuck me around you got another thing coming. If you and your little buddies want to keep what you have just learned a secret from the public then you'd better reconsider your hopes of preventing Baynard and me from leaving. If you force my hand you'll regret you did."

Wearying of my tirade, Lymes explained the situation.

"Mr. Declan, you have this all wrong. I think your incarceration has changed you in ways you don't fully understand, especially regarding your trust of the government—we are not the enemy. Early in your life you wanted what we are. You applied to West Point before going to Butler. You could have easily obtained anyone's position here if you wanted. You have a gift and we need that gift. Your threat, I have to believe knowing your nature, is inevitable. You wouldn't walk in here today without a plan. If we force your hand I'm sure we'll regret it. But before you walk out that door, at least hear what we have to say.

"Marcus, you are the only one in the world right now that has infiltrated an Al Qeada cell this deep. There is a real opportunity in that. We realized long ago we need you a lot more than you need us and unfortunately for you we cannot forgo the opportunity to infiltrate Al Qeada, it's far too good to pass up. We want you to become an operative for us. We need you to go back to jail to continue your investigation into the Buffalo Six."

"You want me to what? Go back to jail? You're crazy. The whole point of me coming here today was to get out of jail and stay out."

"We understand that Marcus, but the fact still remains you are the only person we have. You are the only one with access to them. You're not anyone's first choice, believe me. But look around this room. They realize that you're our best hope. You were the only one to engineer Al Qeada's operatives. So before you make your decision to walk out that door, realize that if you are not with us, you're against us."

"Thank you for the offer but I think I'm going to pass Mr. Lymes. Baynard and I are leaving."

"Is that a fact?" Greene questioned.

I replied, "Yes it is. Now all of you must decide whether or not you value what you all learned here today and whether or not you want anyone else to know."

"That's pretty tough talk from someone that could have just taken his last breath," Middlehouse said.

"That might be true, but even if I come to my demise at the hands of the very government that just asked for my help, I'll still have the last word," I responded.

"How do you hope to accomplish that?" Middlehouse questioned.

"My ace in the whole," I replied.

"What ace would that be?" Lymes asked.

"I knew you would fail to live up to your end of the obligation. So I made sure that if I disappeared, everything would go public. I can play dirty pool, too. I knew when I came here today I might not walk out. I had no delusions about that. Anyway, I'm leaving and so is Baynard. Have a nice day."

I moved towards the doors only to be stopped by two guards. "Move out of my way," I demanded.

The guards looked to Lymes for direction. I turned and addressed Lymes, "Well, what's it going to be?"

Lymes replied, "I get that you don't want to work for us. But what about Teek and his sister, your mattress business they have been running for you in that fancy new building in Arlington? What about your friends back home in Buffalo? How about your friends and family that helped you in Erie County Jail? What? You don't think we'll find them? What about your parents? Oh, and don't think we don't know about your offshore bank accounts in Costa Rica. If you say no, what do you think is going to happen, Marcus?"

I said, "So that's how it's going to be? I knew that I couldn't trust any of you, and that's why I am so glad I covered my ass."

"How'd you do that Mr. Declan?" Greene questioned.

I replied, "What is it you think I was doing this morning when your agents barged into Teek's house? I was recording my trump card. Everything I just told all of you has been recorded, encrypted, and sent out to the web."

"What?" Lymes asked.

"You want the information all for yourselves and I gave it to you. However, if you don't honor our deal, the world will learn what went on in here today and all those little blips up there will learn as well. All those leads you have will go bye bye."

"You're telling me everything you told us here today is out on the web for everyone to see?" Lymes asked.

"Not exactly," I replied.

"What do you mean by not exactly?" Lymes asked.

"Yes. The information is out on the web, but no one can see it yet. The recorded video is encrypted and it is placed in a virus that is set to go off in 48 hours. You have 42 hours left to release me...well you know the consequences.

"Also, if you're thinking or trying to crack it, think again. I used DOD 1024 encryption, so it will take you over 100 hours to crack which is far too late."

The room fell silent. They could not believe I had trumped them. However, the real question was would they be willing to forgo the information's secrecy to punish me for my genius?

"Is there a way to stop it?" Lymes asked.

"Yes, of course. I built in a safeguard so I can stop the information from getting out," I replied.

"Then stop it now," Greene ordered.

"And lose my only bargaining chip? I don't think so."

"This isn't a game. You must stop it or all of this was for nothing," Greene said.

I replied, "I know this ain't no game. You just threatened my life, my family, my friends, and my business...everything I love. You're the ones playing the games, so you can all go fuck yourselves!"

With the situation heated again, cooler minds needed to prevail. They were shocked by my response as I sat with my arms folded. Lymes began to speak, which just enraged me more.

"I think we're getting off track here Mr. Declan. What do we have to do to get you to stop this?" Lymes said.

"Listen I'm done talking. I just want what I was promised—my freedom and Baynard's, too."

The ball was back in their court.

Chapter 91

Awaiting their response, I realized I wasn't standing alone. Baynard, Teek, Karen, my friends, and my family all were besides me. I knew they wanted me to be set free.

Then I realized I had taken liberties with everyone's lives' and livelihoods with my stand. My own future hung in the balance but I was, after all, the one who started all of this with my big mouth. I should have never told Baynard anything.

Lymes and company gathered together as they contemplated my ultimatum. The minutes seemed to pass like hours. I was either headed home to start my new life or to Guantanamo Bay or worse.

"I think we are going to pass on your deal Mr. Declan." My heart sunk.

"You and Doctor Baynard aren't going anywhere except to back to jail," Four Star stated.

"Really, that's how you want to play it?" I retorted.

"Yes. The NSA said they can break the encryption in time. So I guess this is the end of the line for you. You've ended up right back where you started. As for your family and friends, they are all going to be investigated by the FBI, courtesy of Director Greene," Four Star said.

Greene went on, "We might not be able to make anything stick, but you know full well that we can make anyone's life, shall we say, uncomfortable for a very long time. Everyone you love will have their lives torn upside down. How many of them do you think will stick by you after going through that? We will make yours friend's lives so unbearable they loyalties will evaporate."

I replied, "So lock Baynard and I up, and throw away the key. What will the public say about all of this? How will their views change on the government? The public will see me as a normal citizen who did what you could not and see that I did try to help you but you chose to forgo that help. The US is in a fragile state and you are ready to make it more so."

Lymes answered, "You have forced our hand Marcus. You have refused to work with us. No man is more important than the whole. You and Doctor Baynard will spend the rest of your years locked in single cells with no contact to the outside world. You are officially going to be charged as enemy combatants. We have been doing this since before you were born. You're not the first to make this stand. The annals of history will be devoid of any mention of this ever taking place."

My bluff had been called. The guards placed handcuffs on Baynard and I. My future started to look like a tangled mess of cars on the interstate. I had spent time in the box in the Feds and in New York State, but that was only a couple of weeks at a time. After the first day the walls of the cell start to close in on you. You do pushups and read books but your days are marked by the overhead light to the cell being turned on and off. Often, your only access to the outside world is a sliver of a window. Your only aspiration is to become a regular inmate, a sorry empty existence.

Then my family and friends came to my mind. Their lives too would be forever changed by this one decision. This was my cross to bear. I had never asked anyone in the past for help in carrying my burdens, and I wasn't about to start now. With my hands behind my back I realized I had no choice.

"So what is it that you want me to do?" I asked.

Chapter 92

"I want you to come to work for us," Lymes said.

"What do you mean by "us" and what is it that you want me to do?" I asked.

"You would be working for me at the CIA and we need you to go back to prison. We need more information from the terrorists."

I said, "How is this going to work? I'm currently a New York state prisoner. My sentence is up and the terrorists know that. My cover's blown the second I step back into jail." As they pondered the obvious, I thought this was a SNAFU in the making.

Lymes and company had not thought that far ahead. All they knew was that they wanted more information and I was the one that could get it for them. No one in this room had ever been to jail. They just didn't understand.

"You guys haven't thought about this have you? These guys have been locked up for years. What? Do you think Al Qeada is sending carrier pigeons in to give them updates on Al Qeada? I would say their intelligence value is nil. What else could I possibly I get from them?"

Lymes replied, "Ok Marcus, you've got a valid point. What if you missed something in your investigation? Maybe the Six have contact with the outside world other than you. Maybe someone just like you smuggled a cell phone into BOP and gave it to them. We just don't know and that's why we need you to go back in, unless you have a better suggestion."

"In fact I do," I said.

"What would that be?" a clearly bored Greene asked.

"Even if I in work for you, I just can't walk up to the terrorists. They will know something is up. Prison works like this. You get arrested, you go to county jail, and you make your way to reception, then you get bounced around to a couple of jails, and in about six to 10 months you reach the facility where you'll complete your sentence. That's how it works.

"So I would have to finish my sentence at Butler and then go back to Federal prison. I mean we are talking about years here. So, given that, is it worth me going back? It's not like the terrorists, even if I do this, are going to start talking about Al Qeada as soon as I get there. It's gonna take me time to get back in their good graces."

Greene jumped in, "We don't have enough time for all that. Two years is too long for us to wait. Our plan is to send you right back to FCI Loretto to see what you can get out of them."

"What, so I can get labeled as a snitch and end up dead? I told you that's not how jail works."

I looked to Baynard. He understood the stupidity and took his turn with the clowns.

"Declan's right. The terrorists and the other inmates will figure the ruse right away. You have to let him go through the movements to make it legitimate. That's the only way it will work."

Lymes and company discussed what we had just explained but I didn't have time to wait for them to figure it out for themselves. So I posed a question to them, "What if the terrorists weren't in jail?"

This stopped the conversation in its tracks.

"What do you mean?" Greene asked.

"Listen, I told you how jail works and Director Greene has made it very clear that two years is too long for you to wait. I have to agree with that assessment. This leaves us with a difficult choice."

"What do you have in mind?" Lymes questioned.

I replied, "Exactly what I said. You have to believe they would be better assets if they were free."

"So you want us to free the Buffalo Six? That's your idea? That's crazy," Greene exclaimed.

"Is it?" I asked.

"Yes Mr. Declan. There is no way in Hell we're going to release the Buffalo Six. The public would have our heads on a plate. God forbid what the press would do to us. We're still leaching from the Guantánamo photos scandal. The press would have a field day with that one."

"What if it wasn't the government's fault? What if there was someone else to blame?" I questioned.

"I'm not following you Marcus. Are you suggesting that somehow their cases go back to court and they get released?" Lymes asked.

"I have a better suggestion. What if I organized the breakout? Then it wouldn't be the government's fault, right?"

"So you are suggesting we allow Al Qeada's operatives to come into this country and break out the members of the cell. I don't think so Declan. We are trying to prevent terrorism not encourage it," Four Star said.

"But if I were allowed to control the outcome. What if I was the one to break them out?"

The group stood there in silence as they realized what I was suggesting. It made sense. With me controlling the escape the outcome would be planned to Lymes' satisfaction as he and his government cronies would know what was happening every step of the way. I would help the Six flee to the Middle East and I would tag along with them. This was right up Lymes' alley, but would the rest of the group go for it?

Greene asked, "How exactly would you break them out? You're already in jail, and by your own admission you're not even up for parole for another year. So you break out of the State and then you break out the terrorists? Not likely. The other issue to keep in mind is that the terrorists are in a max facility. Your plan is near impossible."

"Nothing is impossible if you help me do it," I said.

"Why would we help you do that?" Lymes asked.

"Because if I broke out the Buffalo Six, they would have no reason not to trust me. I would be beyond reproach. I could become the only American on the inside of Al Qeada," I answered.

Christopher Prior

That statement threw the switch on for the rest of the group. The plan, however crazy, would ingratiate me with the terrorists. Lymes loved the idea, but could he sell it to the rest of the group and the President?

Chapter 93

There was no denying my plan had merit. The escaped Buffalo Six would be held up as conquering heroes in the Middle East. The decision might land Lymes, Greene, and the rest of the men in this room all in prison, but the information they would obtain was very, very enticing.

Baynard and I watched as they dissected my plan. They weighed whether the ends justified the means. The fact that they were even considering my plan showed they had few options.

"Desperate times call for desperate measures," I heard one of them say.

"So if we decide to implement your plan, how would you propose we achieve our objectives?" Greene asked.

I replied, "First off, I can't just go back into the Federal system from State. So we need to do is fix that problem."

"How do we do that? You still have time remaining on your sentence," Lymes said.

"I'll file a Habeas Corpus when I return to Butler, you'll find a judge who will rubber stamp my request for relief from the court. I'll be free in seven days. That's the only way it will look legit."

Baynard looked at me. He knew the extra benefits associated with this motion to the court. It would give me a reversal, clearing my case and record forever, and double jeopardy would apply. Making my illegally siphoned off funds secure.

Christopher Prior

"Ok, so you're out. How do you propose you get back into the Federal system?" Greene asked.

I replied, "Simple. I'll commit another crime and you arrest me for it. A new charge is the only way anyone would believe I went back to a Federal jail. The difference this time is that all of you will be accessories to the crime. I'm not the type of person that would go back to jail on a rinky-dink violation. The crime has to be a good one to make it believable."

"You understand we are the government right? You expect us to help you commit a crime?" Greene asked.

I replied, "You will if you want me to do this. You're asking me to risk my life. I'm not going to do that for free regardless of life imprisonment. We do it this way or we don't do it at all. You're going to help me steal $500 million."

Middlehouse audibly choked.

"You'll arrest me right away, lock me up, and in four to five months I'll get to where the terrorists are."

"Why the money though? Why can't we just send you back without all the drama?" Lymes questioned.

I answered, "I need money, and lots of it, to help them escape. That is unless you want to pay for it. This is the only way anyone will believe that after getting out of jail I went right back in. You know after I break them out there is going to be an investigation and this will separate any connection between all of you and me."

I could see they all had questions. Lymes, though, possessed a boyish fascination of the absurd, "How do you plan to get them out of jail?"

Chapter 94

I said, "As you may or may not know my case appeared in the newspapers. I remembered reading an article next to mine about an executive that found a way to beat the options market. His position gave him control of the way the options were dated. This meant he could change the purchase date of any option to fit the in-the-money position. Meaning that if options were out of the money and not able to be sold or exercised, he would just backdate the options to meet the current market position and rake in huge profits. The SEC was ignorant of this possibility despite the simplicity."

"It's business ethics 101," someone murmured.

"The guy simply found a loophole in the system. He was arrested but only received three years. So, even if you do renege on your deal again, I can do three years standing on my head for $500 million. It's a win-win."

"Oh, so that's it? You just want us to help you steal millions of dollars. That's the equivalent of some third world countries GDP," Greene said.

I ignored this.

"Let's just say for the sake of argument that we go along with your plan. I want to hear how you plan to break them out," Lymes questioned.

"Well Mr. Lymes it's ironic you should be the one to ask that question considering your part in Baynard's rescue in Rhodesia. Your use of helicopters in saving the doctor is what inspired me. Baynard is fond of telling that story."

"What exactly is your idea?" Lymes asked.

"I think a helicopter break out would be the easiest," I said.

"You think you're going land a helicopter in a Maximum facility?" Greene asked incredulously.

I replied, "No, You are. I'm going to be in jail doing your dirty work. I don't care who flies the helicopter and lands it. Hell, make it Jackmann and Sinsel if you want. It doesn't matter to me.

"Here is where the money comes into play. With those kinds of funds it would appear to anyone that I could do whatever I wanted, even hire a helicopter crew to come in and break me out. That's what will make the plan work, and it will keep all of you from being investigated.

"My arrest will be national news and you'll feed the press that you never recovered the money. I'll make my way through the Federal system to the terrorists and present them with a chance to escape.

"The Six will read about my arrest before I get there. They won't suspect anything about me being back in jail for stealing $500 million.

"Then I will present to them a chance to bust out of prison. I'll tell them in three weeks a helicopter is going to land in the yard to fly me out, but I need their help. I'll tell them once I escape from Federal prison there's no way that I can stay in the US. I'll offer a deal to take them with me to the Middle East where there are no extradition treaties."

"That's the craziest plan I have ever heard," Four Star bellowed.

"It's so crazy that it will work," Lymes replied.

Chapter 95

The group clustered again. I was betting on the fact they could understand that escaped terrorists were better than locked up ones that could be easily brought back into the Al Qeada mix. It was no longer who needed who more. It was rather, what was at stake. My plan was a tremendous gamble. In life things often come down to last minute plays. As I waited for the thumbs up or down, I thought back to the last minute play that placed me in this position in the first place.

It was a Friday morning and the Dow Jones was about to open. The day before I had staked everything I had on one stock trying to get back to even after my losses following 9/11. I had jumped out the window, to use a jail colloquialism. All my money and the funds money was placed on margin. The stock was EMLX, a tech hi-flyer that had a history of quintupling or better. I was making educated guesses now. I was transformed from stock broker to gambler.

I bought EMLX on Wednesday, 26th of September 2001 for $10.52 and by noon Friday the 28th the stock had lost $1 a share. Ordinarily a loss of a buck was nothing to worry about, but I had purchased all the stock on margin to buy more of the stock than I could afford, every dollar lost was multiplied by two.

That Friday I lost $2 on every share the fund and I owned. It was almost a 25% loss in a matter of 48 hours. To make things even worse, in the three days following 9/11, I had already lost 72% of everything and this new loss only tightened the noose.

I started drinking heavily and my judgment went south. I spent hours staring at computer screens. My whole world was crumbling but I had to make a decision to either stay with the stock I was losing money on or press the enter button completing the trade that would ultimately send me to jail.

I was nervous EMLX would go down further so I sold it and took the loss. Quite simply I lost my balls and headed straight for Michelle's strip club by the Buffalo Niagara International Airport.

When I returned home four hours later, the stock I sold had tripled. Then and there I knew the ride was over. Easy money was gone. I failed to trust my instincts.

Though, today, I felt like the old me before 9/11. I had convinced the government to consider an outlandish plan of breaking out terrorists from jail and helping me steal $500 million. I had stayed a step ahead of them all.

Lymes broke away from the rest of the group and said, "You got it. We'll do it your way. What's the next step?"

"You're going to need to get all the members of the Buffalo Six to one facility. As far as I know they are all separated besides Tihir and el Barwan who are at Loretto. I'll take care of the rest."

"What do you mean you'll take care of the rest?" Greene asked.

"I'll file the Habeas Corpus motion and you'll see it goes through the court with ease. In the meantime, I'll have a way to steal the money so you can lock me back up. The only thing I need from you is a helicopter I can buy and someone to fly it into the facility. I'm sure Mr. Lymes can handle those arrangements."

"What are we to do with Doctor Baynard? Are we sending him back to jail?" Middlehouse questioned.

I replied, "Yes."

The look on Baynard's face was instant anger. He thought I was selling him out. I explained, "I know you don't want to go back to jail, but I'm going to have them put you in the same place with the terrorists and you can escape with all of us."

"You want us to let Baynard out too?" Greene asked.

"Yes. We're already breaking out seven people what's one more? I need some help on the inside and Baynard is just the man. He's got the relationship with Lymes and I don't trust Lymes but I do trust Baynard."

"Is there anything else we can do for you, Mr. Declan? Possibly a monster truck with a tilting hydraulic body?" Four Star questioned.

"What about the computer virus you sent out?" Lymes questioned.

"Just let me send out the code to stop it dead."

I sat down at the computer and sent out what they thought was the code to stop it, but I was no dummy. I reset the virus to go off in 168 hours, one week from now and told them, "As long as I stay free no one will ever watch the encrypted video. So if you all keep your word, your secrets will stay secrets and I'll help you."

They had no choice. Their main goal was to stop Al Qeada and I was the only one who could give them a chance to get close to the terrorists on the inside.

I said, "So I guess I work for the CIA now. Do I get a business card? Special Agent Marcus Declan, I like the sound of that."

"CIA agents aren't called Special Agents, they're called Operatives," Lymes explained. For the first time Lymes seemed utterly defeated.

Chapter 96

Lymes' correction had given me a reality check. I had gone from high school jock, to scholarship college athlete, to accomplished stock broker, to imprisoned stockbroker, to CIA Operative. In between I had been many other things, a lover, a liar, and a glutton weighing in at 317 pounds. Quite a journey in three decades.

When I was younger I had aspirations of becoming a cog in the government's machine but I thought that pipe dream had long gone. I guess life isn't about waiting for the storm to pass; it's about learning to dance in the rain.

"So what happens now? Do I go home before all this or do I get issued dark sunglasses, a black hat and suit right now?" I questioned.

Lymes was the one to answer my question, "Now that you're on board I see no reason why you can't go home today. Does anyone else have a problem with that?"

The conference room presented a sea of silence.

He continued, "We're going to have to start trusting you, Mr. Declan, and you're going to have to start trusting us."

"Trust isn't given, it's earned," I said.

"Well said Mr. Declan, and it's a two way street," Four Star replied.

"Go home and enjoy the rest of the day. You are to report to Langley in the morning. You do know where that is right?" Lymes asked.

"Yes, I know where it is, but what are we going to do with Baynard?" I questioned.

Lymes replied, "He's going to stay with me and iron out some details. Then we'll send him back to prison."

I shook Baynard's hand and told him I was sorry about not being able to get him his freedom today. His reply was, "Six more months isn't shit when I was looking at ten. Don't worry about it." Always the gentleman.

I made my way around. First Lymes, then Greene, next Four Star, then Trout's boss, the head of naval intelligence, and last but not least, Middlehouse. I shook all of their hands.

I walked out escorted by the guards that had interrupted my lunchtime excursion. They commented I was doing the right thing, the patriotic thing. The taller one said, "Mr. Declan, I would like you to remember one thing."

"What's that?" I asked.

"This is the land of the free, because of the brave. What you have decided to do for your country today is the bravest thing I've ever witnessed. I wish you the best of luck. The entire country is counting on you." I was shocked.

Chapter 97

The guards escorted me to the ground level, where we continued to make our way towards the Pentagon's main entrance. We stopped at the front desk. They shook my hand and walked away in silence, disappearing with their stoic demeanor. I turned towards the doors—my gateway to temporary freedom beckoned—and watched for a moment as the sun's amber waves settled across South Washington Boulevard. I couldn't wait to push on through to the other side and finally smell some fresh air.

I looked around and saw a silhouette in the distance. After maneuvering against the sunlight, I finally recognized Teek.

I held up my hand and he waved back. I was so happy to see him, but how did he know I'd be right here, right now? Ignoring my cynicism, with each step I took towards him, life just felt...justified.

Cresting the embankment to Teek's Hummer, I noticed the Arlington National Cemetery and wondered if I would ever be buried in such a hallowed place. Truthfully, the best I could hope for would be an anonymous golden star on the wall at CIA headquarters and that would have been pushing it. Then again, I was the government's best chance to break Al Qeada; I had achieved, with some help, what no government on the face of the earth had been able to do. I was about to try to become the savior of the world.

God help us all!

Teek was standing in the doorjamb of the driver's seat. As I got to within ten yards I yelled to him, "How'd you know I was getting out?"

Teek held up his phone and pointed, "Got a text from the fish man."

'Trout', I thought. Of course. Last night he was the king pin of perversity and now he had become my PA, organizing taxi rides home.

Teek got down from his perch and slid back into the truck as I opened the passenger door and got in.

"Well?" he said.

I smiled.

"C'mon man?" Teek begged. "Did they buy it? Are you in?"

"Of course I'm in."

As we turned on to George Washington Memorial Parkway, Teek rolled down the window letting in the cold air and screamed, "Whooa! That's what I'm talkin' about."

"Easy buddy, let's not celebrate," I told him. "We can't tell anyone, OK?"

Our electric mood was interrupted by Teek's ringing cell. He showed me the screen—it was my dad. I could face down terrorists, Latino gang members and untrustworthy CIA Operatives, but my father? Well, he scared me.

I grabbed the phone and let out a sigh and said, "Here we go."

"Listen, Whitey's gonna understand," Teek said.

"Understand what? I can't tell him shit."

"Oh, and your lawyer's secretary has been calling me all day. Something about a fax that landed in Mallory's in-box. She seemed really upset."

"Really?" I brushed off the question.

Now, on the fourth ring, I answered the call.

"What's up Leo?" It was the name we always called each other.

"Marcus, you've got some goddamn explaining to do..."

To be continued...

www.ingramcontent.com/pod-product-compliance
Lightning Source LLC
Chambersburg PA
CBHW072054020726
47501CB00003B/591

* 9 7 8 0 6 1 5 4 5 3 0 5 7 *